He brought his hands up to my face, lifted it, then kissed me, deep and hard. I felt the world narrow down. This man. This desire. This time. This night. I put my hands inside the collar of his shirt then yanked.

"You have no idea what I want to do to you. What I'm *going* to do to you, Candace," he whispered, his words a promise that sent shivers down my spine.

I had broken all my rules for this moment—the moment his needs overtook him and he forgot himself.

Quick as lightning, I brought up the hand I had let drop to the side of the couch.

"Actually, I think that's my line, Nate," I said, as I plunged the long, thin stake of silver into his back, driving it all the way through to his black and treacherous vampire heart.

Passionate Thirst

A CANDACE STEELE
VAMPIRE KILLER NOVEL

CAMERON DEAN

BALLANTINE BOOKS • NEW YORK

Passionate Thirst is a work of fiction. Names, characters, places, and incidents are the products of the author's imagination or are used fictitiously. Any resemblance to actual events, locales, or persons, living or dead, is entirely coincidental.

A Ballantine Books Mass Market Original

Published in the United States by Ballantine Books, an imprint of The Random House Publishing Group, a division of Random House, Inc., New York.

This book contains an excerpt from the forthcoming book *Luscious Craving* by Cameron Dean. This excerpt has been set for this edition only and may not reflect the final content of the forthcoming edition.

ISBN 0-345-49253-6

Cover illustration and design by Tony Greco

Printed in the United States of America

www.ballantinebooks.com

OPM 9 8 7 6 5 4 3 2 1

For Jane and Ellen,
long live the triumvirate!

Prologue

Just another night in Sin City . . .

He was the sexiest guy I had seen in Vegas.

Considering how many guys I see in a day, that's saying something.

Not only that, I see all kinds, from sleek high rollers in silk shirts and Italian leather shoes, wreathed in clouds of expensive cologne, to slobs in Hawaiian shirts and flip-flops, oozing bad body odor. As a general rule, casinos don't get terribly exercised about dress codes. Most don't care too much about what you've got on, or what you don't, as long as you can make it through the door to lay your money down. For a guy to make me sit up and take notice like this one did, he had to be something really special.

Trust me, he was.

Though to say sitting up is slightly misleading since I was on my feet at the time. They hurt. But then they usually do. Occupational hazard of my job. I'm on my feet, my high-heeled feet, a good eight hours a day, cocktail waitressing at Vegas's newest mega casino-hotel, the Scheherazade. One of the first things you learn: Do not, under any circumstances, take off your shoes till you go off-shift, no matter how much you might want to.

After shift, however, you can take off anything your little heart desires. Which brings me back to the guy.

"It's so unfair," my coworker Marlene moaned as we shared a rare moment of togetherness while waiting for our drink orders. In our regulation high heels, gauzy harem pants, and pillbox hats, I figure we looked like two *I Dream of Jeannie* clones, Vegas style, though I think even Jeannie would have drawn the line at the pink velour halter tops.

"Who shows up in my section?" she went on. "Guys who look like Beavis or Butt-Head. You get Sean Connery as James Bond."

It was a good description, I had to admit. The man in question was currently at the blackjack table I covered, looking like he owned the place and winning like there was no tomorrow. I spotted him as soon as I came back on the floor from my midshift break. Tall, dark, and handsome with a sort of lean and rangy build that kept him from sliding too far into *GQ* territory. Though his clothing was plainly expensive—charcoal-colored pants and a white cotton shirt so sheer I could almost see right through it—he didn't look as if he had been born with a silver spoon in his mouth. Instead he looked . . . hungry. An alpha-male wolf in designer clothing. As combinations go, it packed quite a punch.

Down, girl. You're still on the clock, I thought.

"You can tell which one is Beavis and which one is Butt-Head?" I asked Marlene as I began positioning drinks on my tray. The one for the guy in question was a very expensive single-malt scotch.

Marlene huffed out a laugh. "Cute," she said. "But you can't fool me. I know you're only trying to soften the blow. It's such a waste. That's the thing I can't stand."

I have very strict personal rules about tangling up the sheets with casino patrons, a thing my coworkers know quite well. Going to bed with strangers may sound exciting. And it is, sometimes. But a girl gets tired of being the thing that happens in Vegas and stays in Vegas.

"And what were you planning to do?" I came right back. "Take him up on whatever it is he has to offer?"

Marlene has a good ten years on my twenty-something, all of which she's spent happily married to her high school sweetheart—a guy with a face so gorgeous it almost has me convinced angels really do walk among us. She was about as likely to take a roll with a customer as she was to flap her arms and fly to Mars.

"That's not the point," she said loftily, aligning

drinks on her own tray. "The point is that somebody's got to. He watches you, you know, when he thinks you're not looking."

I tried without success to keep a satisfied smirk from stealing across my face. "Does he now. . . ."

"I knew it. I just knew it," Marlene pounced at once. "You're tempted. Admit it, Candace. Please, please tell me you're going to cut loose just this once. If you don't, Gloria will get him and we'll all have our noses rubbed in it for weeks."

Gloria, a stacked blond who staffed one of the roulette wheels, was a notorious man-eater of the kiss-and-tell variety.

"Well," I said slowly, no longer making any attempt to hold back the smile. The truth was, I *was* tempted. Very. In a way I hadn't been in quite some time. "He *is* pretty spectacular. And I guess there's not much point in having rules if you don't break them every once in a while."

Marlene gave a whoop of triumphant laughter. "Now you're talking. Have I ever mentioned that one of the things I like best about you is your sense of . . . proportion?"

"Oh, now you're just talking dirty," I chastised.

She leaned toward me, lowering her voice conspiratorially. "Let Mama Marlene give you one little tip. Do absolutely everything I wouldn't do. And for future reference, always remember that Butt-Head is the ugly one."

I was laughing as I plunged into the crowd.

* * *

" 'Night, James," I said to the employee entrance doorman four hours later. I was now officially off the clock.

" 'Night, yourself, Candace," he said, his voice like ground gravel. "Don't do anything I wouldn't do now."

"Wouldn't think of it," I said, and earned a smile.

Cutting around the side of the building, I headed for the Strip. The truth is, I love Vegas at night. Sure, it's loud and bright and phony. But it's also vibrant, colorful, *alive*. I've never seen a place more dedicated to the future than Vegas is. Even the air seems filled with a sense of anticipation. Because the thing about gambling is that you can never quite predict the outcome.

I heard a car horn honk, a voice call out, and I lifted my hand in greeting as one of the city's numerous cabs shot by. Tourists almost never realize this, but there's actually a strong connection among the locals in this town. So many faces coming and going, you get so you notice the ones who stay put. I paused in front of the Bellagio, watching the way the lights flirted with the waters of the fountain.

"That's the first time I've ever seen anybody do that," a voice behind me said.

I felt a cool shiver of anticipation slide straight down my spine. I didn't have to turn around to know who it was. Throughout the rest of my shift, Mr. Tall, Dark, and Handsome and I had played a silent game of seduction. A quick brush of my bare arm against his sleeve as I delivered his drink. The stroke of his fingers along the top of my hand as he set a chip on my tray. Was I interested? Yes, but not in my own casino, my own backyard.

He played blackjack steadily, following the dealer as she moved through her rotation, as if he was convinced she was bringing him his luck. It took him out of my section, not that it made much difference. We kept an eye on each other. It got so I could tell when he was watching me, a feeling like cool air moving across my skin.

"You've never seen anyone do what?" I asked now, and felt him move to stand beside me.

"Daydream at night."

I turned my head to look at him. He was staring at the leap and play of the water, his face in profile. Again, I saw the contrast between his lean, sharp features and that rich, full mouth. Tension began to pool in my belly.

Definitely worth breaking the rules for, I thought.

"That's a nice thing to say," I said, my tone light.

He turned to look at me then, and I could see the way his eyes were dancing with mischief.

"I can be nice."

I laughed. It was such an obvious thing to say.

"Can I ask you something?" he went on.

"Sure," I said.

"What's your name?"

"Candace. Candace Steele," I replied.

I extended one hand in introduction. He took it, but instead of shaking it, he brought my hand to his lips, his eyes on mine. Now, finally, I felt that mouth against my skin. First the lips, then the slow glide of his tongue across my knuckles. Goose bumps danced across my skin. I felt a tug, deep in my groin.

"I'm Nate Lawlor," he said. He kept my hand in his. His thumb made lazy circles in my palm, and I felt my breasts tighten. "Mind if I ask you something else?"

"Twenty questions," I said. "After that, I'm cutting you off."

He grinned, quick and wicked, and gave my hand a tug. Slowly, he began to pull me toward him. One step, then two, until our pelvises bumped.

"Do you like to *play* games, Candace?" he asked. "Or do you just like to watch?"

"Yes," I said.

He laughed then, head thrown back. I watched the way the muscles moved in the column of his throat. Unable to resist the impulse, no longer certain why I should, I took a step toward him, sliding my breasts along his chest, nuzzling at the base of his throat with my open mouth.

He brought his hands up to my face, lifting it, then kissed me, deep and hard. I felt the world narrow down. This man. This desire. This time. This night.

"Come home with me, Candace," he murmured against my lips. "I can play all sorts of games."

"Show me, Nate," I whispered back. "Show me how."

I'm not sure how long it took to reach his apartment. I wasn't exactly watching the clock. Nate drove a BMW convertible, slate gray, top down. The desert air slid across my skin like cool silk. He didn't touch me. Not once, all the way home. By the time we reached his apartment, every inch of my skin was quivering, poised in anticipation.

He held my hand as we walked to the door.

Inside, Nate's apartment suited him to perfection. All cool, hard surfaces, stark and streamlined. Big picture windows looked out toward the mountains, the glass tinted against the glare of the sun. He released me, and I went to stand before them, my eyes on the lights of the city spreading out across the valley floor. I heard the flare of a match being lit. The air filled with the sharp tang of sulfur.

Behind me, Nate moved slowly through the room. Clusters of tall pillar candles sprang to life. Their scent was something I couldn't quite put a name to, spicy and exotic. It flickered through my senses as the candlelight danced across the room. Most guys I encountered rushed through motions like these, as if they were embarrassed by them. But Nate seemed to recognize them for what they were: foreplay.

I liked it. I liked it a lot.

I heard a whisper of sound, so soft it took me a moment to identify it. He had stopped at the living room's media center, turned on the stereo. *That's the sea,* I thought. The rhythm of it seeped into my veins, seemed to move my very blood. Why had I never realized before that the sea makes an erotic sound? Ancient and insistent. Driving in, easing out. And it would never stop. Could never stop. Stamina. Of the most elemental kind.

And then, suddenly, Nate was there, behind me. Running his hands across the back of my tight jeans, then sliding them around to the front. He stroked along the length of my crotch, then eased me back against him, his fingers pressing and releasing in the same rhythm as the sound around us as he nestled my ass against the ridge of his cock. I could feel the thick, hard length of it, pulsing against the constraints of our clothes.

I bent forward slightly and began to shift from side to side, rubbing my soft curves against him. He made a sound, low in his throat. His hands streaked up my body to seize my breasts, thrusting them outward. And then finally, finally, he was doing the thing they had ached for since that moment outside the Bellagio, rolling his thumbs back and forth over my nipples. Shivers danced across the surface of my skin, skittered down my spine. I heard someone take a sobbing breath, and realized I was the one sobbing.

"What do you like to do, Candace?" his low voice sounded in my ear. "Play, or watch?"

"Yes," I murmured as I turned in his arms to face him. "Both." I nipped at his chin. "More." His ear. "Now." His mouth. "Tell me what you want."

He reached between us, stroking between my legs, his eyes on mine. "You really want to know?"

"Tell me," I whispered urgently as I began to move against his hand. "Tell me."

"I want to feel you, Candace," he murmured. His tongue danced along the contours of my ear. "Your hands on my body. Your mouth on my skin. Take my clothes off."

I felt my pulse leap then start to run. *This is why I'm here,* I thought. Why I had broken all my own rules. To feel this need, this power.

"How do you want it?" I asked, though the air felt so thick I could hardly breathe it. "Fast or slow?"

"Yes," he said. A perfect page from my own book. This time I was the one who laughed, low in my throat.

I put my hands inside the collar of his shirt then yanked hard. The thin cotton gave way with a sharp, searing sound. Buttons bounced across the hardwood floor. Beneath the shirt, his skin was taut and smooth, pale as marble, an animated statue of some Greek god. Everything about him was hard. His nipples, dark and erect. I dipped my head and flicked my tongue across them, then settled in to tease and suck. He made a hissing sound between his teeth as his hands moved up to cradle my head.

Why do men have nipples? Because God is a woman and she really wants us to enjoy ourselves, that's why.

My mouth still busy at his chest, I ran my fingers down his arms to undo the cuff buttons, then push the remainder of the shirt away and off. Then slowly, I let my mouth rove across his torso. Teasing, testing. I heard him make another sound, and felt his fingers tangle in my hair as he urged my head lower. I felt the power of his desire sing along my veins. He may have started the game, but the rules were mine now.

Slowly I eased the button of his pants open, slid down the zipper, then pushed the pants off his hips, scraping my nails across his butt. The second his cock was free it pushed forward, straining against the thin silk of his briefs. I kissed it, openmouthed.

With a sound that was almost inaudible, his control snapped. His hands tightened in my hair as he pulled me to my feet, brought my questing mouth to his, and plundered. I felt my knees begin to shake, then buckle. Never taking his mouth from mine, he caught me up, took two steps, then lowered me onto the couch.

Cool leather against my back. His knee between my legs, easing them open. With eager fingers, I reached inside the waistband of his briefs. His eyes stayed locked on mine even as he moved to help me. For a moment, he stood, still as the statue he resembled, eyes glittering as they gazed down.

I let one hand rest limply at my side, as if I lacked the strength to lift it, even to touch him. With the other, I reached and ran my nails up the back of his leg. I saw the way his body jerked, just once. Then he was tearing open my halter top, covering me, his mouth hungry on my breasts, tongue sliding along the length of my neck, teeth biting gently at one sensitive earlobe.

"You have no idea what I want to do to you. What I'm *going* to do to you, Candace," he whispered, his words a promise that sent shivers down my spine.

I had broken all my rules for this moment, too. The moment his needs overtook him and he forgot himself.

Quick as lightning, I brought up the hand I had let drop to the side of the couch. There was a flash of something even I couldn't quite see, though I knew damn well what it was.

"Actually, I think that's my line, Nate," I said, as I plunged the long, thin stake of silver into his back, driving it all the way through to his black and treacherous vampire heart.

One

Three months later

I was on fire.

Blood pounded in my ears. My breath came in shallow gasps, panting in and out. Hands were racing across my bare skin, rough and gentle all at once. I let my body arch to meet them. *Up,* I thought. *Take me up. Drive me to the brink and send me straight over the edge.*

He knew how. I knew that much.

Blindly, my fingers sought his face, and brought his mouth to mine. The kiss was sure and deep, potent as a drug. I let my fingers roam down his body and felt his urgency increase. *Now,* I thought. *I want you inside me now. Don't wait. Don't stop.*

A strange, wild keening filled the room. I heard my lover give a grunt. He lifted his head, shaking it as if to clear it. The sound continued, piercing as a siren. Which, as it happens, is exactly what it was. Just my luck. I was in bed with the only guy in Las Vegas who downloads police sirens as ring tones for his cell phone. His most recent acquisition: one that sounded like those sirens you hear in French films. High low. High low. High low.

Very sexy on the screen. Not so sexy in real life—particularly when sex was the thing that was getting interrupted.

"Dammit!" Detective Carl Hagen said. He drove his fist against the wall behind my head with more than a little force. He looked down at me, his dark eyes narrowed. "Hold that thought. In fact, hold that position. Move so much as an inch and I'll be forced to cuff you."

In spite of the way my entire body was screaming in protest, I managed a laugh. "Promises, promises."

He gave a snort of what might have been amusement, then rolled toward the edge of the bed, reaching for the still wailing phone. As he sat up I saw him wince as he flexed the fingers of his right hand.

"Ow."

"That's what you get for resorting to violence," I remarked.

"Keep it up, Steele," he said over his shoulder. "See what it gets you." He flipped the phone open and the siren cut off. "Hagen," he rapped out.

I watched in silence as the transformation took place. One moment, I had been in bed with a man. Now, I was in bed with a cop. Carl's entire body went on alert, seemed to listen, as if he could absorb information through the pores of his skin. When he tucked the phone against his shoulder and reached for the pen and pad of paper on the bedside table, I sat up. I know serious business when I see it. Homicide detectives don't get all that many happy calls in the middle of the night.

"Give me the address," he said, and began to write. As always, his movements were economical, precise. I don't think I've ever known anyone quite as spare, as direct, as Carl. Absolutely no effort is wasted. Though he can circle around it if he has to, he always has the point in sight. It's what makes him so good at his job, to say nothing of certain other things.

I pulled my knees up and rested my chin against them, watching him work. We were an unusual couple, no two ways about it. Detective Carl Hagen and I became acquainted several months ago, under less than romantic circumstances, when I was questioned in the disappearance of a man named Nathan Lawlor. Though the homicide division was called in, they bowed out in the end, mostly because nobody could actually produce any evidence of foul play, let alone a body.

Nate Lawlor had simply vanished into thin air, which is essentially what happens when a vampire gets staked. The police, backtracking Lawlor's steps, discovered that he had spent his last evening at the Scheherazade. A number of staff members had been questioned, including Marlene and me. When my turn came, I told as much of the truth as possible. Yes, I had waited on Nate, known he had big winnings. Yes, I had found him attractive, so much so that I broke my own personal rule and let him take me home.

But he had been as alive when I left him as he was when I arrived, I informed the police. As to his present whereabouts, I knew absolutely nothing.

That also happens to be the truth. Even vampire experts haven't devoted a lot of time to where vamps go once the undead part of their existence comes to an end. My personal opinion, also my fervent hope, is that they occupy the lowest, most uncomfortable ring of Hell.

Since I was the last person to see Nate alive, I was initially considered a suspect. Fortunately, all my coworkers at the Sher backed me up—Marlene, in particular. I think she felt guilty for having encouraged me to go for the gusto in the first place.

The investigation into Nathan Lawlor's disappearance stalled. Everything about his life was precisely where he had left it. The only thing missing was Nate Lawlor himself.

He was gone. But the attraction the homicide detective and I had carefully sidestepped during our interviews stuck around. About a week after the case was officially considered cold, Carl Hagen strolled through the doors of the Sher and into my life.

Closing his cell phone with an audible snap, he turned back to face me. "You moved," he remarked. His tone was joking, but I could see the way the weariness had risen in his eyes. I knew it had nothing to do with the time of night.

"You started it," I came right back. I scooted forward to wrap my arms around his waist. "And besides, you have to go."

"I do," he confirmed with a sigh. He leaned in for a long, sweet kiss then rested his forehead against mine. "The timing sucks. I'm sorry."

"That makes two of us," I said, but I gave him a smile. He eased back, and I saw the tiny crease running down between his brows and knew what it meant. "You're going to be a while, aren't you?"

"Looks that way."

"Then I'll head out when you do," I said briskly, swinging my legs off the side of the bed, careful to keep my tone light. "Al wants to see me in his office, first thing. Apparently I'm being given some special assignment with regards to Temptation McCoy."

Temptation was the current hot pop diva, and in just a few days' time she would become the newest headliner at the Scheherazade.

Carl gave a low whistle. "Bet every security guy's nose is out of joint."

"You think it's just their noses?" I asked sweetly.

Carl gave a snort.

"Anyhow," I said as I stood up. "I might as well head out when you do. I show up late, Al's never going to let me hear the end of it."

Al Manelli is my boss, head of security for the

Sher. The truth is, cocktail waitressing is just a cover. I actually work casino security, a thing Carl discovered when he ran a standard background check. The thing that's not standard, and that the check didn't reveal, would be the thing that only Al and I and my best friend, Bibi Schwartz, know.

I have a special area of expertise: rousting vampires.

It may or may not come as a surprise that Vegas is home to a thriving vampire community, always assuming that something not living can actually be said to thrive. Vamps love Vegas for the same reason humans do: the excitement. Even if you're undead, Vegas can make you feel alive. Add to that the fact that there's an influx of fresh faces, fresh blood, every single day of the week, and you pretty much have vampire paradise.

Though, as it turns out, there are very strict rules governing the consumption of human blood. Only the vamps at the very top of the food chain get to drink blood from live humans. Lower-echelon vampires make do with animals and the dead. Too much bloodletting tends to produce unfortunate results, such as a shortage of humans and an overabundance of vampires.

"You're sure?" Carl said now, in response to my suggestion that we depart at the same time. "You don't mind?"

"That you have to go, yes," I said, moving to the overstuffed chair on the far side of the room where

I had draped my clothes. "That I do, no." I shimmied into my underwear then reached for my bra. "It'll be easier to get up early if I start from home."

Every relationship has its own rules. Carl and I had established ours early on. Each of us recognizes and respects the privacy required for the other's work, and sleepovers are strictly invitation only. I don't stay at Carl's place if he's not there, and he doesn't stay at mine. They were my rules just as much as they were his. Still, I could tell he felt a little awkward about booting me out in the middle of the night.

"So that works out all right, then," he said, but he was frowning.

"Carl." I yanked up my jeans, fastened them, then pulled a turtleneck over my head. "It's fine." I crossed to where he still sat, buck naked, at the edge of the bed, stepped between his legs, and leaned down for a quick kiss. "Much as I love a man out of uniform, I think you're going to want to put something on."

"Jesus, you're a pain in the ass, Steele," he said, but I could see my tactic had worked. The frown was gone. "Remind me again. Why do I put up with you?"

I stepped back and turned away, giving the ass in question a provocative little shake.

He gave a bark of laughter, got to his feet, and strode over to a chest of drawers. He pulled on a pair of boxers and a T-shirt. He didn't say a word, but I could see that he was no longer smiling.

"How bad is it?" I asked as he continued dressing. I sat down in the overstuffed chair and pulled my boots on. I was skirting the edges of forbidden territory and we both knew it. What the hell. The worst he could do was tell me to back off.

Carl was silent as he slid a brown leather belt through the loops of a pair of faded jeans. "Bad enough," he finally replied. "And if I can't wrap it up quickly, I guarantee you it's going to turn into my worst nightmare. The media is going to go for this one like a school of sharks."

"Why?"

"Somebody just reported a headless body in the parking lot over at Lipstyx."

I sat up straight, one booted foot clunking to the floor. "*What?*"

I could feel my mind begin to race. A headless body was pretty extreme, even by Vegas standards. Not only that, I knew it presented possibilities even more dire than the ones Carl could imagine.

"Okay, wait. Did you say 'Lipstyx'?" I asked before Carl could speak.

"Uh huh," he replied, his tone glum. "So I take it you get my point."

"I most certainly do," I nodded.

Lipstyx was a recently opened after-hours club, of the less-than-savory variety. Which pretty much guaranteed the headlines were going to be absolutely accurate, like somebody's idea of a bad joke, and go a lot like: "Headless Body Found in Topless Bar's Parking Lot."

About half an hour later, I was home and in my private office. And I do mean private. I bought my place in Vegas as a fixer-upper, then made the modifications to the floor plan myself. My dad owned a construction company when he was alive, and I can swing a hammer with the best of 'em. I am also the only woman I know unafraid of drywall. Most of my house is pretty standard. It has a kitchen, a dining room, living room, bedroom and guest rooms, and one and a half baths. The nonstandard part embedded deep in the house's center, its contours concealed by a careful wall arrangement, is a room that's mine and mine alone. Nobody else in the world knows about it, not even Bibi.

Other people have panic rooms—a place to go when they're afraid. I have a place where I go to stave it off. My office is my own personal testament to the notion that knowledge is power. It contains everything I know about vampires.

I stepped in, making sure the door clicked shut behind me, and was engulfed in total darkness. I stood still for a moment, listening to the silence. I had toyed briefly with the idea of soundproofing the walls, then decided against it. Too easy for something nasty to sneak up on me. When I was satisfied that I could account for every sound I heard, I snapped on the light. A special strip at the bottom of the door takes care of any possibility of light spill.

My office is comfortable but spartan. Desk. Chair. Reference library. Weapons cabinet. Mini-fridge stocked with emergency rations and water bottles. The only item that could be considered personal is a sketch of a man's face, mounted in a sterling-silver frame. Every time I look at it, I get the shivers. That's why I keep it around.

His name was Ash. Is Ash. He still exists, as far as I know. We met in San Francisco, which is where I lived before I relocated to Vegas. Once upon a time, I thought what Ash and I had together was true love. That fairy tale ended the night we entered the elevator of my apartment building and indulged in a passionate embrace, and I staggered out six floors later with my own blood running down my chest and his teeth marks in my throat.

If it hadn't been for Bibi, who came along moments later, chances are good I would have bled to death. It took thirty-six stitches to repair the damage. The doctor who worked on me in the emergency room told me later he had never seen anyone lose so much blood and still wake up alive.

I don't forget what happened in San Francisco. I can't forget. Having firsthand experience of vampires has opened up a whole new realm of possibilities for me, most of which I could have done without. It has also provided a positive side effect.

It's given me a tool to fight them.

As I healed, a strange thing happened. I discovered that Ash's bite had left more than just scars behind. It also left me with the ability to tell the vamps from the humans. I know who they are. But no vampire I've ever encountered has been aware that I can tell he or she is not alive. It's how I took out Nate Lawlor. He literally never saw me coming.

For the first full month after the attack, I was a basket case. Unable to sleep. Starting at the slightest sound. I'm not quite sure when I realized there was a reason for this.

I was jumping at sounds because I heard things more clearly, as if all my senses had become heightened. After that, I became less afraid and paid more attention to my surroundings. My vision was better, too. My reflexes quicker. Not that I had superpowers. The best way I can describe it is to say I literally feel as if I have an edge. My nerves may have settled, but my senses are like a jagged piece of glass. Everything about them is sharper.

At the end of the third month, I sensed my first vampire. I locked myself into my apartment for a solid week; not even Bibi could get me to come out. But I wasn't in there shaking in my shoes, at least not after the first eight hours or so. I was doing what I probably should have done in the first place, downloading and printing out everything I could find on the subject of vampires. By the time the week was out, I knew what I was going to do: I was going to spend the rest of my life destroying them.

Not just any vampires. With occasional exceptions, I'm not all that interested in the rank and file. It's the ones at the top of the food chain that interest me. They're the ones who feast on human blood. Encounter one of these guys and you pretty much have three choices: end up dead, undead, or a human mind-slave—a vampire's drone.

Sometimes, as a reward for services rendered, a high-level vamp will give a lower-level one permission to feed on humans, as a sort of twisted reward. The best I can figure, that's what the deal was with Nate Lawlor. It's the reason I went after him the way I did. I could tell he was looking to feed, and that his timeline was short. If I hadn't offered him the possibility of my own blood, I would have had to live with somebody else's on my conscience.

I took a few turns around the room, my feet silent on the carpet, as I let the questions that had driven me to my place of refuge stream through my mind. Though my personal weapon of choice for offing vampires is silver, beheading also has a long history as a method of vampire destruction, particularly among vampires.

The thing is, vampires don't do away with each other very often. They prefer preying on things with fresh, warm blood to preying on their own kind. In those rare instances when a vampire does decide to take out another vamp, they tend to choose dramatic means. Leaving a decapitated body behind sends a pretty unmistakable warning.

So was the body in the Lipstyx parking lot a vampire, or wasn't it? If it was, who was being warned, and why?

I let my feet carry me to the wall directly opposite my desk, then paused. Mounted in the center is an enormous corkboard. You know those TV shows where the cops create a situation board to help them track what's happening in a case? Well, they're not the only ones. I was always good at solving puzzles. Now I do it for my own personal crusade instead of fun.

Like everything else about this room, I designed the situation board myself. It has a tray at the bottom, just like a schoolroom chalkboard. Instead of chalk and erasers, however, mine holds pushpins, red; permanent-ink pens, black; pads of sticky notes, yellow; and three-by-five cards, white, unlined.

I plucked the top three-by-five card from the stack, uncapped a pen with my teeth, and began to write, the stink of the permanent ink sharp in my nostrils. When I was finished I stuck the card, which now read *Headless Body, Lipstyx,* in the very center of the board. I have to admit it did look sort of stupid up there all by itself. But the thing about puzzles is that they all start out the same. You've got to put that first piece down.

I stepped back from the board and checked my

watch. I had been home for a little more than an hour. Depending on what Carl and his team had found at Lipstyx, the body, with or without its head, just might be on its way in for an autopsy by now. I have a contact in the medical examiner's office, one who works the night shift and would be unlikely to freak at the unusual question I was planning to pose. Blanchard would be able to tell me if the Lipstyx beheading victim was a vampire.

The reason for this is very simple: Blanchard Gray is a vampire himself.

Two

"I'm really counting on you, Nerves," my boss, Al Manelli, said the following morning. That is Al's nickname for me. Short for Nerves of Steel, or, actually, of course, Nerves of Steele. He had given it to me the day I officially became part of his department.

We were in his office, deep in the bowels of the Sher. Like most of the newer casinos, the Sher's nerve center is actually underground. Not much of a view, unless you're assigned to watching the feeds from the security cameras. Al's private office is to one side of what the staff calls "mission control." Though I never give a second thought to them when I work the floor, the sight of all the monitors in mission control always sort of creeps me out. It's all just a little too Big Brother for my taste, but then I actually do have things to hide.

I took the seat Al indicated, facing him across his desk. "What's going on? Are you expecting problems with the Temptation McCoy show?"

"Problems? Only a few." Al dropped into his

chair with a force that made it groan. Al is not a small guy. He's built like a fireplug, and his hands are as big as my head. "First, second, and third, we've got Dru Benson, Temptation McCoy's manager. This guy gives a whole new meaning to the term 'control freak.' "

"In other words," I said, "he's an asshole."

Al grinned like a shark. "You said it, I didn't. I *will* say that this is a guy who really likes to throw his weight around. Benson wanted to bypass us completely, bring in his own security detail, and I don't mean just the standard extra bodyguard. I told Randolph, point-blank, that if he agreed to that, he could have my job."

Randolph Glass, the owner of the casino, is the one who sealed the deal for Temptation McCoy to play the Sher.

"The last thing we need is an extra set of hotshots running around, taking orders from somebody on the outside," Al went on. "What we need is one of our own in Temptation's inner circle, monitoring things from within. Someone we can control."

I leaned back, letting the information filter through my brain. "You think you control me?" I inquired.

Al gave a quick laugh. "See?" he said. "That's exactly what I'm talking about. I knew you would pick that up. I don't have to control you, Candace, and we both know it. Because we both know you're someone I can trust."

"So you don't trust Dru Benson but you do trust me," I said. "Thanks very much. What else?"

"Next we have Act Two of her show."

"Wait a minute," I interrupted. "What happened to Act One?"

Al gave a sigh. I watched as he fiddled with the paperweight on his desk, an ugly gray rock with splotches of pink paint on it. It looks like it's got the measles, I swear to God. His daughter, Talia, made it in preschool, about twelve years ago. She's sixteen now, but Al still keeps it around.

"Act One is a known quantity," he explained. "Temptation McCoy's greatest hits, that sort of stuff. Act Two is a great big black hole of mystery, and it's going to stay that way until opening night. The only way we could get Dru Benson to back down on bringing in his own security was if we backed down on knowing the content of Act Two ahead of time. We know the technical details, music, light cues, that sort of stuff. But as to what will actually take place on stage . . ."

He let his voice trail off. This was not good. It was not good at all. In addition to being just plain weird, it's also just plain stupid from a security standpoint. You can't cover your bases if you don't even know where they are.

"Will I have access to rehearsals?" I asked.

"For Act One, yes," Al replied. "For Act Two, no. You've probably seen the publicity that's gone out." He stopped manhandling the paperweight and pushed a glossy flyer across the top of his desk. It touted a show that would appeal to Temptation's loyal fans; at the same time, it promised to reveal a whole new dimension to the star.

"Please tell me she's not planning to take her clothes off."

Al gave a snort. "This is Vegas, so who knows?"

I considered the matter for a moment, rolling possibilities over in my mind.

"You think maybe Dru Benson is deliberately setting us up to take some sort of fall?"

Al blew out a frustrated breath. "That's just the trouble. I don't know. My gut tells me all this secrecy stuff is just a power play. Tit for tat, a way for Dru Benson to get back at Randolph for making him back down on the extra security stuff."

"He doesn't like the terms, then why doesn't he just go somewhere else?" I asked.

"Don't let Randolph hear you ask that question," Al said with the glimmer of a grim smile. "It's disloyal. Everybody knows the Sher's the hottest spot in town. You want my read, it was Temptation's call. She wanted to be the first to headline at the newest theater on the Strip, to set the standard, not follow one. Randolph wants her for essentially the same reason: She's hot and she's never played Vegas before."

"So the stakes are high for everyone," I said.

"Exactly," Al nodded. "Everybody's ass is on the line here, starting from the top and moving right on down the line."

"But no pressure or anything, right?"

Al snorted. "I mean it, Candace. Dru Benson's going to watch you like a hawk. He's a real Svengali type. Been with Temptation since the very beginning. Hardly ever lets her out of his sight. It's your job to watch her. You can be damn certain he's going to be there, watching you."

"So who gives the orders?" I asked.

"Depends on the circumstances," Al said, immediately understanding the ramifications of my question. I was Al's employee, and through him, Randolph's. But what was best for the Sher and what the star wanted might not always coincide.

"You'll be joining their team. You play by their rules, unless you feel your ability to protect Ms. McCoy is being compromised. That's the bottom line. You're there to assure her safety. That's what they wanted, so that's what they got. I know you can hold your own, but feel free to kick it back to me if things get dicey. Way I figure it, I've got nothing to lose. I've already pissed Dru Benson off."

"So when do I start?" I asked.

"Tonight," Al said. He slid open his top desk drawer, withdrew an envelope, and pushed it across the desk. "Randolph's hosting a welcome party up in his penthouse. He wants you to attend. He thought a social engagement would be a good, neutral place to perform the introductions. After that, you'll be on Temptation detail, full-time. You're assigned to her for the duration of her stay in Vegas. No more working the floor."

"My feet thank you," I said. I took the envelope, opened it. Inside was a voucher good for any goods or services provided at the Scheherazade. In any amount. "Wow!" I said. "What's this for?"

"Personally, I would consider it hazard pay," Al said with a somewhat sour smile. "You've just become part of Temptation McCoy's entourage. It may take you out in public a little more than usual. Randolph thought you might need a few things. You know, in the wardrobe department."

I considered feeling insulted, decided against it. The truth is Randolph was right. My wardrobe tends to lean toward the strictly functional.

"So what you're trying to tell me," I said, not bothering to hold back the grin that was slowly working its way across my face, "is that, as part of my new assignment, I am actually *required* to shop?"

"It's in the job description," Al said, his expression serious. "Right below busting the chops of any unknown individual who tries to get too close to Temptation McCoy. Randolph will foot the bill, for the wardrobe I mean, as long as you do your shopping at the Scheherazade. Anything you need outside the Sher, you're on your own."

"I can live with that arrangement," I said.

"I thought you might." Al stood up, signaling an end to the meeting. "So, I'll see you tonight. Nine o'clock."

"Miriam can spare you?" I asked as I moved toward the door. Miriam is Al's wife.

"Yeah," he said. "She's hosting some cooking gadget thing tonight. Don't ask me what. I just hope it doesn't involve too many knives."

"See you tonight, then," I said. I pulled the office door open, stepped through it into mission control. Before Al closed the door behind me, I had my cell out of my pocket and was punching buttons. If I was going shopping for high-class girl stuff, I definitely wanted reinforcements. That meant Bibi.

Need U, I text-messaged. *Must shop. Now.*

"Well that was fun," Bibi said, several hours later. "I am so psyched about the bronze."

"That's because you don't have to wear it," I said, a little glumly. "It has sparkly things on the shoulders."

Bibi gave an elaborate sigh. We were having lunch at my favorite of the casual restaurants at the Sher, one that overlooks a portion of the casino floor. I spotted Marlene, who had switched to days. When she saw the enormous pile of bags around our table, she grinned and flashed me two thumbs-up.

"Candace," Bibi said in a tone of exaggerated patience. "We've been over this before. Sparkly is feminine. Sparkly is good. You have to learn to let your feminine side run wild every once in a while."

"My feminine side ran wild in San Francisco," I said. "I ended up with teeth marks in my throat."

Bibi shuddered. "You don't have to remind me," she said. "I'm the one who found you, if you'll recall."

"Only vaguely," I said. "I was trying not to bleed to death at the time."

We both fell silent. I took another bite of my salad. Bibi sipped a diet soda. "Speaking of San Francisco, how are things on the dream front? Still tapering off?"

I gave a nod.

In addition to my newfound ability to detect vampires, there was one other lasting side effect of the attack in San Francisco. Dreams of Ash and me together. I had them almost every night. Sometimes I dreamed of the time when we were first together, before I knew he was a vampire. Other nights I dreamed of the time after, when I stayed with him even knowing what he was.

Regardless of when they take place, however, all the dreams feature one important element: Ash and I make love. In the cold light of day, my feelings for Ash are incredibly complex. At night, they're simple. All I want is to be in his arms.

Lately, however, the dreams had begun to taper off, so much so that, at long last, I thought I might be getting over him.

Bibi took a breath, as if to ask a follow-up question.

"No more talking about me," I said. "How's it going with you and Randolph?"

Bibi lifted one slender shoulder. "When we're with each other things are great, but he's a busy guy."

In addition to owning the Sher, Randolph Glass happens to be married. His wife spends most of her time on the East Coast. It doesn't take much to understand why Randolph fell for Bibi. She is absolutely gorgeous. Tall, dark, and slender, with a dancer's tight muscular build. I think her legs actually begin right beneath her cheekbones. Me, I pretty much blend right in, a fact of life that used to piss me off but now suits me just fine. Medium build and height. Brown hair, brown eyes.

"You'll be at the party tonight, right?" I inquired.

Since Randolph's wife is usually back East, when Randolph entertains in Vegas Bibi is often at his side.

"Mmmm." Bibi nodded. "I'm really looking forward to it. This is a big deal for me, opening for Temptation McCoy. The whole opening number is built around my solo."

"So what do you think of Ms. McCoy?" I asked.

Bibi's eyebrows rose. "I haven't met her yet. I don't go much for the sexy little girl act myself, but the audiences love her, that's for sure."

"I guess her being here is really important to Randolph."

"Being the first to bring Temptation McCoy to Vegas is a very big deal, Candace. Of course it means a lot to him. He's got huge investments riding on this." She gave me a sly grin. "At least we know Sher security won't let him down."

"I'm glad to hear that," I said. "You're sure I have to wear the bronze?"

"Of course I'm sure," Bibi said. "You'll be gorgeous, but if you don't stop worrying so much, you'll give yourself wrinkles and then you'll need Botox."

"Now *that's* scary," I said.

"You're telling me. Go home. Take a bubble bath. Think calm thoughts. I'll see you tonight."

I stood up, carefully maneuvering my chair around the pile of bags. Out of the corner of my eye I saw Bibi's feet moving out of view.

"Where do you think you're going?" I asked. "Get back here. The least you can do is help me carry some of these. You picked most of them out."

I hefted the bag closest to me. The shoe box inside it slid out onto the floor.

Bibi's eyes widened. "And ruin my perfect exit?" she asked. "I think you have me confused with somebody else."

"There's no one even remotely like you, and you know it," I said as I knelt down.

She gave me a megawatt smile. "You say the sweetest things sometimes, Candace Steele," she said.

I was still struggling with the shoe box as she sauntered off.

Three

Several hours later, I was strolling through the doors of the Scheherazade, all dressed up with someplace to go. It was kind of a kick, to tell you the truth. I might be any other tourist out for a night on the town. And Bibi had been right, the bronze dress was the perfect choice.

Walking into the Sher is like walking into a puzzle box. You begin by sinking into a lush, heavily patterned carpet, as if, simply by entering the front door, you've embarked upon a magic carpet ride. Once inside, the casino seems to swoop off in several directions at once. Most of the walls in the Sher are curved. Sort of a Hollywood version of a sultan's palace, amped up for Vegas. Each room has its own signature color, all of them rich jewel tones. Carefully draped fabric continues the illusion of opulence. In fact, they help camouflage high-tech elements like security cameras and temperature control devices.

The main body of the casino is a single story, flanked by curving towers on either side. The towers house other public amenities like the hotel and the more upscale restaurants, shops, and spas. Randolph's new theater is a great tower in the center of the complex.

Although I work inside it five days a week, every time I step into the Sher I'm always astonished at how much noise a casino puts out. Slot machines beep and clang and flash. Humans squeal and curse and shout. The inside of a casino is like the belly of the beast only with really bright lights. Surrounded by games of chance, there's still one thing every person in the room can count on: There will never, ever be a single dull moment.

I was about halfway across the main casino, on my way to the elevators that would take me to Randolph's suite, when I sensed the vampire.

He was playing blackjack, exactly like Nate Lawlor had been just a few months ago. Sadly for all concerned, the new guy did not have Nate's taste in clothes. He was dressed in khaki slacks that looked as though they could use a good washing, topped by a Hawaiian shirt in particularly lurid shades of orange.

I sauntered closer, making a mental note to suggest to Al that he find Janette, the blackjack dealer and a fairly recent hire, a new spot. She had been Nate Lawlor's dealer of choice, too, if memory served. Definitely not good news for the casino. Vampires love to gamble in general, but they're particularly drawn to games with a human element. You don't find many vamps playing the slots. Not enough interaction with a warm body whose mind they just might be able to control.

Though no vampire I've ever encountered can actually *read* a human mind, most are very adept at the power of suggestion. Vamps even have a term for this ability. They call it "establishing rapport." In its most dangerous incarnation, rapport is what enables vampires to first select, and then overcome, their victims. More often, however, rapport gets used for mundane things like cheating or stealing, encouraging humans to make fools of themselves.

Officially, I could stroll right on past this particular vampire and not feel guilty about it. I had been relieved of my regular duties while assigned to Temptation McCoy. But I didn't think it was going to take much time to roust this guy. I figured it was the least I could do for Randolph Glass. Payback for my new wardrobe.

I glanced quickly in the mirror behind the bar. I had my hair up, a choice I don't make very often. The plastic surgeon who had worked on me following Ash's attack was a genius, but he couldn't get rid of all the scars. To camouflage them I added a tattoo: a small black cross. The symbolism appeals to me. Usually the tattoo is covered by my hair, or by the halter top of my *I Dream of Jeannie* uniform. But with this dress both my neck and my tattoo were exposed.

I reached the table, slid in beside the vamp, and flashed Janette a quick smile.

"I know I can't play yet," I gushed, trying to send the message that she should treat me like a tourist. Preferably, a clueless one. "But I—" I gave a quick, slightly embarrassed giggle. "I just love to watch."

I switched my attention to the vamp, gazing up at him through lashes that had a tendency to flutter. The expression on his face was almost comical, hovering between flattered and annoyed.

"You're winning, aren't you?" I breathed seductively as I leaned closer. The dress wasn't really designed to show off cleavage. But it was thin. I settled for pressing my breasts against his arm. "Don't even try to deny it. I can always tell. And now I've broken your concentration. Please say you'll forgive me."

I gave a little wriggle, moving my breasts against him, then eased back and reached up, as if to tuck up a stray curl that had tumbled down. He never even noticed where my hand went. His eyes were glued to my chest—and they say women can't resist glancing at a guy's crotch. The only guys I've ever encountered who won't look at a woman's nipples are the ones who don't care about boobs anyhow.

Slowly, I eased one of the thin wands of silver I almost always wear in my hair out and into my palm. Then I dropped my hand back down to my side.

"Sure, I'll forgive you, on one condition," he said, and I added halitosis to his list of sins.

I smiled and leaned in a little closer. "What's that?"

"You gotta stick around."

"I think I can manage that," I said. I took a single step that had me right up against him, insinuated my arm around his waist, snuggling in close.

"Oh, for Chrissake," the guy across the table suddenly exploded. "You playing here or pickin' up broads?"

The vamp opened his mouth. Before he could respond, I ran the tip of silver along the unprotected bare skin on the inside of his arm. It really didn't do any more than scratch him, but that was enough. Any contact with silver that breaks the skin is painful for a vampire. Silver is a purifier, restoring the body to what it should be by rights. It doesn't take much, even if the goal is to finish a vamp off. All you need to do is disrupt the body's integrity. You don't even have to hit the heart. A couple of inches usually does the trick. Not that this was what I had in mind this night.

With an oath, the vamp scrambled back. "You stupid little bitch," he said. "What did you do that for?"

"I don't know what you mean," I said, letting my eyes go wide. If I'm really on a roll, I can muster up tears, but this guy was hardly worth the effort. Besides, I was on sort of a deadline. "What are you talking about? What's wrong?"

He held one hand against the place where I had scratched him. Between his fingers, I could see the way the skin had gone dead white. Any minute now, if I was lucky, it would split and start to flake off in great big pieces. It all depended on how long he'd been not-alive. Whatever happened, he was going to have a reaction that he would have a hard time explaining in public.

"Something I can help you with, sir?" a new voice inquired. The cavalry had arrived in the form of Sher security. I could see the vampire waver, torn between a desire to make trouble for me and avoid it for himself. Self-preservation won out in the end. In my experience, it usually does.

"No. No, thank you," he said. "I'm just . . . I don't feel very well." Still clutching his arm, he backed away from the blackjack table then turned and scurried for the exit.

"Oh, for crying out loud," the guy who had spoken earlier said in disgust. "I knew there was something funny about that guy. He didn't even cash out."

Even when I'm not on the clock, sometimes I really love my job.

"It's about time, Blanchard," I said, several minutes later. I was in the elevator, on my way to Randolph's penthouse. No sooner had I stepped inside than my cell phone began to warble. The caller ID read *Gray Skies.* Gray for Blanchard Gray, my contact at the medical examiner's office.

"Where the hell have you been?" I said. "I called you hours ago! Is the headless body a vampire or not?"

"Candace, an-gel," Blanchard's fluty voice sounded in my ear. "Lovely to talk to you, too. Always *such* a pleasure to hear your voice. I'm fine, by the way. Thanks so much for asking."

"I'm very happy to hear that, Blanchard," I said, with a mental sigh. I watched as the floors ticked off, the numbers higher and higher. "You know how I worry about your health."

He made a rude sound.

"I'm in an elevator and I have to get off in about ten more floors," I continued. "I'm sorry to sound impatient, but my time is not my own. If you could just answer my question, I would really appreciate it."

"Well, of course I'll answer," Blanchard said, his tone aggrieved. "Why else would I call? My dear, your instincts have not failed you. The newest resident of my humble work establishment definitely plays for our side."

"Your side, you mean," I said. "I'm still breathing, in case you've forgotten."

He gave a trill of laughter, as if I had actually

said something funny. "My dear," he said, "not very likely."

"Did you recognize him?" I asked, my eyes still on the flashing floor numbers. "Was he a local guy?"

"Negative," Blanchard said. "There was no ID so, officially, he's a John Doe."

"Anything else?"

"Nothing definite," Blanchard admitted, his tone sliding over into troubled. Instantly, my radar went on full alert.

"You want to get together?" I proposed. Blanchard and I don't meet face-to-face all that often, but we've been working together awhile now. I know him pretty well. Well enough to know that if he was sounding worried, something was up. A thing he wouldn't want to discuss over the phone. "What time do you get off?" I asked.

"Honestly, Candace. That's a tad personal, don't you think?" he asked in his usual tone. "I get off *work* about one-thirty. That's a.m., dearie."

"Thanks for the reminder," I said, my tone dry.

I suggested a location. He counterproposed. We settled on a third choice and I hung up. No sooner had I set the phone on vibrate and slipped it back into my bag than the elevator pinged for the final time and the doors slid open to reveal Randolph Glass's penthouse.

Randolph's personal suite has a panoramic view

of the city. In front of me was a great wall of glass. The space is completely unbroken, supported by an elaborate system of trusses above. There isn't so much as a single wall. The first time Bibi brought me up here, I took one step out of the elevator, then stepped right back in again, all my instincts screaming that my foot should be dangling over empty air. It takes some getting used to. After that, it's flat-out gorgeous.

I spotted Al standing over by one of the food tables. He grunted a greeting, and I helped myself to a small plate of hors d'oeuvres, accepted a glass of sparkling mineral water from a waiter with a tray, then took Al by the arm and steered him to a location where we would have an unobstructed view of guests as they entered the penthouse.

Off to my right, I could see Randolph and Bibi working the room. Like Al, and pretty much every other guy present, Randolph was wearing the standard-issue tux. Bibi's dress was a long column of burgundy silk. As always, she looked absolutely fabulous.

"What is it about stars?" Al groused. "They think we've got nothing better to do than stand around and wait for them to show?"

"Actually—" I popped a tiny crab puff into my mouth, chewed, and swallowed. "—I think it's even worse than that. They don't think about us at all."

Al plucked a stuffed mushroom off my plate and ate it morosely. "I just wish they would hurry up."

"Candace, there you are. If I may say so, it's delightful to see you out of uniform," Randolph's voice broke in.

Aware of Al's eyes on my face—he knows I'm not entirely wild about the Bibi-Randolph thing—I turned toward the Sher's owner with a smile. Randolph Glass has a face that makes you want to tell him your life story. Pure Iowa farmboy, a grown-up Opie, only with hair. But he has the cold, flat eyes of a shark. Bibi clearly finds the combination sexy. It gives me the creeps. I do my best not to let it show.

"I hope you'll still think so when you get the bill," I said with what I hoped was a professional yet friendly smile. "Either way, you can blame Bibi. She picked it out."

"I told her that dress was perfect for her," Bibi said, tucking her arm through Randolph's.

I watched the way he reached to give her fingers a squeeze even as he shifted his body away, ever so slightly.

"As always, she was right," Randolph replied. "I appreciate you coming tonight, Candace. Al tells me the two of you have discussed the dynamics of our upcoming situation."

"We have," I answered with a nod. "I understand there are a lot of fine lines. I'll do my best to walk them."

"If you have questions or concerns . . ." Randolph let his voice trail off.

Again, I nodded. "I know where to go."

"Good. Very good," Randolph said. "I know I can count on you. That's why I didn't question Al when he suggested you for the job."

"I appreciate the support," I said.

That was the moment I felt it. A faint chill, sliding across the surface of my skin, as if I were standing directly in the flow of a vent and someone had just turned the air conditioner on. Over Randolph's shoulder, I saw the doors to the penthouse elevator slide open. Goose bumps rose along my arms.

Holy Mary, Mother of God, I thought.

Randolph turned. I don't know if some change in my expression tipped him off, or if he had some other way of keeping tabs on the elevator and its occupants. He pivoted smoothly, releasing Bibi's hand to put his on the small of her back as she turned, too.

"Ah," he said. "If you'll excuse us." His pace brisk but not rushed, he and Bibi moved toward the newcomers.

"Finally," Al muttered. "It's about time."

Together, we watched as Temptation McCoy's entourage swept into the penthouse.

"Tell me who I'm seeing here," I said, grateful that it was an entirely reasonable question. The cold was flowing through the room now. If it had had a shape, I was sure it would have looked like great waves of thick, greasy fog. My whole body felt coated with it.

First into the room was a bleached blond male with well-defined muscles, the kind that involved serious gym time.

"That's Lucas Goldfinch," Al said, his low voice for my ears alone. "Been with Temptation several years now. Former president of the fan club, if you can believe that. Very devoted. Also very protective, but that could just be the job."

"Which is?" I asked. I took a sip of the mineral water I realized I was still holding, savoring the liquid as it slid down the back of my suddenly parched throat.

"Personal assistant," Al said. "Also bodyguard."

I watched as Lucas Goldfinch continued on into the space, saw the way his eyes tracked quickly from side to side. He might look like bulked-up eye candy, but he was good at his job. He probably liked the setup. An open floor plan means no corners where someone can hide.

A trio of thin brunettes in different shades of the exact same dress came next.

"Backup singers," Al said shortly. "Don't ask me which is which. I can never keep them straight. I think they might have numbers instead of names."

"Cute," I remarked.

And then, suddenly, there was Temptation McCoy.

I had seen pictures of her, of course. Music videos. Television specials. But never in person and never up close. Even in high heels, she was small. Hair, so fine and pale it was almost white, streamed down her back like an icy waterfall. Her dress was a slide of inky black. The fabric shimmered, even in the slightly dimmed lighting of the penthouse. I watched as she put her hand into Randolph's, smiled up into his face, her manner hesitant, almost shy.

So that's it, I thought. For the first time I really, truly saw what all the fuss was about. Temptation McCoy might play up her sex-kitten body, but inside it was the spirit of an unspoiled child.

I felt the cold start a long, slow seep into my skin. My arms and legs danced with painful pins and needles. I bit down hard on the tip of my tongue.

Randolph said something. At this distance I had no idea what, and I watched Temptation McCoy's face light up. In the next moment, she moved on to shake hands with Bibi, and the final person in the entourage came into view. The cold had settled into my bloodstream now, forcing its way through my veins like a thousand shards of ice.

"That's her manager, Dru Benson," Al said. "They make quite a pair, don't they?"

I nodded. It was all I was capable of.

But Al was right. They did make quite a pair. Dru Benson was tall where Temptation was petite. Dark where she was light. His face had a sort of Hugh Jackman quality to it: handsome but rough-cut. You might feel excited, but you would never feel quite safe with a man who looked like that. He finished shaking hands with Randolph, flashing a set of perfect white teeth, then stepped to where Temptation still stood, chatting with Bibi, and reached for his star's hand, easing it back to slip it into the crook of his arm.

If I hadn't been watching her so closely, I might not have seen it. The way her body jerked, then settled, as he drew her to his side. As if she'd had to fight her first impulse to pull away. Her mouth tightened then smoothed out. I made a strangled sound.

All of a sudden I realized Al was peering down at me, his face wrinkled in concern.

"Nerves," he said, "are you all right?"

I am not all right. I am nowhere near all right and neither are you, I thought. And there was no way in hell I was going to say so. The last thing Al needed was for me to tell him a vampire had just walked into the room. A strong one. Aside from Ash, the strongest I had ever encountered.

That's what all the cold was about. Though it starts from the outside and works its way in, there's a very simple way to describe what happens to me when I sense a vampire. Quite literally, my blood runs cold. I can actually feel it change. Freezing up. Slowing down.

The more intense the cold, the stronger the vampire.

"Smile," Al whispered. "Here they come."

I locked my best smile into place, the one I wear

when I'm finding some human in the casino truly annoying and am doing my best not to show it.

Focus, Candace, I thought. *Focus on the obvious aspects of the here and now.*

"I think all of you but Ms. McCoy have met my head of security, Al Manelli," Randolph said as the group reached us and Randolph began the introductions.

Quickly, professionally, Al shook hands first with Lucas Goldfinch, then Dru Benson, then Temptation McCoy.

"If we're going to be working together, you'll have to call me Temptation," the diva said as she placed her tiny hand into Al's. I could hear the faintest hint of the South in her voice.

According to one of the fanzine articles I read, Temptation McCoy had grown up poor as dirt in rural Arkansas, given her name by a mother who had apparently decided that her daughter would benefit from a daily, lifelong reminder of how she had started out. But Temptation McCoy had defied her mother and the odds. She had grown up gorgeous and turned the name intended to bring her shame into an asset.

"I appreciate the honor, ma'am," Al replied. "But if it's all the same to you, I think I'll stick with Ms. McCoy. I'm pretty sure that's what Mrs. Manelli has in mind."

Temptation McCoy gave a delighted laugh. *Nice job, Al,* I thought.

"Well, aren't you sweet," Temptation said. "But just so you know, I'm going to reserve the right to call you Al."

"And this is Candace Steele, a member of our staff assigned to your security detail, effective first thing tomorrow," Randolph went on.

"I'll be calling you Ms. McCoy, too, if I may," I said.

"I'm so glad you'll be with us," Temptation McCoy said as we shook hands. Her eyes laughed into mine, inviting me to share in some secret joke. Then she tossed a provocative glance in Lucas Goldfinch's direction. "You'll be such a nice change from all this testosterone."

"Happy to be of what assistance I can," I answered.

Temptation shifted aside slightly, and I switched my attention to Lucas Goldfinch. If looks could kill, I would have been reduced to a pile of steaming protoplasm on the floor.

"I appreciate your willingness to let me assist your team," I said, extending my hand.

He took it, the grip tight enough to break bones. "Whatever Temptation wants," he said, in a tone of voice that made it crystal clear that, in this case at least, he wanted just the opposite.

"This is Dru Benson, Ms. McCoy's manager," Randolph finished up.

"You'll probably be seeing a lot of me, too," Dru

confided as we shook hands in our turn. "I'm very hands on."

I'll just bet you are, I thought. A bolt of cold lightning shot straight up my arm. I clenched my back teeth together, to keep them from chattering.

Dru Benson was the vampire.

Four

The rest of the evening was an icy blur. My bones felt brittle, my brain slow, but my heart pounded like a pile driver. My worst nightmare had just strolled in the door, and I didn't have the faintest idea what I was going to do about it.

The introductions complete, Temptation McCoy began to work the room, Randolph and Bibi two steps behind her, Dru Benson never far from her side. They looked like a couple, though I was pretty sure what bound them together wasn't sex, in spite of the way he touched her. A palm to the small of her back, a quick caress down her hair, his fingers curved protectively around one of her arms. It would have been romantic if I hadn't recognized it for what it was: control.

Temptation McCoy was Dru Benson's drone.

He was draining her, probably had been for years. Drinking her blood by inches. Prolonging his pleasure, her pain, humiliation, and fear. Slowly but surely replacing her will with his own. Only the most high-level vampires get to use humans in this way. Drones are the ultimate status symbol. Fresh blood 24/7. Until the human stops putting up any resistance, and the vamp gets bored and finishes the job. Sometimes the controlling vampire does this. Other times the drone gets handed off to lesser vampires as a sort of bonus snack. This is actually the tidiest way to handle things, from the vamps' point of view, as the drone generally ends up torn to pieces and there's no body to dispose of.

The initial meet-and-greet portion of the evening complete, I watched as Bibi and Temptation chatted together. Dru Benson moved a few steps away to form a loose circle with Randolph and a handful of other casino owners. Acting on impulse, I snagged a glass of champagne from a passing tray and moved a little closer.

"Oh, Candace, good," Bibi said as I approached.

"I wondered if you could use one of these," I said with a smile, offering the glass of champagne to Temptation McCoy. "Making nice with total strangers must be thirsty work."

"It very definitely is," she said. "That's so thoughtful of you. If it hadn't already been taken care of, I would tell you, you were hired."

"My pleasure," I said. I handed her the glass of champagne. Her fingers had barely touched the thin stem before I heard Dru Benson's voice.

"Now, Temptation," he said, his voice smooth and parental. "Honey, what have we talked about?"

She made a face. "For heaven's sake, Dru, it's

just a glass of champagne." She rolled her eyes at Bibi and me. "Managers," she mouthed.

He moved to stand beside her, wrapping his fingers around the body of the glass as if to take it from Temptation's grasp. She held on.

"Precisely my point," Dru Benson said. He switched his dark gaze to me, and I felt a spurt of pure adrenaline. The last thing I wanted was to attract his attention or cause trouble for Temptation McCoy. All I had wanted was to get a little closer, see if I could gauge the extent of his power over her.

"There's no way you could have known this, Ms. Steele," he said as he wrapped an arm around Temptation's waist. "But, as a general rule, Ms. McCoy does not drink alcohol at public functions. That's why she's going to give that glass of champagne right back to you." He smiled down into her face. "Aren't you, honey?"

"Of course I am, Dru," Temptation said. Beneath her carefully applied makeup, her face had gone dead white. "Thank you," she said as she extended the glass toward me. "It was a lovely thought."

"I apologize," I said. I took back the glass, hoping my own fingers didn't tremble in the process. I had wondered just how strong his hold over her was. Guess I knew that now. "May I bring you something else, Ms. McCoy? Mineral water, perhaps?"

"That would be delightful," Temptation said. "Thank you so much." She sounded like a Stepford wife.

"If I could just have a moment with Temptation?" Dru Benson said, addressing Bibi.

"Sure," Bibi said. "Of course."

Together, we moved off.

"Well, that was certainly weird," she said. She took the champagne glass from me, and downed a slug as I located a glass of mineral water. "If Randolph tried to pull a thing like that with me, I'd tell him to go fuck himself."

I turned a little, angling myself so that I could see Dru and Temptation over Bibi's shoulder. He had a hold of her elbow now. Leaning in close, speaking to her intently. She kept her eyes on his, her face fixed in the parody of a smile.

"My guess is she would like to do the same thing," I said.

"So what's holding her back?" Bibi snorted. "She's the star."

It was on the tip of my tongue to tell her. Instead, I bit down on it, hard. Bibi was going to be spending a lot of time with Temptation McCoy in the immediate future. Until I could clearly see my course of action when it came to Dru Benson, the best way to keep Bibi safe was to keep the fact that Temptation's manager was a vampire to myself.

The more people who knew what Dru was, the

greater the chance it would leak out. And that would put us all in danger.

I shrugged. "Love can be a complicated thing," I said.

Bibi choked on a sip of champagne. "You think that's love?"

"You tell me," I said. Bibi turned around.

Temptation was smiling up at Dru Benson now. A real smile, this time. Full of warmth and affection. I felt my stomach roil. Temptation's sense of self-preservation clearly urged her to fight Dru's control. But did she also long to surrender to it? Was it possible that she both longed to be free and longed to give him whatever it was he wanted because she loved him?

If Ash hadn't lost control that night in the elevator, if we had stayed together, would I have become like Temptation McCoy?

"You know what, I think I'm going to call it a night," I said.

"Oh, no," Bibi said at once. "You're blowing this champagne thing all out of proportion, Candace. Don't go."

"I've done what I needed to do," I said, with a shake of my head. "And remember, I'm not really here to socialize. You have a good time. I'll see you at rehearsal tomorrow."

"Well, if you're sure," Bibi said reluctantly.

"I'm sure. And you were right about the dress, by the way. It's dynamite."

Bibi smiled. "Sweet dreams," she said.

Nice thought, but not likely, I thought as I stepped away and caught Al's eye. He lifted a hand.

I breathed a sigh of relief as I stepped into the elevator alone, and the doors whispered shut. I closed my eyes, and visions of Dru Benson danced in my head. My eyes sprang open. *Make that altogether out of the question,* I decided.

Given the choice between dreaming of Ash or dreaming of Dru, I would have to go with door number three.

Insomnia.

I cranked the car's heater up to full blast all the way home. If I had ever been happier to see my own front door, I couldn't remember when. Call me cowardly, but what I wanted most was to go inside, run a bath so hot it turned my skin lobster-red, then soak until the cold leached out of my bones.

I pulled into the driveway, switched off the car, then sat for a moment, listening to the engine tick as it cooled down. I love my house. It's just your basic fifties bungalow. Nothing anybody else would go into ecstasies over. But it's mine, and mine alone. With every sheet of drywall and every coat of paint, every bouquet of flowers or picture on the wall, I built a barricade against the past. I had been vulnerable and just plain stupid. No more. Not ever again.

I got out of the car, giving the door a satisfying slam behind me, and moved up the front walk. I unlocked the door, stepped into the entryway, and let the door swing shut as I silently set my purse and keys on the table by the door. I stood for a moment in the dark. Your eyes can deceive you. Mine did. So I prefer to use my other senses when I first get home. Satisfied with the entry, I moved into the main body of the house.

I was halfway into the living room before I felt it. A sucker punch of ice, straight to the gut. I stopped dead in my tracks. Fought to pull just one startled gasp of air down into my lungs. *No, it can't be,* I thought frantically. *He can't be here.*

I'm not certain what I would have done next. Begged or screamed. I never got the chance to find out, because in the next moment, strong hands seized my shoulders, swung me around. And then his lips found mine.

All the cold vanished in an instant. I was burning up now. Burning with a fire I had banked so low I'd actually managed to convince myself it had gone out. Instead, it was going to consume me, blazing from the inside out.

Ash, I thought.

Hunger. Had I ever felt such hunger? A desperate craving that only this touch, these lips, could satisfy. Was it his or was it mine? A thousand fevered images were speeding through my brain. Our bodies moved in the dance of seduction, then joined. Had we already done those things together? Or were these the promises of what was still to come?

His lips left my mouth to roam across my face, his hands busy with the fastening of my dress. I felt air on my bare back, and then his fingers were racing across my skin, leaving trails of fire. My hands fisted in the back of his shirt. I heard him moan, deep in his chest, and made a sound of my own. To this day, I can't tell you if it was a laugh or a sob, denial or a plea for more.

"Candace, Candace," I heard a low voice chant in my ear. A mantra. A prayer. The lips were moving down my throat now. And suddenly I knew that if I let him get that far, if I let his lips touch the place where he had fed on me once before, one of us would simply cease to exist. I had a very bad feeling about which one of us it was.

"Ash," I whispered. I began to twist inside his embrace, desperate to get away now, my instinct for self-preservation finally kicking in. "Ash. Don't. Stop!"

I felt his lips lift, his hands pause. A second instinct flooded through me and I ceased to struggle; I stood perfectly still in the circle of his arms. There are some hunters for whom the struggling of the prey only increases the enjoyment of the hunt. A silence more profound than any I could remember filled the room. Then, gradually, I became aware of a sound I recognized: the frantic beating of just one heart.

"Why on earth would I want to do that?" Ash finally inquired, his tone mild.

I felt a shudder along the entire length of my spine. How many nights had I dreamed of hearing that voice? How many nights had I dreamed of what my own would say if I ever got the chance? *You dirty, rotten, undead sonofabitch,* I thought. *I don't give a damn what you want. We both know what that is, in the end. You showed me that clearly enough.*

"Because it's what *I* want," I said, my tone steady as a rock. *Stay calm. Stay calm. Stay calm,* I was chanting to myself. Stay with what Ash was himself: in control. In spite of the fire he could kindle, he was cold, as cold as ice. I could never afford to let myself forget those things about him. Not even for an instant. Instants added up. I needed every single one of them I could get if I was going to stay alive.

"What did you think was going to happen?" I asked now, my tone mocking. "You would just materialize like some phantom and pick up where you left off? It's been more than a year, Ash. I have a new life. I don't want you anymore. Now let me go."

He jerked back, as if I had struck him. His hands dropped away. Cold flooded back through my veins. I welcomed it even as I fought the impulse to shiver.

"You don't want me," Ash mocked, all the mildness, the gentleness gone from his voice. "Is that what you tell yourself? Would that be before you fall asleep and dream of me inside you, or when you wake up in the morning, weeping because you're not in my arms?"

I felt my temper teeter then start down the slope. My fear went along for the ride. Bad as feeling his teeth in my neck had been, even that paled beside the fear that had walked beside me, more constant than a shadow, ever since that San Francisco night. The fear of Ash inside my head, manipulating me like a puppet. Like Dru Benson and Temptation McCoy. Had Ash sent the dreams? Or had he merely given what was already in my mind a nudge in the direction he wanted it to go? Long-distance rapport.

"You fucking bastard," I said. "Stay out of my mind. Stay out of my life."

"I can't," he said simply. And, suddenly, there it was. A truth so pure it penetrated my anger. A truth so pure not even he could keep it from his voice. One that gave me both fear and hope.

He turned and took a step away, as if our proximity had abruptly grown too close. With quick fingers, I reached behind me to refasten my dress. I felt naked enough.

"I can't escape you, Candace," he said as he

turned back. "Any more than you can escape me. We belong together. I'm yours. You're mine."

Don't listen. Don't believe, I thought. The words were an echo of the first night we had been together. The night I welcomed him into my body and my heart for the very first time. He told me then that I belonged to him. And I welcomed the knowledge, fool that I was.

"That's very sweet," I said. "Is that how you've spent these last few months, reading Hallmark cards in your spare time? You left out two items, Ash. You're dead. I'm alive. I plan to stay that way, just for the record. Not that you paid much attention when I said that the last time."

Not waiting for an answer, I crossed the room, reached for the control panel on the wall, and gave the dial a vicious twist. Instantly, the entire room was flooded in hot, white light. There was not a single corner where anything even vaguely resembling a shadow could hide.

"What are you doing here, Ash?" I demanded as I turned back around. I was feeding my anger with both hands now. The longer I stayed angry, the longer I could put off dealing with what I had just done. What I had just felt.

"You think you can walk back in here and put your hands, your mouth, on me after what you did?"

I could see his eyes now, a thing that almost made me wish I had left the room dark. Ash's eyes are a color I've never seen on any other creature, alive, dead, or undead. A blue so pale they look almost silver. The flash of the sun on water. The beautiful, ice-cold light of the stars.

Those amazing eyes focused on the tattoo on my neck, and his voice became gentle. "Will it do any good if I say that I'm sorry?"

"No."

He laughed then, a sound that always catches me by surprise. It sounds so open, so free, so alive. I had fallen for him, more than a little, the first time I heard that sound.

"God, I've missed you, Candace," he said. "You have no idea how much. You're the only one who resists me. Sometimes I think the reason I love you is because you're the only one who can."

"You don't love me," I said. It was true. It had to be true. "Love is a thing that breathes and grows. You can't do those things. That makes you incapable of love."

He took a step toward me then caught himself. But I saw the way his hands curled to fists at his sides. I might actually have believed I had hurt him, if I still believed he could be hurt.

"All right, Candace," he said. "You say you don't want me. What do you want?"

"I want you out of here," I replied, without a moment's hesitation. "Out of my house, my mind, my life. I want you to walk out that door and not come back. I do not want *you,* Ash, in any way, shape, or form. Is that clear enough?"

Before I could so much as blink, he moved, closing the distance between us to jerk me forward into his arms. His lips descended in a kiss designed to punish, and arouse. Tongue thrusting deep into my mouth, as if to demonstrate how easy it was to get inside me. I felt his teeth scrape against mine. He released me, and I staggered back, one hand rising to protect my throat.

"You want me to go? I'll go," he rapped out. "For now. For tonight. But make no mistake, Candace. I don't give a damn what you tell yourself you do or don't believe. Do or don't want. I know the truth. *You. Are. Mine.* I've come to Vegas for you and I won't leave without you."

He took a step back, a smile twisting those thin, sensuous lips.

"And unlike Mr. Jagger," he said. "I always get what I want. Why don't you try dreaming about that?"

He turned and was gone, and I don't mean out the front door. Damn all vampires and their supernatural tricks. *Damn you, Ash,* I thought. He may have left the room, but he had left me nowhere to run, nowhere to hide. He was untrustworthy. Undead. These things were undeniably true.

So was the fact that he was the one, the only one, who made me feel alive.

Five

San Francisco, a year and a half ago

"Hey, Candace," a voice said. I looked across the room to where Mark Simpson, the proprietor of the Library, my favorite haunt, stood polishing glasses behind a dark-wood bar.

"Hey, Mark," I answered in kind. I slid out of my coat, hung it on the rack near the door. "Cold night. I thought you would be busier."

To my right, a bright fire burned cheerfully behind a wrought-iron screen decorated with fanciful animals. On a couch before it, a young couple sat with their heads together, pints of dark Guinness resting on the coffee table in front of them.

There were a few more people scattered at tables throughout the room, but, for the most part, Mark and I had the place to ourselves.

Occupying the downstairs of a renovated Victorian, the restaurant/pub was informal, inviting, and cozy, particularly on a foggy San Francisco night. As its name suggested, bookshelves, most of them original to the house, lined the walls. Customers borrowed what interested them, then returned the books when they were done. Often, they brought in personal favorites to add to the collection. One young woman had borrowed *Pride and Prejudice*. When she returned it to the shelf, she brought along *Fight Club*.

"I thought so, too," Mark said now, with a rueful shrug. "But it's pretty thick out there tonight. Guess it's just bad enough for people to decide they would rather stay home."

"Can't see to the corner," I concurred, as I made my way toward him. Mark turned to punch the "on" button on an electric teakettle. "You want the usual, right?"

"For now," I nodded.

I wanted my usual location, too, one of a pair of wing-backed chairs tucked to one side of the bar. A low table sat between them. I plunked my always-heavy backpack down on the table, then slid into the chair that faced the room.

"It's cold. You should move closer to the fire," Mark suggested, arranging tea things on a tray.

I shook my head. "The usual spot is fine. Besides, it might get busy later. You never know."

Mark gave a chuckle as the kettle clicked off. "How anyone can be a psych major and an optimist at the same time is beyond me," he remarked with a smile.

A moment later, a teapot, my favorite mug, a

small pitcher of milk, and a plate of oatmeal cookies jostled for position with my backpack on the table. Satisfied with his work, Mark stepped back, tucking the tray under one arm. "You want anything else, just let me know. You eat any dinner?"

I smiled. "Not yet, Mom. I just want to get these ideas down on paper, first. Then, we'll see."

Though he was only a few years older than I was, Mark had a definite tendency to mother, which was interesting considering he had no family ties of any kind. It was one of the first things we discovered we had in common. The "no family" thing, I mean. My mother died when I was six. My father and brother had died together in an automobile accident shortly after I got my B.A.

In another few months, if all went well, I would graduate from Stanford with a Ph.D. in psychology. I had a small one-bedroom apartment in the city with easy access to transit. I took dance classes and worked out at a local dojo to stay in shape. But I had no plants. No pets—not even a goldfish. In short, I lived alone. The closest I came to actual friends were Mark himself, and Bibi Schwartz, who always seemed to show up in whatever dance class I was taking and, in addition to that, lived right down the hall. It was Bibi who first introduced me to Mark and the Library. I liked both, right off.

I settled into my chair, pulled my notebook and

pen from my backpack, propped the notebook on my knees, and began to write.

I worked steadily for an hour or so, drinking tea, munching cookies, while the pub slowly filled up around me. As it turned out, I had been right. Eventually, the fog made people go a little stir crazy and decide they would rather not be trapped at home. By the time I was ready for a break, the Library was humming with activity.

I got up to stretch, then decided I would carry my dishes to the bar. I went around back to set my dirty dishes in the sink full of hot sudsy water. Then, seeing no reason not to, I rolled up my sleeves and started to wash. "I told you so," I said.

Mark, who was pulling a glass of the amber brew San Francisco was known for, made a rude noise.

"There must be a clinical name for that sort of childish remark," he observed. "And what the hell do you think you're doing?"

"My own dishes," I said. "You looked busy enough."

"You're a customer," he said, making shooing motions with his hands. "You belong on the far side of the bar."

"I'm a friend. I can help," I protested with a laugh.

"You cannot," he said. "You want to get me busted by the health department? Their undercover spies are everywhere. You never know when one is going to walk through the door."

At precisely that moment, the front door opened.

"See?" Mark said triumphantly as he gave me a push. "I told you so."

"Um, Mark," I said, my eyes glued to the newcomer. "I really don't think so."

There was no way this guy was an undercover anything, for the simple reason that he could never enter a room without attracting every single female pair of eyes. Considering we were in San Francisco, he was likely to get everybody looking his way.

It was his build I noticed first, but then I have this thing for tall, rangy guys. There's just something about a pair of long, long legs. I always wonder what they'll feel like tangled up with mine. His were encased in a pair of faded jeans that looked as if they'd gotten like that the old-fashioned way—by actually being worn. A pair of battered cowboy boots adorned his feet. An oatmeal-colored cable-knit sweater topped by a brown leather bomber jacket covered a pair of appropriately broad shoulders. It should have been too *GQ* for words, but somehow it wasn't. I think it was the hair, this amazing color, gold sand with dark flecks. Just a shade too long, a little unruly, it kept falling down into his eyes.

He skirted the edge of the room, as if he preferred the more circuitous route to a direct approach. As he neared the place where I had been sitting, that one unruly lock of hair tumbled forward. Impatiently, he gave his head a toss. The next moment, a young couple pushed past him on their way to the bar and gave him a little shove that carried him right into the table that held my research materials. The table rocked. My papers teetered then began to slide toward the floor.

I was around the bar in a flash, just as he muttered an oath and knelt down.

"It's okay. I can do it," I said as I frantically began to gather them up. "Don't bother, honestly. And don't worry about it. It's all my fault. I shouldn't have left them just sitting there."

Way to go, I thought. *Babble like an idiot.*

He rocked back on his heels, brushing at the errant lock of hair with one hand. I looked up into his eyes and I swear to God I felt time stop. His eyes were a blue so pale they looked almost silver. I had come in for tea, oatmeal cookies, and a quiet place to work and ended up gazing at a guy who literally had stars in his eyes.

"I think the fault is mine," he said, his words ever so slightly formal in a way I suddenly discovered I found absolutely charming. "My mother may be right. She always was after me to get a haircut."

"Oh, I don't know," I said, uttering the first words that popped into my head, then blushed. That's when it happened. He smiled. Not a preening, "this is great, she's really into me" sort of smile. Just . . . a smile. Quick and genuine, lighting up his whole face, kindling those already starlit eyes. I could see myself reflected in them. I felt my heart do a long, slow roll.

"I'm Ash," he said.

"Ash," I echoed, as if words of one syllable were all I was capable of.

"Ashford Donahue the Third, to give you the whole sad truth," he went on. "My friends take pity on me and call me Ash. I hope you will, too."

I felt behind me for the chair, sat down in it, trying to ignore the way my knees were beginning to quiver. He slid into the chair on the opposite side of the table.

"I'm Candace Steele," I said. "My friends call me Candace."

He gave a quick laugh. "No reference to sweets allowed, I take it?"

Full points to you, Ashford Donahue III, I thought. I felt myself begin to settle. Yes, he was gorgeous, in a totally unexpected way. But it was nothing to lose my head over.

"Absolutely not," I replied. "The last guy who called me 'Candy' ended up taking an unexpected dip in one of the ponds in Golden Gate Park."

Ash nodded, his expression serious. "Good to know."

All of a sudden I realized I was still clutching my

dissertation notes to my chest. Embarrassed, I loosened my grip and reached for my pack. He moved to hand it to me at precisely the same moment. Our fingers touched. A jolt of pure energy speared straight up my arm. I felt Ash's fingers curl around mine, then tighten. If the room had been a little darker, I was sure I would have been able to see the sparks. He released me and we both sat back, my dissertation papers completely forgotten.

"Please tell me that you felt that," Ash said after a moment.

I stared across the table at him. Who was this guy? Come to think of it, who was I? My reaction to him was totally out of character. Sure, I feel attraction just like everybody else. But it doesn't usually strike me like a bolt of lightning.

"What?"

Ash rubbed a hand across his forehead, as if he was just as surprised as I was.

"Could I possibly buy you a drink, Candace?" he asked. "Or maybe even dinner? The thing is, I . . ." He made an impatient sound. "It can't be helped," he said. "There's no way I can say this without making it sound like the world's worst pickup line. When I touched you just now, I *felt* something. I want to know what. I want to know why."

"There's always static electricity," I said. But my chest felt funny, sort of hot and tight, the way it does when you tell a lie. I had felt something, too.

And though it might involve friction, I knew all too well it was likely to be of an altogether different kind.

"Just say you'll let me buy you dinner," Ash urged now. "There's a great little Italian place, not very far."

"If you're talking about the Trattoria Carnesi," I said, "it's fabulous and I love it."

"Is that a yes?" he asked.

"It's a yes to dinner," I replied.

A yes to a start. Whether or not we had dessert, only time would tell.

Trattoria Carnesi looks exactly like the clichéd Italian restaurant. Wood paneling, candles in those weird bumpy red holders, red-and-white-checked oilcloth tablecloths. With decor like that, the food should be lousy. It's not. It's pretty much to die for. I thought I had been there often enough that I knew what to expect.

I was wrong. That night, with Ash, was like nothing I had ever experienced before, in more ways than one.

"I have an idea," I said as we settled into our table. I was beginning to feel as if I had my balance back. We were just two people, following an attraction. Nothing less, nothing more. And there was most definitely nothing cosmic about that sudden, strong connection. I had just been so focused on my studies I hadn't had much time for guys lately.

The trattoria's owner, Signore Carnesi, showed us to our table himself, beaming at me as if I were his own daughter who had just brought home an unexpected beau. Then he bustled off, promising to return with the perfect bottle of wine, on the house.

"You have an idea?" Ash prompted.

"I do," I nodded. "It's kind of hokey. Just think of it as the perfect counterpart to the world's worst pickup line."

On the far side of the table, Ash shot back: "You're not going to hold that over my head forever, are you?"

"No, not forever," I answered, and was rewarded with that devastating smile.

Conversation paused as our waitress arrived. She handed out menus, deposited a basket of fragrant, crusty bread, then poured a stream of green-gold olive oil into a dipping bowl. She promised to give us a few minutes then hurried off.

Ash opened the menu. "I'm still waiting to hear that idea."

"You've been here before, right?" I asked.

He nodded. Setting the menu on the table, he picked up a slice of bread and dipped it into the oil. Then he held it out toward me. "Open up."

I admit to opening my mouth, but it was to

protest being bossed around. Ash was quicker, though. Before I got out so much as a word, he popped the bread into my mouth. A drop of olive oil settled on my lower lip. Acting on instinct, I licked it off. My tongue encountered his thumb.

Ash went very still, his eyes riveted to where his finger rested against my still-parted lips. The room seemed to telescope down to that small place, the feel of his hand against my mouth. His skin was slightly rough, as if he worked with his hands. I eased my tongue back. If I closed my lips, I would be kissing his thumb. Ash rubbed it across my lower lip, as if determined to make sure no oil remained, then leaned back. I exhaled a long, slow breath I hadn't even known I had been holding in.

I swallowed, suddenly aware of every muscle in my throat. Who was I kidding? I was aware of every muscle, every inch, of my body. All of them screaming for the exact same thing: more of his touch.

Get a grip, Steele, I thought.

"So here's my idea," I said, pleased when my voice came out sounding normal. It was one thing for me to know I had gone from zero to a hundred at just one touch. Letting him know I'd done it was quite another. "I order you my favorite thing on the menu, and you order me yours. That way, we can see how compatible we are."

Ash took this under advisement. "You are absolutely right," he said, after a moment, his expression completely serious. "That is an excellent counterpart to the world's worst pickup line."

He laughed, then. Just like before, I found myself completely captivated by the sound. It was as if something deep inside him, a thing he had forgotten was still there, had broken free, slipped its bonds.

He reached across the table to capture my hand. The energy of his touch was still there, different every time. Slowly, like honey flowing through my veins, I felt the impact of it work its way up the length of my arm. My pulse beat with a visible motion against the inside of my wrist.

"This feels good," he said. "It feels right. I'm glad we did it."

I looked at the way our hands fit together, not quite able to meet his eyes. If I did, I was sure he would see what I felt: desire.

"We haven't done anything, yet," I countered.

His grip tightened. "Look at me, Candace," he said.

I took a breath and met his eyes. They gleamed like polished metal in the candlelight.

"You don't really believe that, do you? You can't believe that."

Fortunately for me, I was spared the need to answer. At precisely that moment Signore Carnesi came back with the wine.

* * *

"You don't have to keep feeding me," I protested some time later as I let a thin slice of prosciutto all but dissolve on my tongue. Throughout the evening, Ash had continued to offer me morsels from his plate, feeding me as if I were a child. "I do have food of my own. It bears a striking resemblance to yours, as a matter of fact."

We had ended up ordering the exact same dish. Pasta all'Amatriciana, a spicy tomato sauce. Deceptively simple and straightforward. Goes down easy then packs a punch.

Ash stretched, as if relaxing. Beneath the table, his leg brushed mine. A long, slow tingle inched its way upward to settle at the junction where my legs met. I crossed them, then wished I hadn't. All I had done was increase the pressure. I took a sip of wine.

"Do you come from San Francisco?" I inquired, trying not to squirm in my chair. A legitimate question on a first date, and not quite as inane as commenting on the weather.

"Born and bred," Ash said with a nod. "You?"

"A little farther inland. San Joaquin Valley."

"That's pretty country."

"If you go for flat as a pancake and hot as hell in the summertime," I said. "Actually it is quite pretty, but I haven't been back there in years."

"Family?" Ash asked.

I shook my head. "None."

"I'm sorry," he said. "That must be tough."

"I'm used to it," I said with a shrug.

He glanced up quickly, eyes on my face. "I'm sorry," he said once more. I could hear the genuine regret in his voice. "I didn't mean to wander into forbidden territory."

"You didn't," I answered, slightly embarrassed now. Wondering if I could make him understand. "It's just . . . I just don't talk about it very much, not right off, anyhow."

"Entirely reasonable," he agreed, then smiled. "What?"

"I guess I expected you to keep pushing me," I admitted. "You know: try to get to the bottom of things and heal my soul."

He was silent for a split second longer than the time allotted in my comfort zone. "That sounds awfully ambitious," he said drily. "Besides, what's the point of pushing you? If there's something you want me to know, you'll tell me when the time is right."

I set my fork down. "I knew it. I knew you were too good to be true," I cried. "You're gay, aren't you? No straight guy I've ever met has said a thing like that and gotten away with it, particularly not on a first date."

"What I am," said Ashford Donahue III, his strange eyes lighting up with mischief, "is full of surprises."

* * *

He walked me home through the fog.

It had gotten even thicker while we ate. I could barely see ten paces in front of me now. Full-bodied and needy, the fog hugged the city like a lover who won't let go. Moisture clung to my eyelashes, beaded the surface of my skin and coat. Most people find it claustrophobic, isolating, but the truth is, I love the fog. Particularly when it's thick like it was that night, it accomplishes two seemingly contradictory things at once. It makes me feel like I'm in another world, and at the same time it heightens each of my senses.

Walking with Ash, I could almost believe that the world was ours to create. That nothing else existed except the space through which we passed. I could feel every single place where his body touched mine. One of his arms was slung casually across my shoulders, pressing me in close to his side. When we had stepped out of the restaurant, I began to shiver in the damp cold. Without a word, Ash had unfastened his jacket, taken one of my arms, and eased it around his body, under his jacket, to keep me warm.

He turned toward me then, so we were chest to chest, the position throwing me ever so slightly off-center, giving me no choice but to lean against him for balance. I felt the way his knee slid between my legs, a move that did absolutely nothing to relieve the pressure that had been building there all night.

He's going to kiss me, I thought. *I just know it.*

I had no intention of stopping him.

But it seemed Ash hadn't been joking when he claimed he was full of surprises. Instead of a kiss, he slowly reached back to where my hand, under his jacket, was tightly gripping the back of his shirt, and guided it gently downward and further around his waist. The pressure between us increased as I leaned forward to accommodate the change in position.

Oh, my lord, I thought.

Ash nudged my fingers into his front pants pocket, then shifted his weight so that we once more stood side by side.

"How far did you say your place was?" he asked.

I swallowed past a suddenly dry throat.

"Not far. Just a few blocks." Assuming I could remember how to walk.

We moved in silence, our hip bones bumping together as we progressed through the streets. I felt Ash in every part of my body now. Inhaled him with every breath I took, a spicy scent of leather and something else I couldn't quite identify. It swarmed through my senses, more heady than the wine. There was no one but him. No one but me. No fixed place in time but only the moments we created, passing through the fog. Had I really only met him a few short hours ago? It felt like forever. A lifetime.

"This is me," I said, several blocks later. We

halted before a nondescript apartment building, practical over scenic, sort of the way I had chosen to live my life. A steep set of steps marched up to the front door. It's a secure building. You can't get in unless you're invited.

I eased my hand out of his pocket, took a couple of steps back, suddenly awkward, aware again of the world around us.

"I had a good time tonight, Ash," I said, my words coming out in a rush. I wanted to say this, before anything else happened, or didn't. "I wasn't sure I would, but I did. So, thanks."

Not the world's most poetic speech, but it got the job done.

Ash gave his head a quick shake. "I should be saying that," he replied. "The thank-you part. I wasn't worried about the rest. I always knew we would have a good time."

I lifted my chin. "I look like a good-time girl, is that what you're saying?"

He gave a quick laugh, reached out, hooked his fingers into the lapel of my coat, and gave a quick tug. I took one step, then two, till I felt our knees bump. Slowly, his fingers traveled to my chin, tilted it up. He lowered his head.

The first time Ash kissed me, I had my eyes wide open.

I kept them focused on his, while, beneath his lips, my mouth warmed, then parted. He eased his tongue inside, the tip playing along the roof of my mouth. My head fell back, accepting, inviting, as his arm came up to support it. I sucked his tongue deep and saw the change come into his eyes. That strange, contradictory alteration, a shine and a haze together, that always signals just one thing: the onset of desire.

He eased his tongue from my mouth to run it across my lips, as if savoring the flavor he discovered there. At long last, I let my eyes drift closed.

"Sweet, so sweet . . . *Candace,*" he murmured against my mouth.

When I opened my eyes again, he was gone.

"Gone? What the hell do you mean, gone?" Bibi demanded the next morning over our weekly Wednesday-morning coffee ritual.

"I mean gone," I said, wincing as I downed a too-big sip of too-hot coffee. "Corporeally unavailable. Not present and accounted for. Vamoosed. Vanished into thin air, though come to think of it, it was actually pretty foggy at the time."

"You're saying he kissed you brainless in the middle of the sidewalk, then just disappeared?" Bibi clarified.

I nodded. "Pretty much."

"That dirty, rotten sonofabitch."

"You better not be making fun of me," I said, eyeing her across the table. "I'm feeling stupid enough."

Bibi was silent for a moment, munching her way through a bite of cranberry-orange scone. I always looked forward to our Wednesday mornings. Bibi and I didn't really start out as friends. Friendship sort of found us. Not long after I moved into the apartment building, we started running into each other all the time. In the elevator in the building. At dance class—dancing is what Bibi does. What I've come to appreciate the most about Bibi is that I know she'll tell me the truth.

"You really want to know what I think?" she inquired now.

"I really want to know what you think," I replied.

"Then here it is: Lighten up. You feel stupid this morning. Totally reasonable. But you had a great time last night. You had a romantic dinner, a fabulous good-night kiss. Then the guy vanishes like a puff of smoke. Kind of a short-term relationship, I admit, but you still got one pretty-close-to-perfect night out of it."

Before I could give that the answer I thought it deserved, she sat up even straighter in her chair, as if somebody behind her had just poked her with a pin.

"Okay, wait a minute," she said, her tone excited, as she waved one arm across the table toward me. "I've got it. He's totally on the relationship cutting edge. You know this whole 'friends with benefits' thing? Well, he's taken it to a whole new level. He's pared it down to dinner and a kiss."

"In other words," I said, "not really friends, and no real benefits."

"Exactly!" Bibi exclaimed.

I think we lasted for a count of three before we both burst out laughing.

"I just wish I didn't always fall for the guys with commitment issues," I said when I stopped laughing. "I admit we met under extremely hokey circumstances, but the bottom line is, I really liked Ash."

"You are not allowed to use the term 'bottom line' when speaking about romance," Bibi said, her tone severe. She frowned. "Back up a minute," she said. "You never said anything about falling for him."

"I haven't," I said quickly. "Fallen for him, that is. I'm just saying it would have been nice to see him more than once."

She narrowed her eyes.

"What did you say he looked like, again?"

"Tall," I answered immediately. "That was the first thing I noticed, in fact. He has that cowboy build I always seem to go for."

"Kinda sandy hair and eyes of a color impossible to describe?" Bibi interrupted.

Now I was the one who sat up a little straighter in my chair.

"How on earth did you know that?" I asked.

She gestured to the window at my back. "I think he's standing right outside. Don't—" She began as I twisted in my chair. Sure enough, Ashford Donahue III was standing on the sidewalk outside the coffee shop.

"Don't what?" I asked as I watched him raise a hand then head for the door.

"Turn around," Bibi said.

I did so, facing her once again.

"No, I mean don't turn around."

"What in the world are you talking about?" I asked.

She put her head down into her hands with a sigh. "I was trying to encourage you not to turn around in the first place," she said. "It's a sure tip-off we've been talking about him."

"Of course we've been talking about him," I said. "He kissed me senseless, then disappeared into thin air."

"I thought you said it was brainless," Bibi corrected.

"That, too," I said. "Obviously."

Ash reached the table. In one hand, he was holding a bunch of wildflowers: columbine, foxglove, black-eyed Susans, the flowers you see in a meadow.

"Candace," he said. "I was hoping I'd see you. Hi."

"Hello, Ash," I said, trying to keep my voice

cool and calm. I have no idea how well I did. I could barely hear myself think over the sudden rush of my blood. My brain said I was absolutely furious with him. My body was remembering what it felt like to have his lips on mine. It made for a confusing combination.

I don't take to confusion very well. I like to understand things. To be well-organized. From across the table, I heard Bibi clear her throat.

"I'm sorry. I'm being rude," I said. "Do you two know each other?"

"I don't believe I've had the pleasure," Ash said. There it was again. That slightly old-fashioned sound.

"Ash, this is my friend Bibi Schwartz. Bibi, Ashford Donahue III."

"Please," he said as he extended one hand to shake Bibi's. "Just Ash."

"Hello," Bibi said, her tone as frank and appraising as her gaze. She stood up. I saw Ash's eyes widen ever so slightly as her height came close to his own. Bibi is tall and slender, then usually adds several inches with heels.

"I have to dash," she went on. "But it's nice to meet you, Ash. Candace was just filling me in on what an interesting evening the two of you shared last night."

She offered a hand. Ash took it, and I watched the way they assessed each other across the handshake. The very firm handshake. If they'd had their elbows on the table, I would have called it arm wrestling. Abruptly, I felt my mood improve. There's just something about knowing somebody else is on your side, no matter what. Now Ash knew it, too. He knew I wasn't alone.

"Candace, I'll see you in the usual," Bibi said. "Thanks for the coffee and scone."

"My pleasure," I said. Which was true. She slung the oversized tote bag that had been hanging on the back of her chair over one shoulder, then strutted off. Ash stayed where he was, standing by the side of the table. I picked up my coffee, took a deliberate sip, decided I would give it a moment before I invited him to sit down. Not quite as big a gesture as leaving someone standing all alone on the sidewalk, but at least it felt as if I were getting a bit of my own back.

"Would you like to join me?" I finally inquired.

"These are for you," Ash said. He held the flowers out as he slid into the seat. Somewhat awkwardly, I took the bouquet. I caught their scent—wild and sweet, faintly spicy.

"They're lovely," I said, telling the absolute truth. I held them to my face and inhaled their fragrance. "Where did you find flowers like these in the middle of the city? Did you grow them yourself?"

"My next-door neighbor," Ash answered with a shake of his head. "But they hang over onto my side of the yard, so . . ."

"You figured they were fair game," I filled in. I set the flowers between us, on the table. "Is that what you thought about me?"

His head gave a little jerk back. He turned it into a brisk nod. "Okay," he said. "I guess I deserved that. Anything else you want to say?"

"To tell you the truth," I answered. "I'm not so sure I want to be talking to you at all."

Ash leaned forward, his eyes on mine. "I made a mistake, Candace," he said. "I shouldn't have ended our evening the way I did. It was thoughtless, and I'm sorry. My only excuse is—" He broke off, closing his eyes for a moment then opening them again. "I got carried away."

"Carried away," I echoed. "By what, space aliens?"

Ash let out a reluctant laugh.

"Actually, I'm afraid it's more basic than that," he said. "Pure desire. I wanted you. I think I wanted you from the first moment I saw you. But I thought, if I pushed things too soon . . ."

"So you thought I would feel better if you just left me standing on the sidewalk?"

He smiled. "By the time that moment rolled around, I'm pretty certain actual thinking was no longer possible. Let's say I was hoping to come off as the mysterious man of your dreams. It seemed better than a lust-crazed maniac. I got about a block away before it hit me. You agree to go out with a total stranger, who leaves you standing on the sidewalk in the middle of a good-night kiss. I wouldn't feel all mysterious and romantic. I would feel . . ."

"Played and pissed off?" I suggested sweetly.

"That was never my intention, Candace," Ash said, his eyes on mine, face intent.

I stared down at the flowers lying between us on the table. Beautiful. Romantic and unexpected—like Ash.

"So where do we go from here?" I asked.

"That depends on you," Ash answered quietly. "I'll walk out the door and promise never to bother you again if that's what you want. I really hope it isn't."

"I think what I want," I said, choosing my words carefully, "is to go slow. To get to know you, Ash. Last night had its romantic moments, I'll give you that. But being left standing on the sidewalk with my eyes closed is just a little too junior high school for me. I didn't enjoy junior high at the time. I sure as hell don't want to live through it again."

"Okay," Ash said at once. "I get that. I can go slow. There's just this one thing."

"What's that?" I asked.

"I'd really like to kiss you again. Would that be moving too fast?"

"Right here in the coffee shop?"

"Right here in the coffee shop."

"Then I guess it would depend on the kind of kiss you have in mind," I said.

Slowly, he leaned across the table and reached to tangle one hand in the blousy shirt I wore over a tight-fitting tee, easing me toward him. He kept his eyes on mine. I could have pulled away if I wanted to. He gave me plenty of opportunity. I didn't, though. Instead, I kept my eyes open until the very instant his lips found mine.

His lips were gentle, yet insistent. Seducing, laying claim. He didn't try to take the kiss too deep, but I felt his desire for it just the same. It was there in the way his lips moved, in the way they didn't. In the tension in his fingers as they gripped the front of my shirt. I had never had anyone want me like this. Enough to have to hold it back.

He had done no more than touch his lips to mine, but when they lifted, my whole body felt the loss.

"How's that for slow?" Ash asked.

"Slow enough, for now," I answered.

His face still just inches from mine, I saw the smile come into his eyes. "Good," he said. "Now when can I see you again?"

"I thought we would try someplace new," Ash said.

We were in his car, a sleek black Mercedes. Not a sportscar. I'm talking one of the big four-door guys that looks like it's just dying to eat up some lonely stretch of road. The first time Ash pulled up to the curb outside my apartment and invited me to get in, I told him I would do it only if he was willing to faithfully swear the trunk did not contain a body or machine guns. In what I was beginning to learn was typical fashion, he just smiled and popped the trunk. It was empty. Not only that, it was spotless.

I don't think it was until I was eye to headlights with the Mercedes that the coin really dropped. Ash had money. A lot of it. Not that he flashed it around. It was more in the way he didn't, in fact. He did what he wanted to do, went where he wanted to go, absolutely certain there was no door he couldn't open. But he never chose a place that made me feel out of my league or uncomfortable. The result: I had just spent the last month being romanced in a way most women only dream about. There was only one thing missing to make it perfect.

He almost never touched me.

Actually, that's not quite right. He did touch me, casually, all the time. Toying with one of my stray curls as we sat together in a darkened movie theater. Capturing my hand as we walked together in Golden Gate Park. The press of his fingers in the small of my back as we steered our way through a crowded restaurant, the gesture intimate, possessive. *You can look, but don't even think about touching. This one's mine.* His kisses were so heady they literally made my head swim.

Every single time we kissed good night—actually, who am I kidding, anytime we kissed at all—I thought, *This night will be the one.* The one he'll ask to come in or invite me back to his place. The night we both end up where it was pretty damn plain we wanted to go. But every single time, he pulled back. If he didn't make a move soon, I was going to jump out of my skin or go out of my mind. Probably, I'd do both.

"What kind of someplace new?" I asked now. "Mark's going to think I don't love him if I don't start showing up a little more often."

Ash downshifted as we approached an intersection. As he lifted his hand from the gear shift, he brushed his fingers lightly over my hand. *There you go, again,* I thought. But even as I thought it, I felt the way his caress lingered on the surface of my skin, then sank deep, slowly working its way throughout my body.

"Mark knows you're still his best customer," Ash remarked. The light turned red just as we got to the crosswalk. Ash braked. "But the Library is better for weekdays, don't you think? We ought to do something special. It's Saturday night."

"Traditional date night," I said lightly. "I suppose it's too late to say that I have other plans?"

Ash cut me a look. "Like what?"

"Washing my hair," I said. "Isn't that what girls are supposed to say?"

Before I knew what he intended, he reached toward me, spearing his fingers through my hair, flexing them against my scalp. I felt the power of it shoot straight down through my groin. I gave a little moan and let my head fall back. Ash shifted in the seat, and brought his lips to mine. Light and teasing, he danced them over my mouth, then across my cheek to nuzzle at my ear.

"You smell good," he murmured. "You always smell so good. Fresh. Alive."

I turned my head and captured his earlobe between my teeth. Bit down not too gently, and felt the hand holding my hair tighten.

"It's just hair products."

He laughed beneath his breath and brought his mouth back to mine. Behind us, a horn sounded. Three quick, impatient taps. Ash lifted his head. I saw the intense glitter of those strange, compelling eyes.

"You've got a green light," I said.

And watched them smile.

The someplace new turned out to be one of those membership-by-invitation-only clubs. It was down on the Berkeley waterfront. Called the Villa, it was a place I had driven by, never guessing it was there. From the outside it looked precisely like the old warehouses around it.

"But surely that's part of the point," Ash said with a smile as I pointed this out. We got out of the car. He handed the keys to a discreetly waiting valet parking attendant then took me by the arm. "If everyone could see it for what it was, it wouldn't be special."

As we approached the building, a single door sprang open on its own, sending a shaft of light spilling out onto the sidewalk.

"Okay, well, that's special," I commented. "Also slightly bizarre."

Ash stopped immediately, an action that brought us both to a halt. "We don't have to do this. We can go someplace else if you like."

"I'm not saying I don't want to go here," I said, already beginning to feel slightly foolish. "I'm just expressing surprise. I wouldn't have figured you for the members-only-club type, Ash."

"I don't know that I am," Ash replied. "What I am," he said slowly, as if thinking it through, "is interested in experiences of all kinds. I've never been here, either, just for the record. I'm a new member. I've sort of been saving it, thinking it might be something we could try out together."

Way to act like a jerk, Candace, I thought. I was standing on the sidewalk next to a guy who had pretty much given me anything I asked for over the past few weeks, and I was dragging my feet about going into a nightclub.

"I'm sorry," I said. "I didn't mean to get all

weirded out. You're right. We should give it a shot."

"If you decide you're not comfortable, we don't have to stay," Ash said.

"Okay," I said. "Thanks."

The single bar of light lay quiet and waiting, an invitation across the dark sidewalk. I took the first step toward it. Ash and I stepped across the threshold together. As silently as it had opened, the door swung shut behind us.

Once past the enclosed entryway, where we checked in and shed our coats, the inside of the Villa lived up to its name. Beyond the bright entry, the interior of the warehouse was atmospheric, dim. It had been completely gutted and a replica of a Roman villa created in the center. In the low light, it wasn't possible to see the entire layout, no doubt precisely what the designers had in mind. Instead, I was left with a series of sensory impressions. The glimmer of soft light from lanterns and sconces. The splash of water from elaborate fountains. The faint smell of earth as if the darkness around us was filled with things that grow.

A slim, dark-haired woman materialized as if from nowhere, the outline of her body clearly visible through the thin fabric of her toga, backlit by the lanterns beyond her.

"Welcome to the Villa," she said in a melodic

voice. "We hope you'll find your stay with us a pleasure. If you'll be so good as to follow me?"

She turned, and I saw the soft sway of her breasts. Beneath the toga she was completely naked. She began to lead us farther into the space, the flow of her garment now revealing, now covering, the shape of her body. Her sandals whispering across the floor. Ash glanced down at me, his expression inquiring. I nodded. We followed.

At first glance, the floor plan of the Villa seemed open, but the farther Ash and I progressed, the more clearly I began to perceive the cleverness of the illusion. Dozens of small rooms fanned out around a central courtyard. Their levels varied, sometimes only by a few steps. Not enough to break up the flow of the space, but enough so that each room would feel like its own world, intimate and private.

Fabric only a little thicker than that of the toga our guide was wearing drifted down from support beams overhead, creating divisions, the illusion of walls. And, like her garment, the fabric both concealed and revealed. No individual room could be directly viewed from any other, but there were tantalizing glimpses as the fabric moved and swayed. Flickers of light. Snatches of sound. Abruptly, I realized I was holding my breath, as if in anticipation.

The entire room was one big come on.

Our guide stopped, stepped aside, and made a welcoming gesture with one arm. Apparently, this was the place. Ash stayed back, allowing me to enter first. I stepped forward into a room that was long and narrow but still managed not to feel confined. A single lantern hung above a low table. Several plush area rugs and a scattering of pillows both plump and small nestled invitingly on the floor. A fountain played gently in the shadows at the back.

"Your meal will arrive in just a moment," our guide said. Then, in a whirl of fabric and honey-colored skin, she was gone.

"Did you know the Romans ate reclining?" Ash asked as he settled to the floor. He reached up, captured my hand, and gave it a little shake, as if to urge me to follow his example. I was still standing, somewhat bemused. Truth to tell, I was right on the edge of my comfort zone. Still, I wanted Ash and Ash wanted this. Now, if only I knew what *this* was.

"I did," I admitted as I sank down beside him. "They stuffed themselves, went away to throw up, then came back for more, as I recall."

To my surprise, and relief, he threw back his head and laughed, then leaned forward to kiss me. Hard.

"That's one of the things I like best about you, Candace," he said. "Everywhere you go, there you are."

"In other words, I'm a smart-mouthed pain in the ass," I said.

Ash smiled. "Sometimes," he acknowledged. He leaned down again, the kiss slow and lingering. His tongue explored the interior of my mouth then played along the contours of my lips, like a kid savoring his first ice cream cone of the summer. Favorite flavor.

"The thing is," he murmured, "I really, really like your mouth."

"It can do all sorts of things," I said, and watched his pale eyes darken. I enjoy being romanced as much as the next girl, but there was nothing that said I couldn't do a little boundary expanding of my own.

"I wonder what you mean by that," Ash said, though we both knew he didn't. Not at all.

I was just deciding what to answer when our meal arrived.

An hour later, I'd gotten over my initial discomfort. The Villa was turning out to be the sort of place where you got out fast, or stuck around and went with the flow. I was sated and happy, sort of drowsily aroused. We had dined on sumptuous finger food, feeding each other. Every bite had meant another touch. When we were finished, a silent waiter had come and taken the eating table away, replacing it with a small round one at the very back of the room. The lantern had been blown out, then hoisted up. The only light now came from a small oil lamp resting on the new table and the soft glow of the lights from the central courtyard.

Ash and I lay sprawled together among the pillows, I on my side with him stretched behind me, the length of his body pressed against mine. With one hand, he supported his head. The other was draped across my body.

If we'd been in my apartment, I would have suggested he have me for dessert. As it was, I stretched my arms above my head, arched my back, and pressed my ass against his crotch. There was nothing that said I couldn't give him a little taste of what he was missing. Ash didn't make a sound. But the arm that lay across me shifted, the fingers found my breast. Instantly, my nipples tightened. Lazily, he moved his thumb across one, sliding back and forth, then plucking as the nipple hardened. I felt a sudden flush of heat.

Your mouth. I want your mouth there, Ash, I thought. Teeth. The liquid gliding of his tongue. I stretched again, thrusting upward toward his hand, my nipples exquisitely sensitive now. From somewhere in the shadows outside our room, I heard what sounded like a gong.

"What's that?" I managed to ask as Ash's fingers continued their lazy explorations. "The signal for the floor show?"

I felt the soft brush of his hair as he bent his head to mine. The tip of his tongue slid along the curve of my ear. Goose bumps rose on the surface of my skin.

"Watch."

A group of toga-clad young women now entered the central courtyard. They tittered together, like a flock of excited birds. In their midst was a single man, well-muscled, stripped bare to the waist, wearing only a loincloth. A length of white cloth was tied around his eyes. A woman I suddenly recognized as the one who seated us led him by the hand. The group looked as if they were about to play a naughty round of blindman's buff.

I opened my mouth to say as much to Ash then closed it on a quick intake of breath. While I had been watching the courtyard, Ash's hand had slipped beneath my shirt. Only the thin fabric of my bra was between my breast and his questing fingers now. He continued to stroke in slow, lazy motions. I felt my breath back up at the base of my throat.

Without warning, the man in the courtyard made a sudden lunge. With a peal of laughter, our guide dropped his hand and danced away. As if that action had provided a signal, soft music began to filter through the air. The high tone of a wooden flute, the soft pounding of a drum. The women linked hands and began to circle around the man in time to the music. With every turn, they came a little closer.

Then the one who had been our guide broke

hands with her neighbor to run her fingertips across the man's shoulders as she passed by. Soon, all the women were reaching out to brush him with their fingers as the circle wove itself, tighter and tighter, around him. One ran a finger across his lips, another, the front of his chest, a third, the tops of his thighs. The stirrings of his cock became plainly visible beneath the thin loincloth.

Ash's hand eased lower. He slid a single finger out from under my shirt, down the length of my skirt-clad belly, straight down through the notch in my thighs. Even as my pulse leaped, I turned to face him, half-intending to voice a protest. We were in public, more or less, after all.

Before I could so much as get a word out, Ash brought his mouth to mine. His teeth pulled gently at my lower lip, urging me to open. The moment I did, his tongue swept inside. I could feel his hand slide beneath my skirt, begin a long, slow glide up the inside of my thighs. Parting them gently, he began to stroke between my legs, moving the silk of my underwear back and forth across my clit. I groaned, openmouthed. The sound seemed to echo around the room, inside my head. Had I really made all those sounds myself? Slowly, through the haze of pleasure, I realized what was happening.

I wasn't the only one who was aroused.

In the rooms around us, other couples were taking advantage of the privacy the Villa provided.

The Romans hadn't just been good at eating. They had been good at orgies, too.

"Ash," I murmured, suddenly uncertain. His eyes, those gorgeous, dangerous eyes, gazed down.

"You feel so good, Candace," he murmured. He slipped a finger inside my underwear, teasing around the edges of the place he'd stroked before, and I felt my whole body arch up toward his touch. "Let me show you how good you feel." Gently, he turned my face until I was facing the courtyard once again. "Feel. Listen. Watch."

I did what he asked. Not just because he asked it, but because it was what I wanted now. His hands on my body. His skin on my skin. It no longer mattered where we were. All that mattered was that Ash finish what he started.

In the courtyard, the women had stopped taking turns. They were touching the man together, in carefully concerted movements. Two stood behind him, one on either side, their hands reaching to glide, open-palmed, across his nipples. I could see the way his skin glistened in the flickering light. The man reached out again, and this time the women let him touch them. Taking turns exchanging kisses. Guiding him, turning his head from side to side. In front of him, the one who had been our guide dropped to her knees and slowly ran her hands up the front of his legs until they reached the loincloth.

I felt Ash hook a finger into my underwear, draw it smoothly down my legs and off. Again, my pelvis arched. Revealing the depth of my need and my desire. Proclaiming more clearly than any words I could have chosen that even the time it took for him to complete this simple act was too long to be away from his touch.

Then his fingers were back, in a deep, firm stroke. I gave a little cry. Ash's fingers were warm and slick, as if, before he'd touched me again, he'd brought them to his mouth. My breath began to come in short, hard gasps as I moved against his hand, rocking, rocking as his fingers worked their magic. I twisted my head from side to side in almost mindless pleasure.

More. Give me more, I thought.

As if he'd read my thoughts, Ash took the next step. He slid his fingers inside me. My whole body spasmed, my legs locking around his hand, urging him deeper. With his other hand, he urged my head back so that his mouth could feast on mine. The kiss ended, he nuzzled at my neck as he began to move his body in the ancient rhythms of need. Thrusting his erection against my rump even as his fingers probed deep inside me. The pad of his hand pressed, hard, against my clit, then released as his fingers eased back out. Each time they did, Ash hesitated just a little longer before pressing in again, until all my consciousness narrowed down to that place where his hand moved, feeding but refusing to satisfy my desire. His teeth nipped against my neck, just a little short of pain.

"Come for me, Candace," I heard him whisper in my ear. "I want to see you come undone."

"Make me," I gasped out.

He took my mouth in a searing kiss, tongue plunging deep even as his fingers surged inside me. I felt them widen, flexing and fluttering against my very center, and exploded. I cried out inside Ash's mouth, my body bowing upward, nerve endings screaming with pleasure, and still he didn't stop. His fingers continued to stroke and delve, sending me to a place I had never been before. A place I hadn't even known existed.

He'd done it. He'd made me come undone.

The crest over, I collapsed back against him. His mouth left mine to roam kisses across my face and I pulled a ragged breath into my throat. Without a word, Ash turned me gently so that I faced the courtyard once more. His fingers no longer inside me, but continuing to stroke my most sensitive place, ever so insistently and softly. Heat coiled, deep in my belly, a tension, a possibility that would not be denied. The man in the courtyard was naked now. The loincloth, long gone in an action I had missed. His eyes, open wide, his body, spread-eagled upon the floor. And the women were everywhere, sampling as if he were a feast. As I watched, the one who had shown us to our room parted her skirts, straddled him, then sank slowly down.

The second orgasm seemed to come from nowhere, swift and dazzling as a lightning strike. Lifting me up, carrying me to a place so intense that pleasure could no longer describe it. A place so elemental that all I could do was feel. And all I felt was desire.

It took a very long time to come back to myself. When I did, I found I was still lying amid the cushions with Ash at my back. His hands brushed gently along my hair, the way you would stroke a sleeping child. I tried to think of what to say and discovered my mind was an absolute blank. I simply didn't have the words to cover it. Maybe if I had walked a little more on the wild side before I met him. . . . Would I have known what to say then?

Somehow I doubted it.

Then Ash surprised me, speaking first.

"I knew it," he murmured. "The first time I saw you, I knew you were the one."

"The one for what?"

He shifted then, easing upward so that I lay flat on my back amid the cushions with him gazing down.

"For me," he said. "The only one."

"You have got to be kidding me," Bibi all but shrieked during the next dance class we shared. "He said that, *did* all that, then wouldn't even come in when you got home?"

Together, we executed a series of high kicks. I seriously considered aiming for her head. "Say that a little louder," I suggested, trying not to pant. "Then the whole world can know."

She spun expertly then landed in a sexy position, hip cocked. I followed suit. We paused, counting time, then executed a series of head rolls. I felt my hair, straining to break free of its ponytail. Until Saturday night, I would have said that my hair was the wildest thing about me. No matter what I do to contain it, it always busts out as if determined to have a life of its own. Now, however, I had to figure it was entitled to come out and play. The rest of me certainly had.

"Sorry," Bibi panted as we continued the series of moves choreographed by our jazz instructor. "I'm just trying to get my mind around it."

"You and me both."

"He really wouldn't come in?" she asked.

I paused as we executed a quick shimmy. "I never even got to the invitation part. Just as we pulled up in front of my apartment, he got some emergency business call on his cell. Some client in Southeast Asia who had to be dealt with right away. He kissed me good night and drove off."

"Huh," Bibi huffed out a breath. "Remind me what he does."

"Imports and exports," I said. "Specializing in antiquities."

"Oh, right," Bibi said. "I remember now. He has the big bucks, right? He's probably money laundering."

"No wonder I spill my guts to you," I said. "You are such a big help."

The dance sequence came to an end. Along with the rest of the class, we moved to one side of the room to towel off.

"Okay, so I'll help," Bibi said as she mopped sweat from her chest. "You want my advice, here it is. You want him. Show him."

"I've been trying," I all but wailed.

Bibi shot me a look. "Then stop it. Stop trying and make the fact that you want him in bed absolutely crystal clear."

"And how would you suggest I do that?" I asked as the instructor fired up the CD player for the next series of steps.

Bibi grinned. "Simple," she said. "Make him an offer he can't refuse."

"Oh, Ash, I'm so sorry," I said into the phone. He was outside my building, on the intercom. "There's a thing I need to take care of before we can go. Listen, why don't you just come on up? It'll only take a second, but there's no sense you standing out there in the cold. I'll buzz you through."

Depressing the button that released the lock on the building's front door, I hung up the phone. Then I stood still, my hand hovering over the receiver. I half-expected Ash to call back, say he would wait downstairs or in the car, but the phone stayed silent.

So far, so good, I thought. Now if only I didn't lose my nerve or things didn't go horrifically wrong. If Ash took one look at me and headed for the elevator, I was going to feel awfully stupid. Then again, that might not matter. If that was the reaction my plan evoked, I would never be able to face him again anyhow. I had decided to take Bibi's suggestion to heart. Tonight, I would make Ash an offer I sincerely hoped he couldn't refuse: me. I pulled in a breath, and took one last, quick glance at my apartment.

I had no idea what Ash's place looked like. Given what I could gather of his financial situation, I was guessing more opulent than mine. My apartment was a good reflection of my grad-student status: IKEA furnished, except for a few items I kept from the house I once shared with my dad and brother. The result was slightly impersonal though comfortable. At some very basic level, I wanted a home. I just didn't know what kind yet.

I had done my best to set the mood, though. It sounds like a cliché but, as far as I'm concerned, there's no denying the power of candlelight. Rather than go for the candles everywhere effect, I had settled for artful placement. Less obvious, or so I hoped, not to mention easier on the budget. I clustered holders of long tapers together to create pools of light, separated by bands of shadow. I was hoping the whole effect would look inviting and mysterious, rather than like there had been a sudden power outage.

After I dressed the apartment, I dressed myself. I had splurged on a sumptuous silk kimono the color of ripe plums. The sash and lapels were a rich and lustrous gold, so that I really did look like a piece of fruit begging to be opened, its inner riches explored. I pinned my hair up, then gave my head a quick shake. As always, half a dozen curls came tumbling down. I left my face plain. I'm not much for makeup anyway, and I didn't want to look all tarted up. I wanted to look like a woman ready to be loved.

Three quick, decisive knocks—Ash's knuckles against the wood of my door. I felt my pulse kick, anticipation and fear combined. *You can do this, Candace,* I thought. From the moment we met, I had let Ash set the pace. It was time to generate a little momentum of my own. On bare feet, I crossed the room and opened the door.

In the glare of the hall light, Ash's expression was uncertain, as if, even standing outside my apartment door, he was seeking to come up with a good explanation for why he should go back down. I felt my nerves settle on a long, smooth slide. He might be uncertain. I wasn't. I knew the second he understood the reason I had asked for the change in plan. His eyes, those strange and wonderful eyes, blazed so pure a blue it was almost blinding.

"Thanks for coming up," I said, deciding I would simply ignore the inadvertent double entendre. "Come in."

I stepped back, opening the door a little wider. Ash stayed right where he was.

"You're inviting me in," he said.

"I'm inviting you in," I echoed his words, pressing down, hard, on the panic that was trying to claw its way up the back of my throat. Something seemed to be happening, a thing I didn't altogether understand. But I was determined now. If he didn't want me the way I wanted him, he was going to have to say so.

"I'm tired of only seeing you in public places, Ash. I want you here, in my home, in my bed. If that's not what you want, all you have to do is say so. I'm a big girl. I've heard the word 'no' before."

Still, he stayed motionless, as if frozen in place. "You think I don't want you?"

"No, as a matter of fact, I don't," I said. "I think you do want me. So far, it's been on your terms. Tonight, I want it to be on mine."

I leaned forward, reaching through the doorway to capture one of his hands, then stepped back, drawing his arm with me, across the threshold. I felt a shudder pass through his body, and felt sure I'd won.

"I want you, Ash," I said. "I want to feel *you*

come undone. Inside my home. Inside my body. Come be with me tonight."

I gave his arm a little tug, and he was through the door.

The second he was across the threshold, he exploded into action. Whirling, he pulled me to him even as he moved me backward so that my own body closed the door. He pressed me up against it, mouth ravenous on mine. Hands roaming over the silk, then parting it, hands on my breasts.

"More," I panted as his mouth left mine to rain kisses across my face. "I want more, Ash. I want it all."

With frantic fingers, I yanked the jacket back off his shoulders, and felt his arms drop away, heard the sound the leather made as it hit the floor. Then my hands were busy, working the buttons of his shirt. Tugging it up and out of his waistband, then stripping it off. He dropped to his knees, his mouth feasting even as my fingers reveled in the feel of his bare skin. I felt his mouth begin to move down my body. A blade of pure fire shot up through my groin.

"No," I gasped out, my fingers tangling in his hair. "No, Ash. Not yet. I want you inside."

I twisted away and he reached for me. The kimono slid off to pool around my feet. There was nothing but skin underneath. Ash made a low sound. He turned me back toward him. Eyes on mine, he eased me down. He shed his pants in a blur of motion. I saw the man I wanted as much as my next breath naked for the very first time.

"Oh Christ, you're prettier than I am," I said. "It's so unfair."

I watched the laughter and desire tangle in his eyes. He was absolutely gorgeous. And, as always, Ash surprised. His skin was so pale I could see the blue veins running underneath. I'd gone and fallen in love with the marble statue of some long-forgotten god.

Oh, Candace, Candace, Candace, I thought, even as my own eyes closed. Ash's hands and mouth began to work their magic once again. *What have you done?* I had planned an evening of seduction and ended up being seduced myself. I loved him. I was in love.

I felt Ash's knee nudge mine and let my legs fall open. You can scoff at the missionary position all you like, but for me, there's nothing like opening your legs for the very first time. Power and submission all at once, an invitation for everything that is to come.

"You understand, don't you?" Ash whispered, even as I felt the head of his cock press against the opening of my body. I arched upward, urging him deeper. "Look at me, Candace. This is important. I need to know you understand."

I looked up. The expression in Ash's eyes was all but blinding. I gave a sudden sob. As if that was all the answer he needed, he threw his head back, even as his cock surged forward. Never had anyone else gone so deep, so fast, to a place beyond reason. Beyond thought. I moved against him, with him, wanting nothing more than the feel of Ash inside me. Now. Tomorrow. All the tomorrows that were to come.

"Mine," I thought I heard him whisper as our bodies climbed together. "Sweet, sweet Candace. Now and forever, you are mine."

"Yes," I whispered. "Yes."

And then he took me to a place where no more words were possible.

Six

Las Vegas, present

Beside me, on the desk in my office, my cell phone suddenly came to life. Startled out of my reverie, I jumped, my hand flying out and striking Ash's picture in its silver frame, knocking it to the floor. I heard the sharp crack of glass as it hit the corner of the desk on its way down. *Great,* I thought. The phone continued its insistent summons, wailing like an abandoned child. I ignored the picture and snatched the phone up instead.

"What?"

"I think you mean where, don't you?" Blanchard's petulant voice came through the phone. "As in, where the hell are you? The night only has so many hours, you know. I do have a social life. For the record, it does not revolve around Ed's Diner all night."

"Sorry, sorry," I said. I forgot I was supposed to meet Blanchard after the party. *Well, shit,* I thought. Ash had only to show up to throw me off.

"I'm on my way," I told Blanchard. "Stay right where you are."

"Someone is killing my people!" Blanchard wailed a short time later. "You've got to make them stop."

I shoveled a forkful of eggs into my mouth, deciding this was hardly the time to remind the vampire sitting opposite me that killing his people was a particular specialty of mine. The location we had mutually agreed upon, Ed's Diner, was a local dive, greasy spoon all the way, and one of my favorite twenty-four-hour spots. Even the air has grease particles in it. I had ordered breakfast, which always tastes just the same no matter what time of day you order it, as if the same cook is always on the line. Maybe he's a vampire, too.

I swallowed the last of the eggs then took a sip of water. "Tell me what you know."

"Not much," Blanchard said gloomily. He shifted on the vinyl banquette seat, as if suddenly uncomfortable, an action that caused the black leather he was wearing to make those sexy little scrunching sounds. Probably why he chose it, I thought. Though I had to admit, it did look good on him, such a nice contrast to his pale skin and bleached-blond hair. I had met Blanchard during my first week in Vegas. He didn't notice me right away, but then he had a perfectly good excuse. He was too busy fighting for his life at the time.

Before Blanchard—and after the elevator incident with Ash—I had encountered other vamps but always of the low-level kind, the kind I didn't bother with. The vampire making a meal out of the human—who I later discovered was Blanchard—was something else entirely: the kind who feeds on human blood. Seeing another human being treated as food, the way Ash had treated me, flipped some switch deep inside my psyche. I didn't even stop to think. I just ran. Toward the vampire. In my hand, one of the silver chopsticks I had specially made to wear in my hair. Silver is my favorite weapon in my self-proclaimed war against vampires.

I skidded to a stop behind the vamp, tapped him on the shoulder. "Turn around."

He didn't exactly leap to do my bidding. Big surprise. I tried again, thumping him on the back with my empty fist to get his attention.

"I said *turn around,* you undead asshole."

With a snarl, the vamp lifted his head and spun toward me. He let the body drop to the asphalt that lined the alley, limp as a rag. In some sane portion of my mind, I felt regret for the human I didn't know. He had fought so hard, and now he was dying. I was too late to save him, but I could still take care of his murderer. Maybe he would take some comfort in that.

"You have a death wish, pretty girl?" the vampire asked softly.

He was the most disgusting piece of former humanity I had ever seen. Blood completely covered the lower half of his face and stained the front of his snow-white shirt. My guess was he had worn white on purpose. Vampires are big on contrast: Now you're living. Now you're not.

"No," I said. I was in some sort of fugue state now. Fear simply did not exist in the world I inhabited. "I just wanted to look you in the eye when I shared the following news flash."

Disgusting as he was, I thrust my face right up into his, looked him straight in the eye.

"You. Do not. Exist."

Quick as a snake, I slid my hand up between our bodies, the chopstick clenched in a fist, then made one quick jab outward, punching the silver into the very center of the vampire's bloodstained chest. I had time to see his eyes fill with horrible realization before his body shattered into dust. I was left standing in the alley with a motionless corpse at my feet.

Except he wasn't. Even as I knelt down beside him, certain there was nothing I could do, Blanchard threw back his head with a horrible, wrenching gasp. His desperate hands caught my shoulders, dragged me closer, then released me to claw at his neck. The sounds he made were truly terrible, mewling and wet, as he tried to make his body take in air. It refused to cooperate, already understanding what his mind had not yet fathomed.

There are some things you just can't do when you're dead.

"Please," he said, his head twisting from side to side, eyes starting from his head in sheer, unadulterated panic. "Please, I need—"

"You need to feed," I said. I recognized the symptoms. I had read about them in my research. And I had seen them firsthand in an elegant house in the Berkeley Hills.

The thing beside me in that alley wasn't fully a vampire. Not undead. Not yet. He had to feed for that to happen. Only his first taste of blood would make the transformation complete. If this didn't happen . . . Abruptly, my mind shied away from the things I had read. He was still human enough to feel pain, and there would be a lot of it before the end.

"Please," he said again. "Help me. I don't want to die."

As gently as I could, I spoke the truth. I figured he deserved it. "You're already dead."

But even as I said it, I remembered how hard he had fought. Just as hard as I had. If I were kinder, I might have finished things right then and there. But, kneeling beside Blanchard in the alley, I discovered something unexpected. I simply didn't have it in me to do that. Killing vamps who come to embrace their existence, no problem. But I could not end even the compromised existence of someone I had seen fight so very hard to live.

"Listen to me," I said. I reached to take him by the shoulders now, shaking him to make him focus. He didn't have much time left. If he didn't feed soon, he would start to shut down as his brain finally understood that his body had no blood. There are a whole lot of cells in the human body. He would feel the death of every single one.

"There is a way that I can help you, but if I do, you'll become like the one who attacked you. You'll need blood, you'll be a vampire. Do you understand?"

He made a weak, broken sound, like an infant whimpering, but his eyes told me he understood. And he was ready to accept any terms.

"And you'll owe me for this," I added, "for as long as we both exist."

"Anything," he sobbed. "I'll do anything."

I sat back, rolled up my sleeve, and held out my arm. With a cry, he fastened his mouth onto it and began to suck.

That night Blanchard got some version of his life back, and I got a set of eyes and ears in the vampire underground. We don't exactly hang out together. I have no desire to compromise Blanchard's existence, or my own. You could say our time together is strictly "need to know." I tap him only when I can't get the information any other way. He doesn't ask what I do with the information or why I want it. And we never talk about the events of that first night. The thing about a need-to-know basis is that you have to recognize there are some things you don't.

Now he sipped at a cup of strong tea, his expression indignant. "Why didn't you tell me when you called that the victim was a vampire?"

"I wasn't sure," I said honestly. "All I knew was that a decapitated body was found in the Lipstyx parking lot. Has it been identified yet?"

Blanchard shook his head. "No. But word that it's one of us is already out. It didn't come from me. I swear to God," he added quickly.

"I didn't say it did, Blanchard," I said, as patiently as I could. Blanchard is always kind of high-strung, but I had never seen him quite like this. Genuinely nervous.

"Blanchard," I said. "What's going on?"

He fiddled with the silverware on his side of the table. "I don't know. The Community is on edge, kind of"—he gave an expressive shrug—"wired for sound. First Nate Lawlor disappears. Now there's a real live dead body in the Lipstyx parking lot. You know the way things work. We don't do away with our own."

"Did you know Nate Lawlor?" I asked, as casually as I could.

Blanchard shook his head. "Not really. Just around. Not my type, in more ways than one. I'm happy being small-time, but Nate Lawlor had delusions of grandeur. He wanted to play with the big boys."

"You think that's maybe why whatever happened to him happened?" I asked.

There had to have been a better way to phrase that. For the life of me, I couldn't think what it was. But the fact that the Community, which is how the vampires in Vegas refer to themselves, perceived some connection between Nate Lawlor and the headless, nameless body in the Lipstyx parking lot was definitely news to me. There wasn't a connection, as far as I knew. I'd taken Nate Lawlor out myself.

"Maybe," Blanchard said.

"You know," I commented, "you usually have more to say."

He threw up his hands in one of his favorite dramatic gestures. Being undead hasn't put a single crimp in Blanchard's style. Who you are when you were living is who you are when you're undead. There's nothing in the rule book that says you can't be a drama queen and a vampire all at the same time.

"I told you the body in the morgue was one of us. What more do you want?"

"I want to know what's making everyone so nervous," I said truthfully.

Blanchard threw up his hands again. "Well, so would I. Somebody talks, you'll be the first to know. But frankly, dearie, I wouldn't hold my breath."

"Well, I would appreciate anything you can find

out," I said. There was no sense sending him away with his nose out of joint. "Anything happens you think I should know . . ."

I let my voice trail off. He was already sliding from the booth, eager to be gone.

"I know, I know," he said, his voice sarcastic. "I'll use the bat phone."

I paid the tab then headed for my car. I started the engine, pulled out of the parking lot, and turned in the opposite direction from home. I needed to drive, to clear my head, which was suddenly way too full of vampires.

I needed Carl.

Simple as a prayer, the thought slid through my mind, and I knew the truth of it right off. It wasn't just physical, a way to exorcise some of the sexual tension seeing Ash had aroused. I wanted Carl, himself. Wanted him for his direct, no-nonsense approach to just about everything. Wanted him for the fact that Carl was precisely what he seemed: alive.

I pulled up to a red light, rummaged in my bag for my cell phone. The clock on the dashboard informed me it was just after two a.m. In any other town but Vegas, things might be shutting down for the night. In the town that parties 24/7, two a.m. is just about time to get a second wind. I had left Carl's house at about this same time last night.

Given everything that had happened in between, it felt like a lifetime.

I punched the autodial for his number then tucked the phone under my chin as I accelerated through the green light. Generally speaking, I seriously dislike people who phone and drive. They're more of a menace than most vampires I encounter. But even I break my own rules every once in a while.

"It's Candace," I said when Carl picked up. "I happened to be out driving, thought I might head the car in your direction, if that's all right."

"That so?" I heard Carl's deep voice ask. I was pretty sure we both noticed he didn't specify which part of my statement had generated the reply. For the first time in what felt like way too long, my lips curved into a smile.

"But I could just as easily go somewhere else," I said.

"No," Carl answered. "Come on over. I was just thinking about you, as a matter of fact."

"That so?" I asked, and rang off to the sound of his low laughter.

He was waiting for me when I pulled up, opening the front door as I came up the walk, silhouetted from behind by the single light that illuminated the interior of the house. Just before I stepped across the threshold, a car turned the corner, then continued down the street, catching Carl's face in the sweep of its headlights. And in that quick glimpse I saw that I could put aside any hidden fears my need was one-sided. I wasn't the only one with unanswered questions and ghosts to lay to rest.

I stepped into the house. Carl closed the door behind me. Then, in one motion, as if we had rehearsed it, we moved together, straight into each other's arms. Carl's lips were gentle as they roamed across my face then drifted to my mouth. I parted my lips in response to his urgings, welcoming the sweep and play of his tongue, no teeth involved. *Welcome back,* the kiss said. Maybe even, *welcome home.* It ended, and I let my head drift down on his shoulder, nuzzling a little as his fingers ran through my hair.

"I'm glad you called."

I lifted my head, looked into my human lover's eyes, and spoke the truth. "I'm glad you were home."

"You want anything?" Carl Hagen asked.

"Just you," I replied.

He kissed me again, then, more urgently this time. Hand in hand, we moved toward the bedroom. With the streetlight filtering in through the window, we made long, slow love, different from any rhythm we had ever set before. Simple, direct, as uncomplicated and unconditional as it could be between two people who sometimes have things to hide. I felt myself rise up on that sudden crest of pleasure, hurtle over the brink, then begin the long, slide down, all the while aware from the way he moved inside me, from the tension of his back beneath my fingers, that Carl wasn't far behind. And something seemed to open, to blossom deep inside me, a thing I hadn't expected to feel, not on this night nor any other: joy.

Carl slept deeply through the hours of that night, his body curled toward me in sleep, arms wrapped around me, holding me tightly. But, tired as I was, I did not close my eyes. Instead, I listened to my lover's slow and even breathing, felt the warmth of his body and the strength of his arms, and watched the window until the first morning light dazzled through it.

Then, and only then, did I close my eyes.

Seven

"Let me see if I understand you correctly," I said, carefully, the next morning. I was standing on the lip of the stage in the Sher's theater, trying not to let my alarm and my irritation show. "You're denying me access to the backstage areas. Am I getting this right?"

Lucas Goldfinch gave me an unpleasant smile.

Temptation McCoy's first rehearsal wasn't officially scheduled to begin until eleven a.m., but I was in the theater early. My job was to make sure the star was safe. As far as I was concerned, that meant doing my own security check of the theater. Apparently, Temptation's head of security didn't agree.

"I'm telling you that an additional backstage sweep is unnecessary," Lucas Goldfinch replied. *Just like you are,* he said with his eyes. "I conducted my own search, which means no further action is required, by you or anyone else. Temptation likes her privacy." His voice took on an exaggerated Southern politesse. "So if you would just confine yourself to the front of the house areas, I'm sure she would appreciate it."

"And I'm sure Mr. Glass would appreciate it if you would let me do my job."

Lucas took a step closer. We were literally toe to toe. I had only been on the job about five minutes, and already I was involved in a major pissing contest with Temptation's head of security. Some girls have all the luck.

"I'm not here to make sure you can do your job, Ms. Steele," Lucas Goldfinch said. "I'm here to protect Temptation McCoy. If you can't handle the way I do that, that's your problem."

I raised my hands, the way people do when they acknowledge they have lost a fight, took a step back. "Fine. Have it your way," I said.

"I intend to," he said. "You can count on that."

He turned and headed toward backstage. I headed in the opposite direction, toward the middle of the theater.

I wasn't about to count on anything. Math has never been my strongest subject.

A couple of hours later, I had to admit I was impressed. Temptation McCoy worked hard. Not only that, she was a total team player. She might be a star but in rehearsals she insisted on being treated like one of the corps. She arrived dressed simply in dance pants, soft-soled shoes, and a leotard. Her face largely without makeup, her pale hair pulled back in a ponytail, all of which made her look even more like a child.

The rehearsal had started with a dance warm-up that included both Temptation's regular dancers and those who made up the opening act from the Scheherazade. As they all lined up behind Temptation's choreographer, Temptation linked arms with Bibi, tugging her over to stand at her side. They went through the warm-up together, laughing when Temptation got her feet mixed up during a complex sequence and ended up moving in the wrong direction.

Temptation and Bibi made quite a pair. The star's head barely came up to Bibi's shoulder; she was so petite and Bibi so tall. Without makeup, Temptation was pale, almost ethereal. Bibi's angular face doesn't really need makeup to stand out. I could tell from the look in her eyes she was pretty much in heaven, dancing with Temptation McCoy. A fact that made me even more determined not to do anything to spoil the situation for her. This was a big deal for Bibi, a very big deal. She ought to be able to enjoy it without having to hear the word "vampire."

The warm-up ended and the dancers took a break. Temptation and the choreographer walked down the stairs that connected the stage to the auditorium, reviewing the schedule following the break. By the time Temptation's quick conference was over, I was ready. If I couldn't get close to her one way, I would try another.

"Thought maybe you could use this," I said, offering a water bottle I had snagged along the way.

"Well now, that's just what I call sweet of you," Temptation said. I handed the water bottle over, and she took a long, slow drink.

"In a moment, I may be almost human," she said. She took a final swig of water, her eyes watching me as she swallowed. "You're Candace, right?"

"That's right," I said. "Considering all the people you meet, I'm impressed that you remember."

"I'm good with names," Temptation said, with a slight shrug. "It's important to me, I guess. People deserve the courtesy of being remembered, don't you agree?"

"I most certainly do," I said.

"Of course," the star went on with a slight smile, reaching her hands overhead in a stretch, "when you've got a name like mine, remembering other people's names could be considered nothing more than self-defense."

On the surface, she seemed completely relaxed. But I saw the way her eyes kept flicking to the back of the theater to where I knew Dru Benson was. Dru hadn't shown himself much during the warm-up, but it's not as if I needed my eyes to find him.

Again, her eyes cut toward the back of the theater. Whatever she saw there seemed to make up her mind.

"You know what?" she asked suddenly. "I think I'm going to change out of these things. I really worked up a sweat. The last thing I need is to catch a chill. Anybody wants to know where I am, I'm in my dressing room. I wonder . . . will you do something for me, Candace?"

"If I can," I said.

"Just let Dru know where I am. He tends to worry if I'm not in plain sight."

"Will do," I said. The last thing I wanted to do was get close to Dru Benson, but if I could run a little interference for Temptation, buy her even a minute or two away from Dru's direct control . . .

"Thanks," Temptation said. She leaned forward to squeeze my arm, her grip just a little too tight. "You're a doll. I know this isn't quite what you were hired to do, but . . . just a couple of minutes alone."

"I understand," I said. *More than you know.*

"Great. Back in a sec."

I watched as she climbed back on stage then vanished into the wings. I turned around then, toward the back of the theater, and walked straight into Lucas Goldfinch's muscle-bound chest.

Oh, for crying out loud, I thought, taking a step back. This sort or behavior was going to get old real quick. Matter of fact, it already was.

"Where's Temptation?" Lucas barked out. "What did you say to her? Where did she go?"

"She went to her dressing room to change clothes," I replied, working to keep my temper in check. "I was just on my way to inform Mr. Benson, at Ms. McCoy's request."

Lucas's face gave an angry flush. *Don't like it when you're the one taken out of the loop, do you, pal?* Without another word, he brushed past me, hurrying down the aisle. Now my eyes could see the thing my other senses had already told me. Dru Benson was standing right behind him.

"I'm afraid I have to apologize for Lucas," Dru Benson said, with what I'm pretty sure he intended to be a charming and reassuring smile. The cold emanating from him covered me like a second skin. "He's very attached to Temptation. It may make him appear overprotective at times."

This was a man accustomed to women finding him attractive, I reminded myself. Hell, I might have, too, if I hadn't known what he was.

"No apology necessary," I said, with what I hoped was a halfway decent smile of my own. "I'm sure Mr. Goldfinch is just doing his—"

A commotion cut me off. I heard a sharp cry, followed by the sound of raised and angry voices. Without a moment's hesitation, I turned and sprinted toward the stage.

By the time I was taking the rehearsal stairs two at a time, I had my gun out of its holster, arms extended low and in front of me as I made my way into the wings. It was only then that I realized that Lucas Goldfinch's refusal to allow me backstage meant I didn't know which of the backstage dressing rooms belonged to Temptation McCoy.

I settled for the closest one, figuring you wouldn't want the star to have to go far to change her clothes. I heard Lucas's angry voice as I approached.

"I said get down! You try to move again and I swear to God, I'll blow your fucking head off."

Adrenaline sang through my veins. *Go slow, Candace. Go steady,* I chanted to myself. I eased toward the open dressing room door. I could see Lucas Goldfinch now, reflected in the bank of mirrors that lined one wall. He was standing in the far corner of the room, his gun pointed straight down at the head of a man crouched on the floor, wearing what I immediately recognized as a Sher janitor's uniform. Not surprisingly, the man had his hands up, his face turned away. I couldn't see who it was.

"Ms. McCoy? It's Candace Steele," I called out as much for Lucas's benefit as Temptation's. "I'm coming into the room. I am armed."

I stepped all the way into view then braced as Lucas pivoted, the gun pointed directly at me now.

"Lucas, for God's sake," Temptation cried out, her voice a hysterical sob. "Put that gun down. Put it away."

"Like hell, I will," Lucas Goldfinch snarled. "For all I know, she's in on this."

I held my hands over my head, gun pointed toward the ceiling, deliberately disarming myself. "I'm not in on anything," I said. "I'm just here to secure Ms. McCoy."

"Lucas," Dru Benson's voice sliced through the tension in the room. I felt the sheer, cold power of it shoot straight down my spine. "You will follow Temptation's instructions. Put the gun away. *Now.*"

Lucas Goldfinch's jaw clenched. The knuckles on his gun hand gleamed white. One wrong twitch, and he would pull the trigger. He wanted to. I could see it in his eyes. The only thing that wasn't clear was who he wanted to shoot more: Dru Benson or me. Then, with a spasm that looked almost painful, he pulled the gun up and holstered it.

"Ms. Steele, I want you to take Temptation out of here," Dru Benson said.

"No!" Temptation said. "I'm fine. Honestly, I am. It was all a misunderstanding. I'm sure of it. Please, Dru. Let me stay."

"Who is this man? Do you know?" Dru Benson asked me.

"Let's find out." I stepped away from Temptation and moved toward the man in the corner, still crouched on the floor.

"Sir, my name is Candace Steele. I'm with Scheherazade security. I have my gun drawn, and

I'm not going to put it away until I know who you are. I'm going to ask you to turn toward me slowly and identify yourself."

The man on the floor gave what can only be described as a terrified sob. He lowered his hands and turned his head in my direction. I felt relief and dismay flow through me in equal portions. This wasn't some unknown intruder, a rabid fan who had somehow managed to sneak backstage in a God-knows-how-he-acquired-it Sher uniform. It was someone I knew. Someone I liked, who was now in a shitload of trouble.

"Jesus Christ, Charlie." I stepped back and, at long last, holstered my own gun. "What the hell is going on?"

"You know this man?" Dru Benson asked at once. He had come all the way into the room to put a protective arm around Temptation's shoulders. She leaned against him, as if welcoming the support.

"His name is Charlie Johnson," I nodded. "He's a member of the cleaning crew."

"I didn't mean anything by it," Charlie Johnson began, his voice shaking. "An autograph for my granddaughter, that's all. Ever since she heard Ms. McCoy was coming to where I worked, she had her heart set on it."

"But you had to know the dressing room would be off-limits," I said.

"What do you mean off-limits?" Charlie asked, starting to regain his composure. "I clean up here every day, don't I? And I know better than to just barge right in. I knocked on the door. I heard it clear as day. A voice said 'Come in.' So I did."

"Do you remember hearing Mr. Johnson's knock? Did you give permission for someone to enter?" I asked Temptation.

"What difference does that make?" Lucas broke in before Temptation could reply. "This man should be taken away and dealt with. He had no business being backstage. He frightened Ms. McCoy."

"In the regular course of his duties, he does have business here," I said. I knew Charlie Johnson, knew he wouldn't hurt a fly. "Though I agree he shouldn't have been here this morning. Clearly, there's been some sort of communications breakdown."

"I think we would all have to agree it's much more than a communications breakdown," Dru Benson said, his voice a shower of icy calm. "I'm afraid I don't think much of your security measures, Ms. Steele, and I intend to inform Mr. Glass of my concerns as soon as possible."

All of a sudden, I'd had enough. I'd tried to be a team player, and this was where it had gotten me.

"You do that," I said. "And after you inform Mr. Glass of your concerns, I'll voice a few of my own. For example, the way your staff denied me access to areas I should have been permitted to enter. If I had been allowed to make my own sweep of backstage prior to the rehearsal, this whole situation might have been avoided."

A suffocating stillness settled over the room.

"I think," Dru Benson said slowly, "that you had better explain that remark."

"Ask *him* to explain it," I said, jerking my head in Lucas's direction. "He's the one who refused, point-blank, to allow me to perform my own search of the backstage area. You want to look for something more than a communications breakdown, I suggest you start with your own staff, not the staff of the Scheherazade."

"Oh, Lucas," Temptation said. Just three syllables, but every single person in that room could hear the disappointment in her voice.

"It's my job to keep you safe," Lucas pleaded as he turned toward her. "You gave it to me. It's *my* job."

"Then I suggest you do it effectively," Dru cut in, giving Temptation no time to reply. Lucas's eyes jumped to his face, filled with a hatred so pure, no laser beam could have touched it. Guess that settled any question about how Dru and Lucas got along.

"With your permission, Mr. Benson," I said, "I'll escort Mr. Johnson to Mr. Manelli's office."

"Fine," he snapped. "Get him out of here."

"Come on, Charlie," I said, easing him to his feet. "Let's go."

"I didn't mean to cause trouble," Charlie said. "I didn't mean to scare anyone."

"I think we all understand that," I said.

We were almost past her, into the doorway, when Temptation McCoy suddenly spoke up.

"What's your granddaughter's name?" she asked.

Charlie and I stopped, turned around. "Mary Ellen. Her name is Mary Ellen," he replied.

Without another word, Temptation turned toward her dressing table, shrugging off Dru's protective arm. She rummaged in an oversized shoulder bag, came up with a pen and small pad of paper, wrote, tore off the page, and handed it to Charlie.

"You give her that from me," she said.

Charlie Johnson opened his mouth, closed it, then opened it again. "Ma'am," he finally managed to say, "I appreciate it. And I'll tell you this, my granddaughter's gonna be over the moon."

"People make mistakes, Mr. Johnson," Temptation said with a gentle smile. "There's no reason to hold it against them if they make things right."

Together, Charlie and I headed out of the theater.

"Jesus, what a mess," Al said a short time later.

Al and I were alone in his office. The meeting

with Charlie was over and done. Charlie had been relieved of his duties at the Sher but reassigned to one of Randolph's smaller properties. Most guys in Al's position wouldn't have done that much. But a review of the schedule had shown that Charlie was out sick the day his own supervisor had covered the schedule tweaks that would occur during rehearsals for Temptation's show. Yes, Charlie had exercised somewhat poor judgment when he realized Temptation was backstage, but the fact that he was there in the first place wasn't his fault.

"So, other than all this, how's it going?" Al asked.

"Oh, just dandy," I said. *If you overlook the fact that Dru Benson is a vampire.* "If you overlook the fact that Lucas Goldfinch hates my guts. Right this moment, though, it's a toss-up which one of us he would rather turn into his own personal voodoo doll: me or his boss."

"Hey," Al said. "He screwed up. He's in trouble with Benson; he's not going to get any sympathy from me."

"Me, neither," I replied. "But it doesn't exactly make things easier, in either the long or the short run."

Al was silent for a moment, his fingers tapping on the top of his desk. "So what aren't you telling me?"

In terms of time elapsed, Al and I haven't

worked together all that long. But we know each other pretty well, and Al is one of the few humans I know who also knows about vampires. He doesn't make a big deal of it, just says when you've been in Vegas as long as he has, you see everything.

"Nothing," I said now.

Al grunted.

"Nothing I can't handle," I amended, and prayed I was right. It was a calculated risk, but I had decided Bibi wasn't the only one I should be keeping in the dark about Dru Benson's true nature. I wasn't going to tell Al, either. If they knew what he was, there was a good chance that Dru Benson would be able to sense it, and that would greatly decrease their life expectancy.

"I mean it, Al," I said now. "The minute anything changes, you'll be the first to know. Meantime—"

"I know, I know," Al said, with a wave of his hand. "I should leave you alone to do your job. It's just I feel responsible is all."

"I know you do," I said. Another reason not to mention that a powerful vampire had taken up temporary residence at the Scheherazade. If Al thought he was deliberately putting me in major danger, he would do his best to yank me right back out. Then we would have no one keeping an eye on Dru Benson, no one who knew what he was.

He gave me a reluctant smile. "Just watch your back is all. And keep me posted."

"Will do," I nodded. "See you around."

He walked me out of his office. I left him standing in mission control, gazing at the banks of monitors, as if he were going to watch my back himself as I made my way out. Though, frankly, given the way vampires kept cropping up, I had to figure my back was one of my least vulnerable body parts.

Eight

Temptation's rehearsal schedule called for the afternoon to be devoted to the mysterious Act Two. No outsiders allowed. I took the opportunity to take care of some of the business of everyday life. Running errands, grocery shopping, laundry. Even fearless vampire hunters require clean clothes. I made myself my favorite simple dinner of pasta with olive oil, parsley, and just a touch of sautéed garlic, then ate out on the small patio in my backyard with a salad and a glass of cool white wine.

Though the weather in Vegas can get pretty brutal when temperatures rise in the summertime, I like to work in the yard, a legacy from my paternal grandmother. That woman had not just a green thumb but a green hand. I like the old-fashioned flowers the best. Marigolds with fat golden heads. Rainbow snapdragons rising thigh-high. Geraniums in every color I can find. The pots that surround my deck oasis are bold and splashy, bursting with life. Which is, after all, the point. My garden is just like the rest of my personal space in Vegas: a testament to staying alive.

I finished the last of my wine and considered my options. I can't say they filled me with delight. I was assigned to protect a major star, and a major Sher investment, whose handler just happened to be a major vampire. And, as of yesterday, Ash was officially back in my life. Not the way he wanted to be, maybe, but back nevertheless. There was no sense in lying to myself. Sooner or later he would show up again. He had told me as much last night. I had no doubt he meant every word. It was just a matter of time.

Time. That commodity that always seems to run out on the living. And I was wasting mine.

Not only that, I was breaking one of my cardinal personal rules. I was brooding over vampires in what was supposed to be a vampire-free zone. So I headed for the place I should have been doing my thinking: my office. It was time to add a few more items to the situation board.

Ash's name went up first, at the top of the board to the right, followed by Dru Benson's, same position on the opposite side. Then, right below Dru's, I added Temptation's name, and Lucas Goldfinch's.

I paused. Then I put a card with Nate Lawlor's name on it alongside the very first one I had put up, the one for the headless vampire in the Lipstyx parking lot. I knew the two weren't connected, because I'd killed Nate myself, but according to Blanchard, the Community thought there was a connection. And if one of them stumbled onto the truth, I could be in big trouble.

I stepped back for a moment, to survey my handiwork, then winced as something crunched beneath my foot. What the hell? I turned, then knelt. Ash's picture, the one that usually sits on my desk, was on the floor. I had knocked it from the desk when Blanchard called, then neglected to pick it up. Now I had completely smashed the glass in the frame.

Carefully, I picked it up and turned it over on the surface of the desk, shaking the glass out. The silver frame was old, ornate. The image was a sketch executed in charcoal, not a photograph, a gift from Ash in San Francisco. As gently as I could, I pulled the frame away, brushed away the shards of glass, then lifted the paper. Now that Ash's image was facedown I could see something I'd never noticed before. On the back, in the lower-right corner where it would have been hidden by the frame, was a vivid splash of color. Before I could stop it, my hand jerked back, and the paper floated down to rest upon the desk. At first glance, it looked exactly like a drop of blood.

I picked up the paper again, ran a finger over the red spot. *Not blood,* I thought. This wasn't something that had soaked into the paper but something that had been added on top. Beneath my fingertips, the tiny red image was raised ever so slightly, as if it had been embossed. Feeling curious now, I opened the top drawer of my desk, pulled out the magnifying glass that had come with my OED, and focused on the red spot as the image came to life before my eyes.

It was a man with the head of a bird. *Egyptian,* I thought. It even looked vaguely familiar, as if I had seen it somewhere before. This being Vegas, the most likely possibility was probably the Luxor. The bird's face had smooth feathers. The beak was long and curved downward, sort of like a scimitar. I turned on my computer, was about to start looking up Egyptian gods, when—

Whoa, Candace. Slow down and focus, I thought.

Finding out there was something other than Ash's picture on that paper might be a big deal. It might not. Either way, it had nothing to do with what was going down at the Scheherazade. Ash was my personal business. Letting him sidetrack me was a luxury I could not afford. With quick, decisive motions, I put Ash's picture and its frame in the bottom drawer of my desk then swept the broken glass into my wastebasket. The mystery insignia had been in my possession for more than a year, and I hadn't known. It could remain a mystery a little while longer. Discovering the best way to protect Temptation and my friends from Dru Benson, however, was something that could not.

I left the office, moving briskly to my bedroom

to perform a quick change of clothes. Maybe it was time for me to catch a glimpse of a different sort of Vegas nightlife. Sure, I already knew Lipstyx was a topless bar. That didn't mean there wasn't more to it than met the eye.

Nine

Lipstyx lived up to its name when it came to decor. The main dance floor was lit by bands of different colors, radiating out from a central location, timed so that they illuminated in graduated steps, growing larger and brighter, before suddenly going dark. The dancers were in gold cages around the perimeter of the room, suspended above the floor. Each was illuminated by a colored spotlight, matching the brief outfit she wore, assuming you can actually call high heels and a g-string an outfit. Lipstyx was never really going to be my kind of place. Then again, I have spent evenings in worse dives.

There weren't many vampires. In fact, there were none at all. Not so surprising, I suppose. Fortunately for the club's owners, there were plenty of humans willing to fill up any available space. I hadn't realized it when I set out, but tonight was Lipstyx's first night back in business following the discovery of the body in the parking lot.

After a little more than an hour, I was seriously contemplating heading for home. I wasn't really learning anything, and I had an early breakfast date with Bibi the next morning. I began threading my way through the pulsing dance floor in the direction of the entrance, when Lucas Goldfinch walked through the door.

Lucas strode into Lipstyx the same way he had entered Randolph's party, like he was on a security sweep. I felt a bolt of pure electricity shoot through me as his eyes met mine. The hostility in them was palpable, even across a crowded room without much light. Much as I hated to give the appearance of running, sometimes it's better to just get the hell out of Dodge.

Lucas waded into the seething mass of bodies on the dance floor. Instantly, I countered, edging my way toward the perimeter, trying to work my way around him to the door. I was almost there when I felt strong fingers wrap around my arm. Bastard must have doubled back. Instead of jerking me toward him, he pulled me forward, toward the door. The bouncer opened it. I let the momentum carry us all the way outside before I spoke.

"You really want to let go of me," I said, swinging around and jerking my arm out of his grasp.

Lucas's bleached-blond hair all but glowed in the halogen lights that now illuminated the Lipstyx parking lot. Over his shoulder, I could see that the bouncer had gone back inside but literally left his foot in the door. No doubt he had been asked to make sure nothing else too nasty went down in the parking lot.

Lucas's lips curled back in what could only be called a sneer. "Or what?"

"You think I can't take you?" I asked. Though, frankly, I was far from certain of the answer to this question myself. "So nature designed you to pee standing up. Big deal. That just makes your vulnerable parts more obvious."

To my surprise, he gave a quick laugh.

"You really are a total pain in the ass," he remarked with something that sounded almost like affection. He leaned forward, his face right up in mine. "Stay out of my way," he said. "Stay away from Temptation. She's mine."

"Happy to," I replied. "But you have to let me do my job. That's not the same as wanting yours."

He eased back, his eyes considering. "Okay," he said. "All right. But make me look stupid in front of Temptation again, and you'll live to regret it."

"I wasn't the one who made you look stupid the last time around," I snapped.

Then I turned and set off for my car.

The parking lot had been full when I arrived at Lipstyx. As a result, my car was a couple of blocks away. Once away from the glare of the parking lot, the streets were trenches of darkness broken by the occasional streetlight. This was not the usual tourist part of town. I walked briskly, my shoulder bag dangling from one hand, my keys thrust through the fist of the other.

I was about half a block away from where I had parked when I heard it: the sound of footsteps behind me. Too many to identify the number of people clearly but definitely more than one. I fought the impulse to pick up my pace. There's nothing predators like better than to run their prey to ground. Quickly, I judged the number of steps it would take me to reach the closest streetlight. *Ten,* I thought. That's where I would make my stand. I was not going to make a mad dash for the relative safety of my car. Too easy to get forced inside and taken somewhere out of the way.

I reached the pool of light, took one deep breath, then spun around, actually managing to catch them off guard. *They* were half a dozen guys in their late teens. Leather jackets, tight jeans, and T-shirts, like they had just finished watching a community theater production of *West Side Story.* Not truly street tough, I thought. I didn't see any weapons, which wasn't quite the same as knowing they didn't have any. Still, it looked like they figured they could take me on math alone.

"He said you'd turn and fight," the one who faced me said.

Guess that answers that question, I thought. The obvious one. No wonder Lucas Goldfinch had let me walk away. The sonofabitch had set me up. Slowly, easily, I slid the strap of my bag over my head, leaving one hand free. I kept my keys clenched tightly in the fist of the other. The punks were fanning out now. Spacing themselves around me, forming a circle of their own, just outside the circle cast by the streetlight.

"I hope he's going to pay your hospital bill," I said.

The leader smirked. "He also said you had a smart mouth." He made a funny motion with his right arm, and I heard a sound I couldn't quite identify. A moment later, a heavy chain dropped down from his fingers. He had carried it concealed in the sleeve of his jacket.

Well, shit, I thought. If they all had toys like this, I was in very big trouble. I could only hope they didn't all come for me at once. It would be the smart move, but young and cocky doesn't always equal smart.

"I've got more than just a smart mouth, little boy," I said, my voice a sneer. "Why don't you come and show me what you've got?"

He lunged forward on a shout, letting the chain fly out in front of him, a quick and vicious punch of metal. I raised one arm to shelter my face, bent low, and charged. The chain sailed over my head then landed heavily on my back just as I whipped my arm down to let my head connect solidly with the lead guy's stomach. He made a sound like a balloon deflating and went down, hard. The chain slid off my back and I reached for it, yanking back. He hung on, pulling in his turn, and I stumbled forward.

I heard him cry out, felt my ankle turn, had a flash of adrenaline-inspired intuition as I understood the cause. I lifted my foot, and stomped down, hard, a second time, driving the spike heel of my shoe straight down onto his hand. With a scream, the punk let go. The chain was mine.

Instantly, I pivoted away, twisting my wrist to wrap the chain around it and letting the end fly out all at the same time. I felt it connect, the force of it singing up my arm. With a cry, the guy to my right went down. I had a hole now. I danced around the leader, out of range, into the street. The four who remained standing moved together to form a semicircle, facing me. We eyed one another. By now, the leader was on his knees, swearing, cradling his mangled hand against his chest.

"You stupid fucks!" he shouted. "Get in there and finish her off. What the hell are you waiting for?"

I danced backward another couple of steps, dangling the chain in front of me in the street, and heard the squeal of tires as a car rounded the corner, prayed it wasn't Lucas, come to check on his boys. I heard a second squeal as the car jerked to a stop behind me, the opening of a door.

"Hey, Nerves," a raspy voice called out. "You need a ride?"

I turned, tossed the chain behind me to discourage any followers, and dove for the open taxi door.

"Thanks, Doc," I said, several blocks later. The adrenaline rush of the fight was starting to fade, and I could feel what were sure to be bruises. The back of my shirt had holes where the chain had caught and dragged. I was reasonably certain my shoes had blood on them. "Talk about the nick of time."

"What the hell you doin', girl?" Hank "Doc" Watson asked. Doc is one of the legion of Vegas's cabdrivers, not to mention one of the oldest. To hear him tell it, he was driving a cab while I was still in diapers.

"Believe it or not," I said. "I was just trying to go home."

"Not exactly your neighborhood," Doc observed, which was really just another way of rephrasing the same question.

"Not usually," I acknowledged. "No."

"Okay, okay," he said with a chuckle. "I ain't senile yet. I know when I'm being told to back off. Just figured you had a little more sense is all I'm sayin'."

"To tell you the truth, I figured so, too," I said. "Guess I must be slipping."

Doc made a rude sound. "Slippin' my ass," he said. "You don't wanna tell the Doc your problems, that's your choice. Just don't think you're pulling any wool over my eyes."

"There's nothing to tell," I said. "I pissed somebody off. He figures I made him look bad. I figure he brought it on himself. Then he decided to bring in some friends to work on my perspective."

"Chicken-shit thing to do," Doc said as he took the corner at the end of my street, pulled up in front of my house. "Person's got a beef, he ought to be willing to settle things himself. You watch yourself now, Nerves. Some weird shit goes down in this town sometimes."

If you only knew, I thought. Though, frankly, I was glad he didn't. Hank Watson was one of the good guys. If he went to his grave never knowing about the worst that could happen in Vegas, I could die a happy camper. I leaned forward to give him a kiss on the cheek.

"Thanks, Doc. I appreciate the rescue, and the ride."

"Anytime," he said. "Anytime. Not that I want you to start makin' a habit of this."

"That makes two of us," I said. I reached for my purse.

"Oh, now," Doc said, his voice cranky as an old hinge. "What you want to go and insult me for?"

I gave him a second kiss, got out of the taxi, slammed the door. With a wave, Doc pulled away. I started up my front walk. That was the moment I realized I still had my keys clenched in my fist. My car was across town.

Just great, I thought. But it was too late to worry about that now. I could always take another cab back for it in the morning. All I wanted to do was go inside, take a long, hot bath to ease my aching muscles, then sleep and not dream of Ash or anything else.

I unlocked the front door, pushing away memories of the previous night. I'd had a similar plan then, a plan that Ash's appearance had interrupted. *You don't have to worry about that tonight, Candace,* I told myself. Ash was capable of many things. Repeating himself wasn't one of them.

I shoved the door open, stepped into the entry. A wall of scent, a sweet, rich fragrance, engulfed me. I let the door swing shut, then backed up against it, not wanting to go any farther. Afraid to. I knew what that scent was. *Sweet peas,* I thought. My favorite flower. A preference I inherited from my grandmother, now long dead, the one who taught me how to garden. The house had to be full of them for the scent to be so strong. All the colors of the rainbow, everywhere, unless I missed my guess. There was only one other person on earth who knew how I felt about sweet peas.

He wasn't alive, either.

It seems that I had been wrong. Ash did repeat himself. He had done this once before. Then, as now, it was an apology, a way to try to woo me back.

I felt my knees tremble then refuse to hold me up entirely. Slowly, I slid down the length of the door until I was sitting on the floor. My back to my own front door, my face in my hands, I let the fragrance of the flowers swim through my system till I thought I just might drown.

Ash, I thought, unable to help myself. Unable to determine if I even wanted to. *Oh, Ash.*

Ten

San Francisco, a year and a half ago

"What smells so good?" Ash asked. Standing at the stove stirring onions, I felt his arms wrap around me from behind. He lifted me up and off my feet, his lips nuzzling the side of my neck. I gave a squeal. I was so focused on what I was doing, he had taken me completely by surprise.

"Spaghetti sauce, if you're lucky," I said, my voice warm and teasing. "Now put me down."

"When I'm ready," Ash replied. One arm hooked firmly around my waist, he used the other to tilt my head back. His lips took mine in a kiss that made me forget all about the heat of the stove. The only heat in the whole world was the kind we generated together. The kiss over, he released me in a long, slow slide down his body that left me in no doubt whatsoever about the fact that the arousal was mutual.

"I think you may be on fire," he remarked.

With a cry of dismay, I came back to the present.

"Ash, for crying out loud," I said as, just in time, I rescued the onions. "I try to fix a simple meal and look what happens. Out of the kitchen. Right now. Go open a bottle of wine or something. Make yourself useful. Somewhere else."

"I'm useful in the kitchen," he said, his tone mock-injured. But he did step back. He rummaged in one of the drawers, produced a corkscrew. "It's just that my talents are highly specialized."

"You can say that again," I said. I moved to the cutting board to scoop up sliced mushrooms and dumped them in the pan. "Just give me a minute to get this put together. Then you have my full permission to proceed with the demonstration."

"Mmm," Ash said. He strolled out to my tiny dining room in search of the wine rack. I expelled a long, silent sigh.

Over the past weeks, as our relationship had continued to grow, Ash and I had developed something of a pattern. During the week, we didn't see each other during the day at all. But he often came over in the evenings and we had a meal together. Then he worked on whatever he brought in his ever-present briefcase while I plugged away on my dissertation. Usually, he spent the night. On the weekends, he took me out, fancy or casual, as the mood struck us. I had yet to see his place, but I had given him the keys to my apartment about a week earlier.

I suppose some people might have considered

the arrangement lopsided. When I was honest with myself, I had to admit that there were days when I did, as well. But I wanted to be with him. At the moment, that was my bottom line. If he was more comfortable in my space than his, I could live with that. For the time being, anyway.

I gave the mushrooms another quick stir, then moved to the cutting board to chop veggies for a salad. From the other room, I heard the soft pop of a cork being pulled from a bottle. A moment later, Ash's voice floated through the open doorway.

"What did you do with the wineglasses this time?" He liked to claim I always put them away in a different place.

"They're in here," I called back. "I washed them. It's this strange little ritual I perform each time they get used."

"Ha ha," he said, as he came back in, the open wine bottle dangling from one hand. "Very funny."

"What did you open?" I asked. Ash held up the bottle.

"Ash," I said, trying not to hear quite how much I sounded like a wife about to nag. "That's the one I've been saving for when I get my degree. I told you that."

It was a bottle of Pinot from one of my favorite Oregon wineries. I had been saving it to commemorate my own hard-won personal achievement, to toast my degree with the most expensive bottle I could afford. It sounded sort of hokey, but the gesture meant something to me. My degree meant something to me. My choice, my challenge.

"And I told you, you should have champagne," Ash replied. His tone sounded patient, but I could tell he was annoyed. We had been over this ground before. The disparity in our incomes didn't come up very often, but when it did there were fireworks. I simply could not seem to make him understand that there were some things I wanted to do for myself.

"If you still want this for your Ph.D., I can always get you another bottle."

"I don't want another bottle," I said, hating the way my voice was starting to rise. I turned back to the cutting board, continued to chop the carrots for the salad into tiny little bits, the knife *thunking* against the cutting board.

"I want *that* one, the one I bought myself. I know you can get me anything I want, Ash, and I appreciate it. It's just—"

"Why must you always react this way?" he interrupted. "Just once I wish—"

He broke off as I gave a sudden yelp. In my haste, I had let the knife slip, slicing deep into the index finger of my left hand. I dropped the knife to the cutting board with a clatter, reaching for a dish towel as the bright red blood welled up and out. Even tiny cuts on your hands bleed like a sonofabitch.

But I could see that this one was deep. I couldn't feel it yet. Not a good sign.

Instantly Ash was beside me, our argument forgotten. "What is it?" he demanded, his tone intent. "Candace, what's wrong?"

"I cut myself," I said. I wrapped the towel around my finger, pressed down with my other hand as hard as I could, and watched how quickly the blood stained the clean, white cloth. "Dammit, it's really deep. I'm not sure I can make the bleeding stop."

"Let me see it," Ash said. He reached for my hand and I scooted back out of reach.

"I have to keep applying pressure," I said.

"Let me see it," Ash said again. He closed the distance between us, reached out, and pulled my hands toward him. There was no way for me to resist. He was simply too strong. Before I realized what he was doing, he had peeled my fingers, then the dish towel, away. The cut was an angry line across the pad of my finger, the skin around it, a strange white due to the pressure I had applied. I watched as the blood flooded back, beading on the surface of my finger, then spilling over, flowing down.

It hurt now. It hurt a lot. Without another word, Ash pulled me one step closer and thrust my finger into his mouth.

"Ash," I exclaimed. "What the hell?"

Without warning, my free hand groped against the counter, seeking support. I was dizzy with a sensation I had never felt before. I could feel Ash's mouth close around my finger, pulling it deep inside his mouth as he began to gently suck. All my blood seemed to rise to meet him in one great, slow tide. I could feel it, pounding at my temples. A great ringing filled my ears. The world revolved once, then seemed to steady. I made a helpless, wondering sound.

Slowly, slowly, Ash drew my finger from his mouth, lowered it until it rested, face up, on the counter between us. As if from a great distance, I stared down at it. The bleeding had stopped.

"How did you do that?" I panted. "What did you do?"

"Candace," he replied, his voice filled with an urgency I had never heard there before. I looked up from my hand and met his strange and beautiful starlit eyes. There's a thing it's easy to forget about the stars. Their light looks so pure and cold. They're not cold, not cold at all. Instead, they're made of the purest fire. The same fire I saw in Ash's eyes.

I took one stumbling step forward, then a second, and then I was in his arms.

His mouth was fierce, possessive, searing me straight through to my core. He tasted of a flavor I'd never experienced, one that made my head swim. He deepened the kiss, drawing my tongue into his mouth to suck, just as he had my finger only moments before. *It's me,* I suddenly thought. I was tasting myself, my blood, in Ash's mouth. I pulled back, turning my head away. I couldn't breathe, couldn't think.

"Candace," Ash said once more.

Slowly I turned my head back and met his eyes. The expression in them almost struck me blind. Desire, stripped down, laid bare, in its purest, most elemental form. And layered over it, embedded in it, was my own image. There was no difference between me and Ash's desire. The two of us were one. And I knew in that moment what my own eyes held.

"What do you see?" he rasped out. "Tell me what you see."

"Us," I answered. "I see us."

He took my mouth on a moan. This time I matched him. Stroke for stroke. Fire for fire. *I love you, Candace,* I swore I heard him say. The words, resonating inside my head, echoing in the room around us, though our mouths were fused together. *I love you. You are mine.*

Together, all that night, we fed our mutual desire while the stars wheeled in the night sky, then went out, one by one.

Come on now, Candace, I thought, as I stood on the street, gazing up at the building that housed Ash's office. *Just open the door and go in. Other people do things like this all the time.* Ash had surprised me plenty, right from the very beginning of our relationship. I had decided it was high time I returned the favor.

I'd packed a picnic lunch.

The weeks following the night I sliced my finger in the kitchen had been nothing short of amazing, filled with the promise of new love. The world is a different place when you believe you love and are loved. New love makes adventurers of those it holds in its sway. Every moment brings something to be discovered and explored. When you first fall in love, you are glad the world is round, so many possibilities lie just over the edge of the horizon.

I couldn't imagine a lover more wonderful than Ash. For one thing, he didn't seem to have any fear of those three little words, *I love you,* that so many men have. He used them easily, readily, but never glibly. I believed him every time. And every time he said them, I fell a little more in love myself. There was only one dark cloud in all the universe, as far as my eyes could see.

I almost never saw him during the daytime.

It sounded ridiculous, even when I said it to myself, which probably explained why I hadn't told anyone. Not even Bibi, who teased me about neglecting her, then pumped me for my latest romantic details every chance she got. How could I say out loud that the only flaw I could find in my lover was that, during the week anyway, I almost never saw him between nine and five?

When I questioned him, Ash's answer was always the same: I had my studies and he had his business. Both had their own places in our lives. They should be respected, take priority during the hours assigned to them. They couldn't do that if we allowed our personal relationship to interrupt. It wasn't quite a refusal to combine business with pleasure, but it came pretty close. And in spite of how logical it sounded, it bothered me right from the beginning, though I had chosen to let it go.

The more serious our relationship became, the more it bothered me, as did the fact that Ash tended to change the subject each time I tried to bring it up. So that morning, when I woke to find Ash gone and a glorious, fogless blue sky outside my window, I decided to take matters into my own hands. I was going to plan my very own surprise.

I stopped at my favorite market, picking out delicacies I knew Ash enjoyed, then I packed a picnic basket. Now I stood on the street outside Ash's office building, which was, in fact, a gorgeous old Victorian, on the register of historic places, or so the plaque near the front door informed me. I climbed the front steps, desperately trying to remind myself that other women did things like this all the time, that the female of the species isn't the only one who enjoys being swept off her feet. I hit the button on the outside intercom and my stomach fluttered like a cloud of butterflies.

"Donahue and Associates," a woman's voice answered, professional and prompt.

"Candace Steele for Mr. Ashford Donahue," I said, doing my best to match her tone.

There was a pause. Just long enough so that I was debating with myself about whether or not to ring again, when a buzzer sounded and the door locks clicked open. I pulled the door toward me, then stepped into a tile-floored lobby. From a door to the right at the far end, a young woman was already making her way toward me. She was every inch the professional, from her chic haircut, to her dark, tailored suit and her midsized heels. They clicked briskly against the tiles of the floor. In the crook of one arm, she carried a leather-bound appointment book.

"Good day, Ms. Steele," she said, her voice low and pleasant. "Welcome to Donahue and Associates. I'm afraid I really must apologize. I can't seem to find a record of your appointment with Mr. Donahue in my book. He's busy at the moment and cannot be disturbed. I'm sure the error must be ours. Perhaps you would be so kind as to let me reschedule you?"

"I didn't have an appointment," I said. "I'm a personal friend of Mr. Donahue's, not a professional one." I hoisted the picnic basket, as if this would offer an adequate explanation. "I was hoping to take him to lunch, as a surprise."

The young woman's face—I could only assume she was Ash's assistant—went absolutely blank.

"A personal friend," she echoed, precisely as if the thought of Ash having one had literally never occurred. "Lunch."

"People do experience both, on a pretty regular basis," I said, then bit my tongue. I get a little sassy when I'm uncomfortable, but alienating the dragon guarding Ash's lair was hardly my best course. "If you would just tell Ash—Mr. Donahue—that I'm here, I'm sure the whole thing can be straightened out."

"I can't do that," she said, actually falling back a step, hugging the appointment book to her chest as if she feared I was about to rush her. "Mr. Donahue's instructions are very specific. No visitors of any kind are allowed between eleven and one. I'm sorry, Ms. Steele." Her eyes met mine. In them, I read the last thing I expected to see. Genuine fear.

I didn't want to believe what I was seeing. "Can't you make an exception just this once?"

She shook her head. "If I disregard Mr. Donahue's wishes, I'll lose everything. I'll lose my job."

"Never mind," I said quickly. "Please believe me, I had no idea this was going to cause such a problem." Thoroughly unnerved now, I began to edge my way toward the door. "You don't even have to mention my coming here to Mr. Donahue, if you don't want to."

I reached for the doorknob, then looked into Ash's assistant's eyes one last time. Now the expression in them looked remarkably like pity.

"I won't have to tell him," she said softly. "He'll know."

"What the hell were you thinking?" Ash exploded that night.

All day long I had been telling myself that I had let my imagination get carried away as I stood in the foyer of his office. Okay, so my plan to surprise Ash had backfired. But it wasn't such a big deal. He might be a little annoyed at first, but pretty soon we would be laughing about it. Chuckling over the fact that my showing up had scared his poor assistant out of her wits. Instead, he was furious, bursting into anger the second he came through the door.

"I thought I was going to give you a surprise," I said. "A pleasant one. Obviously, I was mistaken. It won't happen again."

"You're damn right," Ash said. He was prowling my living room, pacing back and forth like a caged tiger. "You're damn right it won't. There are good reasons for the boundaries I set, Candace. You can't just stroll in and knock them all down."

"Maybe if I knew what some of those reasons

were. . . ." I said. I was trying to keep calm. It was true I had made a mistake, but that was no reason to let the situation get blown out of all proportion. Ash hadn't even given me the chance to apologize. He just came through the door swinging. "You lay down rules and expect me to follow them blindly, Ash. Surely you can see that's not a healthy way for a relationship to operate."

He stopped pacing, and swung around. "Don't start with that," he said, his tone cold with fury. "Don't practice your psychology on me. It's not up to me to explain myself. I've told you that I love you, Candace. That ought to earn me a certain amount of trust. Until you're willing to commit yourself to me in the way I need, you're going to have to accept the fact that there are some things you can't know."

"And just what sort of commitment would that be?" I asked, my own tone sarcastic. I was truly stung now. I had known we weren't quite equal, told myself that no couple ever is. But I hardly expected this. I thought he respected my work, if nothing else. "One where we keep score? Four dinners earns you two secrets. I want a partner, Ash. Not an emotional accountant. And for the record, I think you missed a step. We've never discussed a specific commitment between us. Not of any kind."

He went absolutely still, so still I swear I couldn't even see him breathe.

"You don't want to commit yourself to me."

"I didn't say that," I said quickly. "I'm saying we've never discussed it. It's pretty clear we have different ideas about what 'commitment' means. We *should* discuss them. Now. Get them out into the open. Trust goes both ways, Ash. When you keep me in the dark, all you do is prove I don't have yours."

"You have no idea what I want for us," he said.

"How can I when you refuse to let me in?" I all but shouted. I took a deep breath, reined my temper back. From across my tiny living room, Ash and I stared at each other. The tick of my grandmother's clock was loud in the room.

"I've opened up every single part of my life to you, Ash," I said, as calmly as I could. "But you haven't done the same, and I think we both know it. I've never seen where you live, can't do something as simple as drop by your office. You may think those are reasonable boundaries to set. I don't. Certainly not without a more reasonable explanation than the one you're offering. Commitment isn't the same as blind obedience, Ash, and you shouldn't ask it of me."

"You're not willing to accept that I may know best about some things," he said, his voice dull and flat.

"Stop putting words in my mouth," I exploded. "I'm sure you do know best, about a lot of things.

That's not the same as saying you can keep them from me."

"Then there's nothing more to say," he said. Numbly, I watched him stride toward the door. At the very last second, he turned back. "I would have given you anything you asked for, Candace. Things you haven't even thought to ask for. I want you to remember that when I'm gone."

"Oh, fuck you, Ash," I said. I was well and truly furious now. Emotional blackmail and I have never gotten along. "That's manipulative bullshit, and you know it. I'm not asking you to leave. You're the one who's running away. *That's* what I'll remember when you're gone."

I turned my back on him then. In spite of the fact that I meant every single word I said, I wasn't all that sure I could take watching the man I loved walk out my door. I had a pretty good feeling he wouldn't be back.

"This is your last chance, Candace," I heard him say.

"No, it isn't," I answered, without turning around. "It's *ours*. If you can't see that, then you should go ahead and leave, Ash. Try not to let the door hit you in the ass on your way out."

There was a beat of silence. Then I heard my front door open, then close. Ashford Donahue III was gone from my life just as suddenly as he had entered it. I stood in my living room, my eyes on my grandmother's cuckoo clock as it began to chime. As soon as the room was still and silent, I walked to the couch, dropped down upon it, put my face in my hands, and let the tears flow.

"I know this isn't what you want to hear," Bibi began.

"Wait a minute. Don't tell me," I interrupted, doing my best to summon a smile. "You're going to say it anyhow."

"Damn right I am," she said. We were sitting in her apartment, having a glass of wine. Two solid weeks had gone by. Fourteen days without a word from Ash. Not one single syllable.

"Being swept off your feet is all well and good," Bibi went on. "But it's not the same as being compatible. Get ready. Here it comes: You're better off without him."

"I know that," I said. "I do, it's just . . ." I took a sip of wine, set the glass down on a coaster on Bibi's coffee table. "He got inside me, somehow. That's the only way I know to describe it, Bibi. I dream about him every night, think about him when I should be studying. I just can't seem to let him go."

"Oh, you poor baby," Bibi said, setting down her glass to wrap an arm around my shoulders and give me a reassuring squeeze. "You really do have it bad, don't you?"

"You could say that. The funny thing is," I went on, "I don't even think we were having the same argument. I know he was trying to tell me something. I still don't have the faintest idea what it was."

"Ah, a man of mystery," Bibi said at once, her tone mock all-seeing and wise. "Very sexy, till somebody gets hurt." She paused, took a sip of her own wine. "In my mind, the biggest mystery of all is this: How come it's never them and always us?"

"That same question crossed my mind."

"So, tomorrow's the big day, huh?" Bibi inquired in a deliberate change of subject.

"Yep," I said. By the end of the day tomorrow, I would know whether I had a Ph.D. or not. I was trying not to think about all the ways Ash and I had discussed celebrating the big occasion. Hell, I didn't even have my bottle of wine.

"You'll call and let me know?"

"Absolutely," I said. "We'll go out and celebrate afterward. No more school nights."

Bibi grinned. "You're on."

"I better get going," I said. I set down my wineglass and stood up. "Thanks for the wine and the pep talk. I appreciate both."

"Anytime," Bibi said. She reached for the doorknob with one hand then set the other on my arm. "Candace," she said softly, her eyes serious. "It's his loss."

"Thanks," I said. "Thanks a lot."

"Talk to you tomorrow, then," she said.

I heard her apartment door close gently behind me as I walked down the hall to my own.

Late the next afternoon, I walked out of my adviser's office in a state of mild disbelief. I had done it. I had made it through the final step—the defense of my dissertation—with flying colors. *Well, that's that,* I thought. I was now Candace Steele, Ph.D. I could add those three little letters to my name on my checks. I could even call myself Dr. Steele if I wanted. I should have been elated, filled with a sense of my own accomplishment. Instead, I just felt hollow inside. And if I didn't stop wallowing pretty damn soon, Dr. Steele was going to turn out to be someone Candace didn't like very much.

Get a hold of yourself, I thought. *Go home. Put some party clothes on, then call Bibi and share the joy. Go have dinner at the Library. Sit in an entirely new spot. Hang with Mark.* It wasn't as if I didn't have people who cared about me, even if Ash was nowhere in sight. I had a life before he strolled into it. I still had one now that he was gone.

By the time I got back to my apartment building, I was feeling better. The way things had ended with Ash would probably always bother me, but it was time to declare my initial period of mourning for the death of the relationship officially over. I had earned my degree, earned a new beginning. It was time to stop being ruled by the past, in more ways than one. Time to start over. I unlocked my apartment door, stepped inside, then came to a complete stop.

The scent of flowers hit me like a wall. Lining the edges of my tiny entry, extending down the hall toward the living room, were bunches upon bunches of sweet peas, my favorite flower in all the world, in all the colors of the rainbow. Their butterfly-wing heads nodding on thin, wiry stems, the ends of which had been thrust into containers of water. Jam jars. Only one person in the world knew how much those flowers meant to me. Only one person still alive.

I felt my breath hitch as my shoulder bag and keys fell, all but forgotten, to the floor. I kicked the front door closed behind me, then sprinted toward the living room.

"Ash?" I called.

Every single surface of my living room was covered with flowers. Some stood in water. Others were scattered, as if thrown by manic flower girls, over my chairs and couch. In a daze now, I moved to the bedroom. The bedspread was a carpet of petals, all candy-apple red. My nightstand, dresser drawers, and bookcase, topped by jars filled with flowers of a white so pure it seemed to glow. Tucked between my pillows was an envelope with my name scrawled across the front. The handwriting was bold, assertive.

With legs that wanted to tremble just a little more than I cared to admit, I crossed the room, picked it up. It wasn't sealed. Inside was a single sheet of paper. On it were just two words. *Forgive me.*

"Ash," I said again, my voice no more than a whisper, this time.

"Candace," I heard a voice behind me say.

I turned, and was in his arms.

The kiss we shared was searing, more than a little desperate. I could feel it, branding me clear down to the bone. I wrapped my arms around him, holding tightly, a single thought pounding in time to the pulse of blood inside my head: Now that he was here again, I would never let him go.

His hands streaked over me, trailing fire in their wake. I could feel the play of his muscles beneath my hands, taste the strength of his desire on his tongue. He yanked the silk shirt I had worn to my meeting with my adviser, Dr. Dutton, out of my slacks. At the first touch of his fingers against my skin, I gave a cry. I brought my hands to his chest, my fingers frantically working the buttons of his shirt and felt the way his stomach muscles quivered.

It's not just me, I thought. I felt a strange sensation flood me and realized it was relief. Potent as a straight shot of whiskey, heady as the desire building between us, moment by moment, touch by touch. Whatever I felt, Ash felt, too. Wherever we went, we would go together, united until it was done.

I pushed the shirt back from his chest, stood on tiptoe to run my tongue up the V of the T-shirt to lap at the base of his neck. Ash's body jerked, then went completely still. *This is what the eye of the hurricane feels like,* I suddenly thought. Around us swirled all the things that were yet to happen, all the things that had come before. But here, in this moment, as his gaze met mine, there were only three things that mattered. Ash. Me. Our mutual desire.

Eyes still on mine, he took two slow, deliberate steps forward. I took two steps back. I felt the edge of the bed press against the backs of my knees, come up to meet my back as I sank down. Then Ash was there, his hands beneath me, sliding me to the head of the bed, even as his body covered mine. His hands were everywhere at once. Stilling my fingers as I tried to keep up. I felt my slacks slide down and away. The flick of his tongue across my heel as he eased off my thin socks. He turned me then, his legs stradling my body, a roll to my stomach that was gentle, yet impossible to deny. I felt the tug of anticipation, deep inside me, heard the way my breath caught at the back of my throat as his erection pressed against my rump.

How does he always know? I thought. Know the way to tease and entice, make me buck and shudder. Ash eased the shirt back from my shoulders, down my arms and away, then released the fastener on my bra. I drew my arms back and out of the straps, felt Ash remove it. *My turn now,* I thought. Slowly and deliberately, I rolled over.

Ash's face was taut, angular, and clean as new-cut marble, etched with some combination of emotions so varied and complex I couldn't even begin to identify them. In it, his eyes burned, pure and hard as diamonds. I reached, and ran a palm up the front of his pants, saw the way his pupils dilated. He captured my hand, brought it to his mouth, biting the pad with a strength that stopped just short of giving pain.

"Let me look at you, Candace," he said. "Let me see you, just for a moment."

I swallowed against a suddenly dry throat, then watched as Ash's hands moved to my hips. I lifted myself toward his touch as he slid the scrap of silk I wore, the last barrier between us, over my hips and down the length of my legs and off, parting them slightly. Hardly daring to breathe, I eased myself back down onto the bed, then lay, just as I was. Fully exposed. No clothing. No secrets. Just hopes. Just needs. Just love.

"My God, you are so beautiful," Ash said, his voice so hoarse with emotion I almost didn't recognize it. "The most beautiful living thing that I have ever seen, and you have no idea why."

I closed my eyes then, no longer able to bear the expression in his. Instead, I reached up, felt his fingers meet mine. I brought them to my lips, kissing each one in turn.

"Then show me."

"I thought I would never see you again," I said.

I had no idea how much later it was, and I didn't particularly care. Ash and I lay across my petal-strewn bed, folded in each other's arms. My head was pillowed on his shoulder, the palm of one hand gliding back and forth across his chest. The simple truth was, I could not stop touching him. Didn't even want to try.

"And I thought that I could stay away," Ash replied. "I thought I could exist without you. The moment I realized I couldn't, I headed straight for the flower market."

"As romantic gestures go, I think it's one for the record books," I said, and watched him smile. A knot I hadn't fully realized was there loosened inside my chest. I had felt Ash's passion, taken him inside my body with a fierceness that left no doubt about how much we desired each other but, until this moment, I hadn't seen him smile. The last few weeks had taught me one thing if nothing else. I hadn't just missed what Ash and I shared in bed. I had missed—no, I had wanted—*Ash*, whatever that meant. All of what he was.

"I did some thinking, in between fooling myself into thinking I could be without you," Ash said, gazing up at the ceiling. "You were right."

I levered myself up onto one elbow. "About what?"

"About the fact that I never talked about commitment," Ash said, his eyes still focused upward. "What it meant to me, what I wanted. All I did was set boundaries then expect you to respect them."

He turned his head, and his eyes met mine. "I want you to know I'm sorry for that, Candace. I had good reasons for the boundaries I set, but without any sort of explanation, I can see how they might seem unreasonable."

"Thank you," I said softly.

Ash made a strange sound, a combination of laughter and frustration combined. "That's it?" he said. "You aren't going to make me grovel?"

"Well," I said, as I marched my fingers across his chest. "I admit I have always sort of wanted to see you crawl."

He laughed outright at that, then reached to urge my head down, bringing my lips to his in a hard, deep kiss.

"That's what I missed," he said. "The thing I cannot be without."

I cocked my head. "And what would *that* be, precisely?"

"You," he said.

I dropped my head down to rest my forehead against his chest. "You're not real, are you? No guy

I know but you would say a thing like that. Not only that, I actually believe you."

Ash pushed himself upright then, leaning back against my headboard. I sat up and crossed my legs, scooted around so that we faced each other.

"That's good," he replied. "Because it happens to be the truth. I will not be without you, Candace. I want you with me, now and always, and *I will not be denied.*"

I watched as Ash visibly sought to master himself, and it came to me suddenly that I had never seen him like this before. I had seen him in the throes of both passion and anger, but never had I seen him lose emotional control.

"I want that, too," I said.

"Do you?" he asked at once. "I hope it's true, but before you can give me a genuine answer there are things that you must know. Things I have kept hidden, behind those boundaries you were so upset about."

"What is it, Ash?" I asked steadily, though I could feel my heart begin to pound. "What do you want me to know?"

He was silent for a moment, as if deciding the best way to answer. Finally, he held out a hand, palm up. I placed mine into it, understanding the unspoken invitation at once. Without speaking, Ash pushed away from the headboard, sitting up straight and leaning closer. Turning my hand over, he pressed it to the center of my chest, directly over my heart.

"What do you feel, Candace?" he asked, his voice soft.

"I don't understand," I said.

A quick smile lighted Ash's features then was gone. Summer lightning. "That's because you're making it too hard. It's not a metaphorical or philosophical question, it's a literal one. What do you feel?"

"My heart."

He nodded, scooting closer still. He turned my hand around, pressing the palm into the same place on his own chest.

"And now?"

I opened my mouth to give the obvious answer, then shut it with a snap. I could feel nothing, nothing at all. But surely that didn't actually mean anything. The only reason I could feel my own heart was because it was beating so hard.

"I don't understand," I said again.

Without speaking, Ash moved my fingers to the side of his neck, held them steady, his eyes on mine. My own slid away, to fasten on the numbers of the digital clock that sat on the surface of my nightstand, counting down the seconds. After thirty, I snatched my hand away. I pressed my fingers to my own neck, found the thing I sought. Then, I placed them back on his. Shifted position, then shifted it again.

I couldn't find a pulse.

As if my action had been some sort of signal, Ash got up from the bed, moving to where his pants lay in a heap on the floor. He retrieved them, fished in one front pocket, then returned to the bed. In his hand was a small ivory-handled pocketknife. He opened it, the blade locking into place with a soft *snick*, then extended it toward me, handle first.

"Will you do something for me, Candace?" he asked.

"If I can," I answered. I was beginning to be afraid now. And the thing that frightened me the most was that I didn't know quite what I feared.

"I want you to cut me."

"For God's sake, Ash," I began.

"Please," he said. "I don't mean you have to stab me, you know." Slowly, he reached out to capture my wrist, drawing the hand that held the knife toward him until the blade rested against the skin above his left nipple. "Just draw the blade straight across."

"No!"

Acting purely on instinct, I jerked my hand back. The tip of the knife dipped down. As I watched in horror, a tiny red line appeared on Ash's chest.

"Oh, God," I said. My breath hitched, painfully. "Oh, God, Ash, I'm so sorry."

"It's all right, Candace," Ash said, his tone perfectly calm. "Don't say anything for a moment. Just watch."

Mesmerized now—I don't think I could have looked away if I tried—I watched the cut. For a few seconds, the blood welled up and out. Then, it simply stopped. Ash pulled a tissue from a box on the nightstand and cleaned the remaining blood away.

The cut was gone. Only a thin, white line on Ash's chest showed where it had been. Then, even that seemed to fade as I kept my eyes riveted to his body. Ash looked exactly the same, just as perfectly formed as he had been before. As he always did.

I made a sound. Without a word, Ash took the knife from me, reversed it so that he held it by the handle, then, before I had even an inkling of what he intended, plunged the tip of the blade into the pad of my hand. I jerked back with a cry. But Ash refused to let go. Holding my hand steady, he brought it to his lips and pulled my bleeding hand into his mouth.

A great roaring seemed to fill my head. *I've felt this before,* I thought. The tug of Ash's mouth in every single portion of my body. The night I cut my finger and he made the bleeding stop. I could hear my blood, rushing, in my ears. My heart, pounding, pounding, pounding. As though my entire being was being drawn up, channeled down my arm, and into Ash's mouth. As if from a great distance, I watched him swallow.

And then he released me, just as suddenly as he had struck. I snatched my hand back, stared down at it. I could still see the cut. But the skin around it was a pale and lustrous white, the same color as Ash's skin. It no longer bled. How could it? It had been . . .

I pulled a ragged breath into my throat. Clapped both hands over my ears, as if that could block the sound of the thoughts that were hurtling through my mind.

"You might as well say it," I heard Ash say. "It gets easier, after the first time."

"What the hell do you mean it gets easier?" I said as I dropped my hands. "How can it? For the love of God, Ash, *you drank my blood.*"

"I did," he said. And I felt those two words cut me clean through, sharp as any sword. He cocked his head to one side, as if gauging my reaction. "Who drinks blood, Candace?" he inquired. "Don't think. Just answer."

"No," I said, well and truly frightened now. Because now I knew what it was I feared and it was this: that the man I loved was a stranger. I loved him but didn't know him at all.

"Look at me, Candace," Ash said. "Please. Look me in the eye. I want you to know I am telling you the absolute truth when I say this."

"You're trying to punish me, aren't you?" I gasped out. "You want me to be afraid to cross any future boundaries. It's not going to work, because we're not going to have a future if you keep this up."

"Yes," Ash said steadily, his tone never changing. "Yes, we are. But first, you are going to look at me when I tell you the truth. *Look at me, Candace.* Or are you so afraid?"

"Of course I'm afraid," I said. "I'm not a moron." But it worked. I met his eyes. And once I had, I found I didn't want to look away. Because what I saw there was the last thing I expected. There was truth in Ash's eyes. With his whole heart, that organ he didn't seem to possess, he believed the thing he was about to tell me.

"I'm a vampire."

Eleven

Las Vegas, present

I shivered, abruptly realizing that the feel of the flagstone floor of the entryway through my thin pants wasn't the only reason I was cold. I had a sudden, wild impulse to laugh. When one member of a vampire couple returns to the domicile of the undead, does he or she call out, *Honey, I'm home*?

"You're repeating yourself," I said, without looking up. "I find that surprising, somehow."

"I wanted to bring you something I knew gave you pleasure," Ash said, as if it were just that simple. His feet moved into view beside me and I looked up.

"Why?"

Before he could offer to help, I got to my feet, the movement calling attention to every single muscle in my back. The chain that street punk had used was heavy. I was going to be sore as hell by tomorrow.

"Why not?" Ash replied. "We don't have to be

adversaries, Candace. You're the one choosing that path."

"You just keep right on telling yourself that," I remarked. I brushed past him, heading for the living room. This time, I kept things dark. "Was there something specific you wanted, Ash? Or did you just come to fight?"

"Only if we get to make up," he said.

I turned with a speed that startled us both. "Not on your life," I said. "Or mine. I remember what happened that last night in San Francisco. One set of teeth marks in my throat is enough, thank you very much. I don't intend to extend an invitation to finish the job."

"I tried to say I was sorry last time we met," Ash said, and I could hear him fight to keep the temper from his voice. "As I recall, you cut me off. I won't keep apologizing for something I can't undo, Candace. What happened in San Francisco is in the past. It's over. It's the future I want to discuss."

"For God's sake, what for?" I asked, suddenly exhausted. I had already fought one fight that night. I really didn't feel like going a few rounds in another. "There's no point. We haven't got a future."

I flopped down on the couch, unable to stop myself from wincing. In an instant, Ash's whole demeanor changed.

"You're hurt," he said, moving to me swiftly, sitting down beside me. "What happened? What's wrong?"

"It's nothing," I said, pushing his hands away as he attempted to ascertain the nature of my injuries. "I mean it, Ash, hands off."

He drew his hands away, and we regarded each other. The air between us hummed like a high-voltage wire.

"Who hurt you, Candace?" Ash finally asked.

"I didn't actually catch his name," I said as I leaned back against the cushions and gave in to the temptation to close my eyes. "He was just some street tough. I got into a sort of pissing contest at work today. Believe it or not, I actually won. But apparently Lucas doesn't take rejection very well. He hired some street kids to rough me up, sort of even the score."

"Lucas," Ash repeated.

"Lucas Goldfinch," I said. "Personal security for Temptation McCoy. He screwed up. I called him on the carpet; he tried for some payback. That's really all there is to tell."

"Someone hurt you," I heard Ash say, a tone in his voice I had never heard before.

Slowly, I opened my eyes. Something was happening here. A thing I hadn't expected and wasn't entirely certain I understood.

"It's nothing serious," I said, keeping my own tone as neutral as I could. "Just bruises. No broken bones. I'm still all in one piece."

Even in the dim light, I could see the way Ash's

jaw worked, as if clamping down on words he didn't want to utter. His hands were clenched into fists so tight I could see the white bones of his knuckles even through his bone-white skin.

"It's all right," I said, gently. "Ash, I can take care of myself."

He gave a bark of bitter laughter. "Why don't you just come right out and say it? You don't need me to protect you."

"I don't," I said. "I've been on my own for a long time now."

He ran frustrated fingers through his always slightly too long hair. So purely human a gesture I felt an unexpected pain lance through my heart. Without warning, Ash stood, then reached down and plucked me from the couch before I so much as had an inkling of what he intended.

"Impressive," I managed to remark. "Mind telling me what you're doing?"

"Taking care of you," he said, shortly. "You obviously need a keeper. I just elected myself. Don't." I pulled in a breath to argue, and he laid a finger against my lips. "Just don't," he said. "Not tonight, Candace. Let me take care of you, just this once."

"Say *please,*" I said.

I saw it, then. The thing I'd once loved so much. The thing I'd thought I would never see again. He smiled. A genuine smile, one that lit him from within. With gentle fingers, he brushed a few stray curls back from my face.

"Please."

I felt a tremor move through his body. Slowly I lowered my head until it rested on his shoulder, my face tucked like a child's into the crook of his neck. For a moment we simply stayed just like that. Then Ash turned and walked swiftly through the darkened house, down the hallway with its glowing nightlight to the bathroom. He set me on my feet, one arm around me, holding me close to his body. With his free hand, he drew back the shower curtain and turned on the bathtub taps. I heard a clank and then a hiss as he turned the shower on, the water almost blistering hot, just the way I like it.

While the bathroom around us slowly filled with steam, Ash gently stripped the clothing from my body, running his hands over me, as if to verify my claim that bruises were the worst that had happened. Then, satisfied, he lifted me in his arms once more, pivoted, and set me on my feet beneath the spray. As the hot water came into contact with my aches and pains, I hissed a breath out through my teeth. Then I simply stood still, letting the shower sluice over me, and watched the man who had once been my love, my lover.

With the same economy of motion he had used with my clothing, Ash removed his own, then stepped into the tub behind me, pulling the curtain closed around us. He reached for the soap, rolling it between his hands till they were slick with lather, then put his hands on me. Open palms sweeping down, then up my back, careful not to apply too much pressure to the bruises. Fingers gently kneading the stiffness from my neck and shoulders. He knelt and ran his hands over the backs of my legs, lifting each in turn to wash, to run his fingertips over the soles of my feet. Then he turned me toward him.

Erotic images streamed through my brain, too numerous to count, flowing together like the water pouring over me. I looked down. Even through the steam, I could see the way Ash's cock had come to life, jutting up and outward. A remembrance of what it had felt like to take him deep inside jolted through me. Was it the steam clogging my lungs, or was it desire? Abruptly dizzy, I put a steadying hand on Ash's shoulder.

He lathered his hands a second time, slid them up the front of my legs, across my belly. He boosted himself up then to stand upright. Taking the bar of soap, he ran it, rather than his hands, over my breasts, as if he didn't quite trust himself to touch them. I heard the soap make contact with the dish. Then, just for an instant, his fingers brushed along my throat, lingering over the tattoo. Then the touch was gone and I felt his fingers in my hair. Massaging my scalp until the thoughts themselves seemed to blur inside my head. As if from a great distance, I heard him turn the water off.

Ash stepped from the shower, turned to wrap me in a towel, then lifted me in his arms once more. This time, my head drifted to his shoulder as if it recognized its place as he set off toward the bedroom.

"You're dripping water on my hall floor."

"Jesus, you are such a nag," he said. But I could hear the smile in his voice.

In the bedroom, he set me on my feet, gently dried me with the towel. He turned back the bedclothes, folded them over me. I lay beneath the covers gazing upward as, with quick motions, he used the towel on himself then left it in a wet heap on the floor. His lips twitched with held-back laughter as he knelt down beside the bed, and I realized then that he had left the towel that way on purpose, certain of my reaction. Stupid, clueless guy.

This is what I wanted, I thought. *All I ever really wanted.* The two of us together, doing everyday things. What I once thought we could have, before I had known the truth. Before I had known what Ash was, and what he wasn't. Without warning, I felt my throat constrict. *Don't cry. Don't cry,* I chanted to myself. It did no good to cry over things you knew you couldn't have. I had done a lot of things since that night in the elevator in San Francisco, but shedding tears had never been one of them.

"Ash," I said.

Quick as lightning, he leaned down, pressed his lips to mine. I felt my mind go blank. Never had Ash kissed me like this before. Deep and easy and slow. Tender enough to almost make me believe he had a heart. Sweet enough to make me fear that he could still break mine. He lifted his lips from my mouth, pressed them softly against my closed eyelids, one by one.

"No more words, my sweet Candace," he said. "Not tonight. Tonight you are going to sleep, and I am going to do the thing I should have done. I am going to watch over you, to keep you safe."

I heard a whisper of sound as he rose. The dull thud of his heels as he left the room then returned a moment later. I heard him go around the end of the bed, then sit in the chair I keep by the window. I rolled toward the sound. Kept my eyes closed as I listened to my house make the noises it always does as it settles down for the night. When I could hear nothing at all save my own heartbeat, my own breath, I opened my eyes.

Dressed again now, in jeans and a T-shirt, Ash was sitting by the window, steepled fingers pressed against his lips, as if lost in thought. His eyes caught the illumination of the streetlight. Brilliant. Gorgeous. Cold.

"Go to sleep, my love," he said, his eyes never leaving whatever it was he waited for outside my window, whatever it was that haunted the night.

I let my own drift shut.

* * *

When I opened them in the morning, he was gone.

The numbers on the bedside clock said 10:00.

Holy shit, I thought. Not only had I slept, I'd overslept, big time. I bolted upright, wincing as the muscles of my back set up a protest. If I didn't hurry, I would be late; I was already late. Bibi and I have breakfast together several times a week, a holdover from our days in San Francisco. I tossed back the covers, threw my legs over the side of the bed, then gave a startled exclamation as my bare feet found something unexpected on the floor.

Sweet pea petals. Now that I was starting to wake up and my senses were beginning to function, I realized the whole house was still full of their scent, full of flowers. *I am not going to think about that now,* I decided. If I stopped to consider what had, and hadn't, happened with Ash last night, I might as well just send out for a straitjacket and be done with it. I dressed quickly, brushed my teeth, ran a quick brush through my hair, then headed for the door. My hair didn't even look too much the worse for wear, considering I went to bed with it wet. But then, it was so uncontrollable even on a good day, who could tell?

It wasn't until I was actually standing in my driveway that I remembered: I didn't have my car. It was across town, a couple of blocks from Lipstyx. *Well, damn,* I thought. I opened my shoulder bag, yanked out my cell. First I left a message for Bibi, telling her I couldn't make it, apologizing for the mix-up. Then I called a cab. There's one thing about Vegas, there's always somebody more than happy to take you where you want to go.

"Hey, Nerves. How you feelin' this morning?" the driver asked as I slid in behind him. "Not sure if you remember me or not." His eyes met mine in the rearview mirror. "I'm Oswald. I'm a friend of Doc's."

"Sure, I remember you, Oswald," I said. "I'm feeling fine." I waited until he pulled away from the curb, heading unerringly in the direction I needed to go without my having given a word of instruction. "So, does everybody know?"

Oswald gave a chuckle. He was young and skinny, a perfect imitation of a chicken. When he laughed, his Adam's apple bobbed up and down.

"Pretty much," he conceded. "Pretty much. Doc was pretty proud of the way he helped you out."

"I left my car a couple of blocks from Lipstyx. You know where that is, right?"

"Sure do," Oswald acknowledged. His eyes flicked to mine in the mirror then flicked away. "Might be a little bit of excitement over that way this morning."

I sat up a little straighter. "How come?"

"Found another body in the parking lot, on fire this time."

"Did it have a head?" I asked.

Oswald took a corner with a screech of tires. "Now that is just unfair," he said, his tone morose. "You already know my punch line."

"It really wasn't anything at all, Carl," I said, several minutes later, trying not to let emotion of any sort creep into my voice.

Oswald had dropped me at my car, which was still in one piece and precisely where I left it. Maybe that emboldened me, because I then took a calculated but stupid risk and walked the couple of blocks to Lipstyx. Carl had been summoned to the first headless body. Chances were good he would get tagged for this one as well. If he was still at the scene, I was going to have a tough time explaining my presence. This was hardly my neighborhood; I was unlikely to just be strolling by.

I decided it was worth the chance, though. Two headless bodies in the same place in the space of a week was not a coincidence, and not a thing I could ignore. So I had taken the chance, and it backfired. Not only was Carl still there, he was interviewing the night-shift bouncer. Apparently, the bouncer had seen my little interaction with Lucas and was more than delighted when I strolled by. What's the best way to get yourself off the hook, any kind of hook? Point a finger at someone else.

Now I was the one being questioned by Carl.

"So tell me once again," he said with exaggerated patience, "what exactly happened last night?"

"Some guy wanted something I didn't want to give, and it took me awhile to convince him *no* meant *no*, that's all. This is Vegas. That sort of thing happens all the time. You know that as well as I do."

Carl gave a grunt. He was all detective now, jotting down notes as we spoke.

"You get a name?" he inquired.

I shook my head. "No. You don't ask for a name in that sort of situation. Gives the wrong impression."

I didn't like lying to Carl. But if I gave Lucas Goldfinch's name to the police, I had a feeling Randolph Glass would have *my* head.

"Just more lousy timing, I guess," I said, meaning every single word. "I know it makes things messy. I'm sorry, Carl."

"Okay. That's okay," he said. He looked up from his note-taking. I couldn't quite read the expression in his eyes. Standing in the open, I had a sudden sense of claustrophobia, as if all the different aspects of my life, all the things I tried so hard to keep separate, were being pulled together, closing in around me.

"Any luck with the head yet?" I inquired.

Carl shook his own, and I thought I knew him well enough to see the exasperation, frustration, in even this simple movement.

"No."

"When you find it, will you let me know?"

Carl shut his notebook with a soft slap. "Why?"

It was a legitimate question. Too bad it wasn't one I could answer with the entire truth.

"I'm sorry," I said quickly. "That was probably out of line. I was just thinking about the Sher, that's all. Temptation McCoy opens at the end of the week. We're in full-fledged security mode. If there's anything I might be able to tell Al, you know, set his mind at ease . . ."

"Okay," Carl said abruptly. "I'll let you know."

"Thanks. I appreciate it," I said. "So, I guess I'll see you around."

"I imagine you will," Carl said. I turned to go. "Oh, and Ms. Steele," he added. I turned back, caught the faintest glint of humor in his eyes. "The Las Vegas Police Department would appreciate it if you didn't try to leave town."

"What the hell is going on with you?" Bibi pounced the moment I walked through the doors of the Sher.

"Bibi," I said. "Not now." Now I needed a quick bite to eat and a little space to collect my scattered thoughts. I couldn't guard Temptation and deal with Dru Benson like this. I needed to focus and stay clear.

"I know you think I'm acting like a jerk," I went

on as I hurried through the maze of the casino, heading to one of the quieter coffee shops. "I don't mean to, and I'm sorry. If you would just give me—"

"No," Bibi said.

I skidded to a stop. "What do you mean, *no*?" I barked. "You don't get to say *no* if you don't let me finish. You have no idea what I was about to say."

Bibi rolled her eyes. "For pity's sake, Candace. You think I don't know you? If I would just give you a little . . ." She held up one fisted hand, then raised her fingers one by one as she counted off. "Time. Space. Slack. God above only knows what else. But it all comes down to the same thing, and we both know it. You're avoiding me."

"I am not."

Bibi put her hands on her hips, thrust her face right up into mine. "Are too," she said. "How many rounds on the playground do you want to go?"

"Bibi," I said. Most of the time it's great having a best friend, someone who knows you almost as well as you know yourself. Occasionally, however, it is one big drag. "It's for your own good," I finally said. "That's all I can tell you."

"Oh, for the love of—" Bibi began, then cut herself off. She took me by the arm, pulled me out of the mainstream of foot traffic, into what passed as a quiet corner. "You don't want to talk, fine," she said, her voice taut and low. "But you're damned well going to make time to listen."

She cast a quick look around. There was nobody near us. No one to overhear. I hoped whoever was monitoring the security cameras couldn't read lips.

"Would this thing I'm not supposed to know for my own good have anything to do with the fact that Dru Benson is a vampire?"

"Oh, shit—"

If she had whipped out a hand grenade and pulled the pin, I couldn't have been more surprised.

"Shall I take that as a yes?"

"Shut up," I said. "Just shut up and let me think a minute, will you? I haven't even had any coffee yet."

"Oh, honey," Bibi said, instantly contrite. "Why didn't you say so? Let's go get you some. Then you can spill and apologize."

"I might do some spilling," I said as she linked her arm through mine. "But if you want an apology, you've got another thing coming."

"Oh, goody," Bibi said. "Just what I need, another surprise."

"I was trying, am trying, to keep you safe," I said, about five minutes and one cup of very hot, strong coffee later. I was working on my second cup, along with a bagel. We had about fifteen minutes before we both had to be at rehearsal. "That's not a thing for which I'm going to apologize."

"Some people might consider knowledge power," Bibi remarked.

"In some circumstances," I agreed warily. "For instance, how did you know?"

She took a sip of her own coffee, prolonging the suspense. "You told me," she finally said, calmly.

I choked on a bite of bagel. "*What?*"

"It's the way you acted in Randolph's penthouse. You just sort of, I don't know, froze up. You moved so carefully, like you were afraid you would put a foot wrong and break a bone or something. And you watched him, the whole time."

"Great. Well, that's just great," I said. "So much for subtlety. How many other people noticed, do you think?"

"Nobody else," Bibi said, her tone definitive. "People weren't exactly there to look at you, Candace. They were there to see Temptation McCoy. The only reason I spotted it is that I know you so well."

I took the information in, thought it over, prayed it was true. Not that there was anything I could do about it now.

"Them," I said softly, after a moment.

"What?"

"I wasn't just watching him. I was watching the two of them together. Dru Benson and Temptation McCoy."

"Don't tell me you think she's one, too!"

"No," I said, with a shake of my head. "No, I don't. What I'm thinking just might be worse, for her, anyhow. I think he's draining her, that she's his drone."

"You mean, like, his slave?"

"For a while. He's controlling her every move while he feeds on her. It's going to be a very long, drawn-out death, and it won't be pretty."

Bibi fell silent for a moment, her turn to let the information sink in. "Jesus, that poor kid," she said. She shook her head, suddenly, as if to dispel ugly visions. "They've been together for so long."

"Precisely my point. When I see the two of them together, it's like watching my worst nightmare walk around."

"We'll just have to stop him," Bibi said, her tone vigorous. "There must be something we can do."

"*We?*" I echoed. "That's one of the reasons I didn't tell you what Dru Benson was. You cannot walk around and think like that. In fact, you shouldn't be thinking about him at all."

"But we can't just . . ." Bibi began.

I leaned across the table, put an urgent hand on hers.

"I mean it, Bibi," I said. "Dru Benson is *strong*. With the possible exception of Ash, he is not like any vampire you, or I, have ever encountered before. You start thinking up schemes to get in his way, it's going to show up in the way you behave, and he's going to realize that you know. The miracle is, he doesn't know already."

"So what do we do?" Bibi asked.

"What *you* do," I said, extra emphasis on the pronoun, "is nothing at all. You keep all the other things about the situation that are true—how excited you are to be in the show, how much you like Temptation—right there, in the front of your mind. That's all that can be true for you, Bibi, all that you can know. Everything else you lock away, slam the door, and throw away the key. What you don't know can't hurt you. What you know can get you killed, or worse."

She shook her head. "It's not enough."

"It *is* enough," I said, my tone insistent. "Our very best weapon isn't silver or a wooden stake. It's surprise. He doesn't expect us to be able to see him for what he is. That's not an ability humans are supposed to possess. Hell, even Ash doesn't know it's something I can do. You let on that you've made Dru Benson, and he's going to start wondering how you did it. That's going to take him right back to me, and then we're both screwed. You want to help Temptation? Then help me. Stay focused. Stay calm. Stay in control."

If I hadn't been so busy making a speech, I might have noticed that Bibi had gone stone-still.

"What do you mean, 'even Ash doesn't know'?"

"I—" I began.

"Don't you lie to me," Bibi cut in. "Don't you even think about it, Candace. You've seen him, haven't you? Here, in Vegas."

"Yes, I've seen him," I admitted. "Twice. And you can just stop looking at me like that. I didn't issue an invitation, and I didn't exactly welcome him with open arms."

"Well, that's a big relief," Bibi said, her tone sarcastic. "When were you thinking you would share this information? Or maybe you decided to keep it to yourself. Maybe not knowing Ash is back is in my best interests, too. Who the hell do you think you are? You think you have the right to do all my thinking for me just because you've got teeth marks in your throat?"

"Bibi," I pleaded as heads began to turn in our direction. "Look, I'm sorry. Please, will you keep your voice down?"

She leaned forward, her eyes pinning me. With strong fingers, she reached out to grasp me by one arm.

"You want me to keep my voice down, I'll keep it down. But you're going to listen to me, Candace. You wanna know something for your own good? I have dreams, too. Nightmares where I walk out the door of my apartment and see you, lying in the hall in a pool of your own blood. I am not going to go through that, not going to let *you* go through that, a second time.

"Before I let Ash make you what he is, or what Temptation is, I will strangle your scarred neck with my bare hands, I swear to God."

She released me, leaned back, picked up her cup to take a sip of coffee, then abruptly set it back down. Her hands were shaking so hard that coffee sloshed over the rim.

"I'm sorry," I said. "I'm really, truly sorry. I didn't mean to keep the fact that I've seen him a secret. It's just that things have been happening so fast, there hasn't been time. I didn't forget you saved my life. I'll never forget it."

"Prove it," Bibi said. "Put that miserable undead sonofabitch out of his misery if he shows up again."

"Bibi," I said. "It's not that simple, and you know it."

"It should be," she said. "It damn well should be, Candace. And you know *that*."

There were tears in her eyes. I reached across the table, took her trembling hands in mine.

"We are going to get Dru Benson, Bibi. I promise we will. I just have to figure out how. In the meantime, Ash is my problem. Leave him to me."

She gave a weak attempt at a laugh. "I'd say that's a whole lot easier said than done."

"I won't make the same mistake twice," I said. "That's a promise, too."

She pulled in a deep breath, slid her hands from mine. "All right," she said. "All right."

We sat in silence for a moment. "Randolph is not going to be a very happy camper when I deal with Dru Benson. Have you thought about that?" I inquired.

Bibi gave a strangled snort of laughter as she rummaged in her shoulder bag. She came up with a tissue.

"Randolph is not always the most important thing in the world," she said. "Not that you're allowed to tell him I said so."

"Wouldn't dream of it," I said. "It's not like we chat all the time."

Bibi blew her nose.

"I'm sorry you have nightmares," I said. "I would say I was sorry I ever brought you into any of this, but it wouldn't be true. I'm too selfish for that."

"Oh, cut it out," Bibi remarked. "I hate it when you go all noble. It always ends up making me look bad, even when we both know I'm right." She stood up. "Let's go. We don't want to be late for rehearsal."

"We shouldn't go in together," I said. "Dru probably knows we're friends, but there's no sense flashing a neon sign at him."

"Okay," Bibi said. "You go on ahead. I want to stop in the ladies' room, check my face."

"It's still there," I said. She turned to go. "Bibi." She turned back. "About Ash . . . I would never deliberately put you in danger. And I'll do everything I can to keep you safe. You know that, don't you?"

"I believe I do know that," Bibi answered softly. "The question is, will you do the same for yourself?"

Twelve

"We are not changing the schedule. We open at the end of the week, Temptation. You can't call off a rehearsal just because Lucas Goldfinch doesn't show up. Contrary to his own inflated opinion of himself, Lucas is not the star of the show."

Dru Benson's voice was the first thing I heard as I entered the theater. Not precisely raised, but definite, intense. The kind of voice that would make other people think twice about doing anything other than what he wanted, even without his vampire's rapport.

"That's a terrible thing to say," Temptation snapped.

The two were standing together, on the lip of the stage, the rest of the cast and crew in a loose semicircle behind them, looking as if they didn't quite know whether to stand or walk away. The air was so thick with tension, it felt like a sauna.

Quickly, I started down the aisle toward the stage. "Is there some way I can help?"

"Oh, Candace, thank goodness!" Temptation said. "Maybe you can find out what's wrong."

I mounted the steps to the stage and joined them. We formed a triangle. Equilateral.

"What *is* wrong?"

"It's Lucas," Temptation said. "He hasn't shown up for rehearsal this morning. It's just not like him to do a thing like that. He's never been late once in all the years we've been together. He knows how much I rely on him."

"Ms. McCoy would prefer not to continue with the rehearsal until she knows Mr. Goldfinch's whereabouts," Dru cut in. "I've explained that I can't allow that kind of delay. Our schedule is very tight."

"So the fact that Lucas, Mr. Goldfinch, is absent is really unusual?" I asked.

"Absolutely," Temptation said, throwing Dru a defiant glance. "Lucas takes his responsibilities very seriously. He would never just not show up. Even—" She paused and took a breath. "Even taking into account what happened yesterday. He was very upset about that. Dru thinks he's off somewhere pouting, but I don't agree. And I won't feel right continuing with the rehearsal until I know what's happened to him."

"Perhaps we could compromise," I suggested before Dru Benson could speak again. "You proceed with the rehearsal as scheduled, while I check on Lucas Goldfinch's whereabouts."

"Oh, but—" Temptation began.

"You said Lucas has been with you a long time?"

"Well, yes," Temptation admitted, her expression slightly confused. "But I still don't see—"

"Then I'm sure he would agree with Mr. Benson on this," I said. "He would want you to rehearse. He would want your Vegas debut to be a success. And he would feel terrible if he thought anything he had done had gotten in the way of that."

"She's right, Temptation," Dru said quietly, his voice gentle.

"Oh, Dru," Temptation said.

He stepped toward her; I moved back. He eased her head down onto his shoulder. I hated myself for a moment then. But I had done what I had to, the only thing I could, bought myself and the Sher some time.

"You checked Mr. Goldfinch's room?" I asked.

"I called," Temptation said. "There wasn't any answer."

"Do I have your permission to ask Mr. Manelli to have someone go in?"

Temptation straightened up. "Yes, yes, of course. If he's sleeping one off, he'll be furious, but he'll forgive me. I just want to know that he's okay."

"I'll do my best," I said. "I'll let you know the moment I find out anything. In the meantime . . ."

Dru Benson turned to face the cast. "We'll get going in fifteen, everyone," he called out, then turned back to me. "Thank you, Candace. We'll hear from you as soon as you know something?"

I nodded, stepping away. I would call Al first, I

thought as I climbed down from the stage. Get him to go in and check Lucas's room. Though, frankly, I didn't think there would be much point. I had a hunch I knew what had happened to Lucas Goldfinch, and who had done it. My cell phone began to wail. I snatched it from my bag, flipped it open.

"Steele," I said.

"This is Hagen," a voice responded in my ear. "My team just found the head."

My heart began a drumbeat in my ears. "Thanks for the call," I said. "How's the, er, condition?"

"You mean, is it burned to a crisp?"

"That is what I mean," I said. "Is it all right for you to tell me that?"

"Hey, why hold back now?" Carl asked. "The condition is good."

"Male or female?"

"Male. Three hoops in the right earlobe. Bleached-blond hair. Anything else you want to know?"

"Well, shit," I said. I seemed to be doing that a lot these days.

"What does that mean?" Carl asked.

"I think I might know who it is."

"You think you know, or you do know?" Carl said.

"I can't answer that till I get there in person," I answered. "I'll clear it with Al, then be on my way. It's at the morgue by now, right?"

"Right."

"*Morgue?*" I heard a voice behind me gasp. Clearly, I was going to have to add a move to my Godfather repertoire: never answer a cell phone with your back to the room.

"Looks like I'm going to have to get back to you," I said into the phone. "I'll be there as soon as I can."

"You're not here within the hour, I'm sending a squad car."

"That is such a comfort to me," I said.

I snapped the phone shut, severing the connection. Took a deep breath.

"You know something, don't you?" Temptation pounced at once. "Something's happened to Lucas, hasn't it? Something bad."

"I don't know that for sure," I said as I turned to face her. Dru was still on stage, talking to one of the dancers.

"But you think so," Temptation insisted.

"I don't know what I think yet," I said. "But I'm afraid it does appear that Mr. Goldfinch may have met with some sort of accident. If you would just let me confirm . . ."

Temptation began to wail. Dru Benson sprinted toward us.

"What is it? What's happened?" he demanded. Reaching us, he put an arm around Temptation's shoulders. She clung to him. I felt a funny, tight sensation grip my chest, as if someone had wrapped a leather belt around it and was cinching it tighter and tighter, notch by notch. *So many layers between them,* I thought. So much mutual need and torment.

"Candace thinks something has happened to Lucas, but she won't tell me what it is," Temptation choked out. "But she said 'morgue.' I know she did. And now she has to go somewhere. Make her take me with her, Dru. I want to know what's happened to Lucas."

"How much of this is true?" Dru Benson asked.

"A contact in the police department has indicated an accident may have befallen an individual who appears to match Lucas Goldfinch's description," I said. I was trying to sound official and neutral. Instead, I came off sounding like a pompous jerk. "I've said I'll try to identify—"

"No, no!" Temptation interrupted. "If anyone identifies Lucas, it should be me."

"Are you sure you want to do that?" I asked, as gently as I could. "It can be an unsettling experience. Perhaps someone who wasn't quite so close—"

"No," Temptation said again. "Lucas worked for me. I'm responsible for him."

I knew when I was beaten. "It's up to you," I said. "But Mr. Manelli needs to be informed. The decision about whether or not to inform Mr. Glass will be up to him."

"I agree," Dru Benson said. "Pull yourself together, Temptation. Go and get your things. The sooner we find out what's going on, the sooner we can all get back to work."

"You're sure, Ms. McCoy?" Carl asked.

I watched as Temptation turned away from the viewing window, her face devastated. "Quite sure, thank you, Detective," she said. "That's my personal assistant, Lucas Goldfinch."

Carl nodded, and a lab-coated technician on the far side of the glass pulled a drape across the window, hiding what was left of Lucas from view. The M.E.'s team had done a great job, I thought. They actually made it look as if Lucas was still intact. I had a feeling it was not his body under the drape. Not information I intended to share.

"I'm very sorry for your loss," Carl said.

"What?" Temptation said. Her eyes were glazed, ever so slightly unfocused. *Shock,* I thought. "Oh, yes. Thank you, Detective. You've been very kind."

"Just doing my job, ma'am," Carl replied.

"How soon can I bury him?" Temptation asked now. "I want to do that. Lucas didn't have any family. I should do that much."

"We'll release the body to you as soon as we're able," Carl said smoothly. I wondered if I was the only one who noticed he made no promise as to the actual timeline. "I'll contact Mr. Manelli. He can have Ms. Steele let you know."

"Thank you," Temptation said.

As we reached the waiting area where Randolph

and Bibi stood ready to offer support as needed, Dru Benson checked his watch. "I'll phone ahead," he announced. "Tell the stage manager to have the cast assembled by the time we get back."

Temptation stopped. "What are you talking about?" she asked. "You can't expect me to work after something like this."

"I can and I do," Dru said, his tone firm. "We open at the end of the week, Temptation. I'm sorry that Lucas is dead, but we can't let that derail the show. Remember what Candace said earlier. Lucas would want you to carry on."

Thank you so much, Mr. Sensitivity, I thought. Way to make someone else look responsible for the fact that you're acting like an asshole.

"You never liked Lucas," Temptation accused, her voice tearful. "He treated me like a person and you couldn't stand that. All I am to you is box-office dollar signs."

"Temptation," Dru said. He reached for her arm, but she scooted to the far side of Bibi, out of range. "Keep your voice down."

"I wonder if I might make a suggestion," Bibi suddenly interjected, wrapping an arm around Temptation's trembling shoulders. "Surely we could all use a little downtime. Let me take Ms. McCoy back to the Scheherazade. We'll have a sauna, maybe a massage, a bite of lunch. Then, after lunch, some studio time. We can run through your numbers," she went on, addressing Temptation directly. "Maybe you could even give me some pointers on a few dance steps."

"Oh," Temptation said, her eyes filled with tears. "I would like that. That sounds so nice."

"We'll do that then, shall we?" Bibi said, her eyes speaking volumes as they turned to Randolph. "It will be a sort of break and minirehearsal combined."

"It might make getting back on track tomorrow easier," Randolph agreed, looking at his tearful star. He turned to Dru. "An excellent suggestion, don't you think?"

I'll say this much for Dru Benson. He knew when to fold. "Fine," he said, his voice making it quite clear it wasn't fine at all. "If you and Ms. Schwartz will escort Temptation back to the casino, I'll take the opportunity to attend to some additional business." He looked at Temptation. "I'll see you tonight."

Without another word, he brushed past Temptation and Bibi, and walked out. Bibi, Temptation, and Randolph followed, more slowly.

"I would appreciate it if Ms. Steele could remain for a few moments," Carl Hagen said. I jumped at the sound of his voice. I had gotten so wrapped up in the other dynamics, I had actually forgotten Carl was even in the room.

"Of course, Detective," Randolph answered smoothly. "Anything my staff and I can do to help.

When you're ready, Candace, just phone and Al will send a car."

He put a hand under one of Temptation's elbows. Bibi kept her arm around the star's shoulders. Together, they guided her toward the door.

"I think this room is free," Carl said. He gestured, and I followed him down a short hall. He opened a door, held it open for me to go first. As soon as I walked through it, he followed, banged it shut, then shoved me back against the door. He stepped in close, his body pressing against mine.

"Hey," I managed.

"Shut up, Steele," he said. "Don't talk. Use your mouth for something else."

Before I had time to ask what the hell that meant, I found out for myself. Carl's lips crushed down. A take-no-prisoners kind of kiss. Full of flash and fire, demanding a response. Carl released me, stepped back, and I met the pain, the fury in his eyes.

"What was that for?" I asked, praying I didn't sound as shaky as I suddenly felt.

"That was good-bye."

"What?"

I would have moved toward him then, but Carl lifted a hand and stepped away. I felt it then, the swift, hot stab of the knife straight through my heart.

"You know," he said, "I think it would be better

if you just didn't talk. That way I won't have to figure out if you're lying or not. That guy in there—what's left of him—that's the one you tangled with last night at Lipstyx. He wasn't a stranger. He was someone you knew. The fight was personal."

Statements, not questions, every single one. I nodded. There was nothing else for me to do.

"You know anything about how he ended up like that?" Carl inquired.

Slowly, I shook my head from side to side. I had my suspicions, my fears, but it would do absolutely no good to share them with Carl. Ash had asked who hurt me. Now the person responsible for injuring me, for causing me pain, was no longer alive. I was not putting Carl in Ash's path. I liked him way too much.

"You see my problem here, don't you?" Carl asked. He was all cop now. "You've just admitted that you lied to me this morning. Why the hell should I believe you're telling the truth now?"

"I only lied because I thought I had to," I said. "Think about this from my perspective for a minute, Carl. I had no idea who that body in the parking lot was until you described his head over the phone. I didn't tell you I knew the guy who hassled me because it could have meant bad publicity for the Sher. If I don't protect Randolph Glass's interests, I could lose my job."

"Okay, I get that," Carl said. "I know the way things work in this town. The trouble is, protecting your job runs the risk of obstructing mine. That's not a situation I can allow to continue, on any level. I can't, I won't, sleep with someone I don't trust."

I felt the knife in my heart twist.

"I'm sorry you feel that way," I said.

Carl lifted an eyebrow. "But?"

"What do you want me to say?" I asked. "You want me to say I'm sorry, I am. You want me to promise it will never happen again, I can't, and we both know it. If we didn't, we wouldn't be here."

"So that's it," he said, his voice flat. "You don't even think what we have is worth fighting for?"

"Actually, I think it is," I said. "The problem is, you're the one I'm fighting for it. Not everyone who lies is untrustworthy, Carl. The world just isn't that black and white. That's something else we both should know."

"So that's it, then," he said.

"That's it," I answered. "Except for this. I never meant for this to happen. I didn't want it to. I'm sorry, Carl."

He was silent for a moment, gazing into space. "Yeah, well," he said. "You and me both. Trouble is, 'sorry' is just not enough, is it?"

I shook my head. "No. If you have any more questions, you know where to find me."

"I do," said Carl. "You take care, Candace."

"You, too," I said.

I turned and let myself out.

* * *

The rest of the day dragged like a ball and chain. I checked in on Bibi and Temptation. I updated Al, telling him as much of what was going down as I thought I could. It was possible the police would have additional questions for me regarding the fate of Lucas Goldfinch, and Al deserved the professional consideration of being told about this possibility ahead of time.

I replayed the scene with Carl over in my head about a half a million times. It always ended precisely the same way: with me walking out, alone. Maybe I had been stupid to imagine I could have a relationship, even one that might be described as casual, given my past. Given my present. Not a particularly cheery thought. As soon as I could call it quits for the day, I hit the road, driving up into the hills. Sometimes a change of perspective helps.

I drove to my favorite overlook, got out, clambered up onto the hood of my car. Leaning back against the front windshield, I watched the sun go down and Las Vegas come to life. Not that it ever really sleeps, of course. But Vegas is definitely a town that shows to its best advantage in something other than the harsh light of day. My personal preference? The half light. What all those poets they make you read in college English survey courses call the *gloaming*. The waning light of day as it gives way to darkness. Even the neon is more beautiful then, shimmering, like a promise.

Face it, Candace. You've made a mess of things, I thought. And the possibilities for additional screwups weren't over, not by a long shot. Lucas Goldfinch was dead, most likely because of me. Dru Benson was still masquerading as alive. And Candace Steele, Vampire Hunter, was in way over her head. The type of vamp I had made it my personal crusade to destroy had literally walked right through my door, and I still didn't have the faintest idea of what I was going to do about it.

I did know one thing, though. Indulging in a self-pity fest was not going to help. I sat up a little straighter, scooting to the front of the hood to let my legs dangle down. I could really see the pattern of the city now. The outside edges may look kind of ragged, but, at its heart, Vegas is a series of tight, well-organized lines. A pattern you don't always notice when you're right there, in the thick of things. Move back a little, and it's impossible to ignore.

That's what I need to do, I thought, *step back, find the pattern.* I closed my eyes, pictured my situation board in my mind, tried to see it like a street plan, stretched out in front of me. Dru, with Temptation and Lucas just below him, now became the main street on the left side. Ash, the main street on the right. Running in between them, parallel to both, was the first headless body in the Lipstyx parking lot. Mentally, I drew a line connecting

Lucas to the unidentified vampire, then continued the line to Ash's side of the board.

That's what I've been missing, I realized suddenly. Cross streets, intersections. Were there places where, even in conflict, Ash's line and Dru's connected?

I felt something brush against my face. Startled, I reached to push it away, my eyes flying open. In the next second, I let out a yelp of dismay and scrambled back. Bats. The air was filled with bats. They were all around me. Darting toward me, wings beating against my face. I could feel their claws scrabble against my skin, as if they were trying to attach themselves. Crying out again, in both pain and fear this time, I covered my face with my arms and rolled off the car.

I hit the dirt, one hand still covering my head, the other frantically reaching for the handle. Could I get into the car without letting any of them inside? It was bad enough being out in the open. I didn't want to get up close and personal with even a single one of these guys in an enclosed space. Talk about claustrophobia. They were on my jeans now, crawling around, exploring.

Screw this, I thought. I scissored my legs, frantically kicking, desperate to shake as many of them off as I could, then surged to my feet, crashing back against the driver-side door. I spun around, yanked the door open, and felt the sudden sweep of cold. Strong hands caught me in the middle of my back, sending me sprawling, facedown, across the front seat of my car. My head smacked against the passenger-side door. In the next instant, a body covered mine.

Hands roamed up and down me, a horrible parody of passion, then captured my arms. Pulling them back, the angle painful, pressing my face down against the passenger seat upholstery. I was shaking now. Deep tremors that racked my whole body, no way to make them stop. A combination of cold and fear. The thing on top of me, pinning me facedown on the front seat of my own car, was a vampire.

"You're frightened, aren't you?" I heard a voice say. *Male,* I thought. "How nice. But then, you should be." The hand that held my head in place shifted slightly, to brush my hair aside, baring my neck, and I tried to jerk away. I simply couldn't help myself. A moment later, I felt his tongue as he ran it from the base of my neck to my ear.

"I want you to do something for me. Do you think you can do that?"

"As long as it isn't making a donation to the blood bank," I somehow managed to get out.

He laughed then, as if genuinely delighted. "You know?" he said, his tone almost conversational. "I think I'm beginning to see what the fuss is all about. Not that it will make any difference in the end, of course. No, I don't want a donation, tempting as that is. What I want is for you to deliver a message."

Without warning, his fingers tangled in my hair, brutally yanking my head back so that I cried out. Once more, he ran his tongue along my neck. This time I felt his teeth every inch of the way.

"We know who you are," the vampire whispered in my ear. "We can get to you, anywhere, anytime. There is no such thing as a hiding place for you, Candace. No place even *he* can take you that we won't find. I want you to tell him that. Tell him, he is not to interfere. If he does, you will be the one to pay the price. You can do that, can't you? I'm sure you can."

He gave my head a second vicious jerk. "Say yes. Right now."

"Yes," I said.

He let me go. My head dropped forward, crashing against the passenger door for the second time that night.

"I knew you could," the vampire said. I felt his weight lift. "Now, that wasn't so bad, was it?"

Fortunately, I was spared the necessity of answering that particular rhetorical question. By the time I got the door open and finished throwing up in the cool night air, he was gone.

Thirteen

Several hours later, I was taking a drive down memory lane. Vegas's, not mine. I was on the old part of the Strip, where the early hotels once stood and you can still catch a glimpse of the town as it was. My destination was an old movie house called the Majestic, now converted into a retro disco club. According to Blanchard, the Majestic is a key player in the vampire underground. If you want somebody to know you're looking for them, the Majestic is where you go to spread the word. For obvious reasons, I had never gone before. But it was pretty clear the message I was supposed to deliver was intended for Ash. It was equally clear I couldn't wait for him to come to me. Which meant I had to find him.

The good news was that I found a parking place right in front. The bad news was that I had to get out of the car. I did it. As I covered the short distance to the entrance on foot, it occurred to me suddenly that I hadn't asked Blanchard if the Majestic charged a cover. If they did, I could only hope it would be one I could afford.

The entry doors were heavily carved and painted gold. It wasn't until I had the one on the right all the way open that I realized that the new owners had altered the original cavorting cherubs, turning them into angelic-looking, plump baby vampires, complete with fangs. Nice. With a start like that, I could hardly wait to see the rest of the decor.

The light inside was dim. The sound was like a solid wall. Seventies disco. Now that was a music style that should have been allowed to die a natural death. Maybe that was part of its appeal for vampires.

Just past the entry doors sat an old-fashioned ticket booth. It was staffed by a slim, young woman dressed in gold to match the cherubs.

"I need to get a message to someone," I said, half-shouting to be heard above the sound system. The young vampire was motionless for a moment, regarding me with bright, dark eyes. I knew from Blanchard that the clientele of the Majestic included both vamps and humans. It pretty much had to, as most humans didn't know vampires existed at all. Some of the humans would have a vampire connection, drones or errand runners. Others would be completely clueless, drawn to the Majestic by its retro music and decor. I had done my best to dress for the occasion, in one of the tight dresses I had let Bibi talk me into for the nights when we went clubbing. If I was going to be an errand girl, I might as well dress the part.

The vampire in the cage licked her lips, as if wondering what I would taste like. Not that this one was going to get much of a chance to drink blood. She wasn't high enough in the food chain for that.

"I don't think I've seen you before."

"First time," I acknowledged, hoping she would cut me some slack. Sometimes it pays to look more vulnerable than you really are. "Can you help me out?"

"Sure thing," she said, after another moment's scrutiny. "You go on in and I'll pass the word along. Who did you say you wanted?"

"Ash," I said. "I want Ash."

And wished I didn't mean it in more ways than one.

I had no idea how long it would take for the message to go through whatever channels it had to travel to reach Ash. Or even if it would reach him at all. But I had to figure the smart money was on sticking around for a while. Even if Ash didn't show, maybe some member of the Majestic's staff or clientele could provide a clue as to where I could find him. I ordered a drink, Perrier and lime, and hung out at the bar. From there, I could see both the entrance and the dance floor.

After about fifteen minutes, I made a discovery. I now had an explanation for the survival of disco music, after all. It's the beat, like accelerated sex, a human heart about to overload. It gets inside your skin, making you dance to its tune whether you want to or not. *Sort of like the way vampires operate,* I thought.

I sipped my mineral water, my eyes on the dance floor. A headache beat in time to the music, right behind my eyes. My skin felt slightly clammy. Not as bad as it was around Dru Benson. Nobody here was anywhere near that strong. But there were a lot of vampires at the Majestic. More than I had ever encountered in such close quarters. The whole situation made me feel slightly nauseated, like I was coming down with the flu. I thought longingly of my bed at home.

A Donna Summer song ended and the music switched gears. The beat was still insistent, but the rhythm had geared down. A slow dance, disco-style. Out on the dance floor, couples moved closer, bodies sliding together. As I watched, a woman near the edge of the floor lifted her arms above her head, her body pressing back against her partner's. He ran his hands up the length of her skintight dress, palms cupping her breasts. She tilted her neck back, to rest against his shoulder, and he pressed a passionate kiss to her throat.

"Well, well, well, what have we here?" a voice beside me inquired. Even through the music, I could hear the drawl. A Southern vampire boy. He was about my age, jet-black hair, sea-green eyes. The sort of looks that seem too impossible to be real. A pair of black leather pants hugged his lower body like a second skin. He wasn't wearing a shirt at all.

I gave a quick glance back over my shoulder, as though I thought he must be talking to someone else.

"Are you talking to me?" I asked, eyes wide.

He laughed, as if genuinely amused. "Oh, sugar," he said. "You just might be too good to be true."

I gave what I hoped passed for a delighted giggle as I looked him up and down. Maybe he would have something I could use, in the way of information, I mean.

"Same goes."

He gave his head a jerk in the direction of the dance floor. The couple I was watching earlier had changed positions. Now she was the one with her lips pressed to his throat. Kind of gave a whole new meaning to the term "foreplay."

"You want a little of that action?" the vamp inquired.

"Not exactly," I said.

He smiled. "That's okay. I do all kinds. Come on, sugar. Even if you're here on business, nothing says you can't enjoy yourself a little till the work shows up."

So he knew I was looking for Ash, I thought. Did that make me safer, or not?

"You sure I'll enjoy myself?" I asked.

He laughed again then leaned forward to slide my drink from my hand and set it on the bar. He kept my fingers in his, tugging me toward the dancers.

"Why don't you just come on out here and answer that question for yourself?"

He was good. I had to give him that. He danced close but not too close. Not enough to crowd me, or make me edgy, but enough to ignite, then stoke, desire. A soft brush against my breasts as he turned to face me in the midst of the dancers. A quick slide of fingers down the bare skin on the inside of my arm. Without warning, he captured one hand, tugging me a little closer, keeping those impossible sea-green eyes on mine. I tugged back, keeping the distance between us intact, and watched him smile.

He released one of my hands then held his out. For a second, I was sure my face betrayed the confusion that I felt. In the next, I understood. He was beckoning, issuing an invitation. To someone else. I saw a slim white hand slip into his and he pulled a young female vampire to his side. She was absolutely gorgeous, even if her attire did make her look more than a little like a Morticia Addams clone. Fine, pale skin. Lustrous black hair streaming down her back, mingling with the glossy black of the skintight dress she wore. The male vampire dropped the hand he had used to pull her to him, ran it down her body to cup her ass.

He never took his eyes from mine.

Leaning over, he whispered in her ear. She gave a smile then nodded. Sliding from his grasp, she moved toward me, then behind, running her fingers across my shoulders. Then just one, all the way down my back, following the curve of my spine, the feeling like someone had run an ice cube across my skin on a scorching hot day. I felt my whole body tighten in response.

The male tugged me forward, till my breasts bumped against his chest. I felt hers brush against my back as she leaned in close. He released my hand, and she slid hers down the outside of my arms. Gently capturing my wrists, she urged them upward so that my arms were above my head, then slid her open palms down my arms. Lingering on the outside of my breasts before continuing to sweep on down my body, urging me one more step forward just as the boy vampire stepped toward me. I was between them now, pressed up against him, her fingers leaving trails of ice and fire.

The pulse of the music pounded in my veins, driving, hypnotic. I felt the place where Ash's teeth had scarred me burn and throb. The air around me seemed thick, alternating between hot and cold. My breath came in short, panting gasps. Was I aroused, or was I terrified? I felt the female vampire slide her hands across my belly, her hands moving inexorably lower, and realized my neck wasn't the only place that throbbed. I lowered my arms, put them on the male's shoulders, pushed him back, then captured the female's wrists, yanking her hands away from my body. I stepped out from between them.

"That's enough."

For one split second, I thought he would reach to pull me back. I saw the intention in his eyes, clear as day. Then it died away, to be replaced by an expression I couldn't quite place.

"I couldn't agree more," said a voice I recognized. A moment later, I felt Ash's hand beneath my elbow. The room steadied. My breath evened out. That was the moment I realized what the expression on the male vamp's face had been: fear.

"Hey, I just heard she was looking to pass you a message," he said quickly. He raised his hands, like a cowboy in a stickup. "She could have been anybody. I didn't know she was one of yours."

"I'm not one of his," I said. "I'm one of mine."

The expression on the male vampire's face might have been funny if he hadn't looked so terrified. His eyes flicked from me to Ash, as if he expected Ash to teach me a lesson on the spot.

"Know this," Ash said, ignoring my remark completely, his tone quiet, yet cutting straight through the music that still pounded all around us. "I protect what's mine."

The male vamp nodded, as if not daring to risk a reply. Ash jerked his head, and the male vampire disappeared into the crowd. The female was already long gone.

His hand still on my elbow, Ash piloted me through the club, out onto the street, then kept on going for about another block.

"When do we reach minimum safe distance?" I asked.

Abruptly, he stopped. Swung me around to face him. I yanked my arm away, took a step back, though I knew it would never be far enough. Ash was radiating fury.

"What the hell did you think you were doing?" he demanded. "You think this is a game? Time for you to have a little fun?"

"As a matter of fact, I don't," I said. "I came here because I didn't think I had a choice. This day has not been what I would call fun. I started out by helping to identify Lucas Goldfinch's decapitated body. Anything you'd like to tell me about that?"

"I'm sorry for your loss."

My body reacted before my mind could stop it, my hand flying out. I heard it connect in a solid slap, saw Ash's head whip to one side. Before I could so much as draw a breath, he closed the distance between us. Hands wrapped around my elbows to jerk me up and toward him, off balance, teetering on my toes, so that I had to hold on to him, my hands grasping at his upper arms.

"You really want to watch that temper, Candace," he advised, his voice soft. "One day you're not going to like the result."

"I already don't like it," I said. "A man is dead, Ash. *You killed a man.* Because I told you he hurt me, that he had set me up. You may not have a conscience, but I do. You think I want to carry that for the rest of my life?"

"Don't be melodramatic," Ash said. "If it's my action, it's on my head, not yours."

"That's bullshit, and you know it," I said. "Cause and effect. You were the effect but I was the cause. I didn't particularly like Lucas, but I sure as hell didn't want him dead. You had no right, Ash. No right at all."

"I had every right," he blazed back. *"I protect what's mine."*

"I'm not yours!" I all but shouted, desperate for it to be true. "I don't belong to you. I never did."

"That's a lie and we both know it," Ash said. He brought his lips down on mine.

It was like kissing a volcano, so much heat, so much pressure. I wrapped my arms around his neck and deepened the kiss, suddenly desperate to be warm. Our teeth scraped together. His tongue swept into my mouth and I bit down, hard. There was nothing but fire and passion. Nothing that was gentle. Nothing giving or unselfish or slow. There was only rage and need, building to its inexorable conclusion: the moment either or both of us lost control.

With a sob, I tore my mouth from his.

"No," I managed. "No."

He eased my head down onto his shoulder, held me still. "You can't say that forever," he replied after a moment. "I won't let you."

"I won't have to," I answered. "Sooner or later, I'm going to die. And who knows? You might not want me when I'm old and gray."

"I will always want you," he said. "Why is that so difficult for you to believe?"

"It isn't," I said. "That's the problem."

He leaned back then, to gaze down into my face. "Jesus, Candace," he said. "You take my breath away."

"It isn't all that hard," I managed. "You're not actually breathing anyway."

His lips twitched as, unsuccessfully, he held back a smile. "You came because you had a message for me," he said. "What was it?"

I scrubbed my hands across my face, suddenly exhausted. "I need you to answer a question first. Were you responsible for that first decapitated corpse?"

"No," he said impatiently. "Old vendetta between vampires. I promise you that one wasn't tied to anyone you know. Now what was this message?"

"I'm supposed to tell you they know who I am. That they can find me, no matter where you might try to hide me. That you are not to interfere. If you do, I will be the one to pay the price."

He took an involuntary step forward then, pulled me back into his arms, holding me tightly. I could feel the way his hands trembled with emotion, but what the emotion was, I couldn't tell.

"Who said this?" he asked. "When?"

"I don't know. Earlier tonight," I said, answering the questions in order. "Around sunset, I drove up into the hills to try and get my head straight. This whole flock—do bats fly in flocks?"

Without warning, my teeth began to chatter. *Shock setting in at last,* I thought, and suddenly found myself thinking of Temptation McCoy. Did my eyes hold the same expression I had seen in hers earlier that day? The look of someone desperately trying to make sense of a world spinning out of control?

"What difference does that make?" Ash asked. He gave my shoulders a little shake, as if to snap me back to reality.

"I just thought it would be nice to know," I said, "seeing as how I was attacked by one. Hundreds and hundreds of bats. I managed to get into my car, and then there was only one, in human form. He's the one who gave me the message."

"But he didn't say who he was."

"Not by name," I said. "I sort of got the impression that wasn't important. It was the message, not the messenger, that was the relevant part. Do you know who *they* are?"

"Probably," Ash said.

"Are you going to tell me?"

"Probably not."

"For crying out loud, Ash," I said, pulling back. I felt a little better now. I think it was being angry at him that did it. "Don't you think I deserve to know? Don't you think it would help?"

"No and no," Ash said, his voice absolutely calm. "Telling you who they are isn't going to do any good, Candace. All it will do is make you afraid to walk around."

"Gee, thanks a lot," I said. "Your way of not telling me makes me feel so much better."

"And it wouldn't help," Ash continued, precisely as if I hadn't spoken. "Because there's nothing you can do about them anyhow. It's up to me. I'll do my best to protect you, up to a point."

"What the hell does that mean?"

"What you keep insisting," Ash said. "You are not, truly, mine. If you were, I would be able to offer you better protection."

"Truly yours," I echoed. "You mean if I was a vampire."

Ash nodded. "I'm not the thing that makes you most vulnerable, Candace," he said. "It's the fact that you're human that does."

"So what you're saying is that I would be better off undead."

"Something like that," Ash replied.

"That works out nicely for you, doesn't it, Ash?" I blazed. "I wouldn't be in danger in the first place if it wasn't for you. Now you're telling me the only way out is for me to let you have your way, to become what you are. Well, fuck that. I don't need you. I don't want you. I'll find a way to take care of myself."

"And how will you do that?" he inquired.

"What do you care?" I asked. "I'm not your responsibility, since I'm not *truly* yours. And for the record, I would appreciate it if you would stop killing people on my behalf. I don't consider that an acceptable method of problem solving."

"Suit yourself," he said with a shrug. "But don't expect me to come crawling. I'm offering you eternal life, Candace. A life for us, together, filled with experiences you can't even dream of."

"I wouldn't be too sure about that," I said. "I'm the one with the scars."

He took a step forward then. It took every ounce of willpower I possessed to hold my ground. For one split second, I was sure he would simply yank me to him and finish what he had started. That, finally, I had gone too far.

"I'm finished saying I'm sorry for what happened in that elevator in San Francisco," Ash said, his voice harsh and low. "That night cost me, too, more than you know. You came to deliver a message; you've delivered it. Thank you very much. Now go."

"You do not get to do that," I said. "You don't get to treat me like a servant at your beck and call."

"All right, then I'll go," Ash said.

Any other guy would simply have turned around and stomped off. But Ash was hardly any other guy. One moment, he was a man, standing in front of me. The man I tried so hard, so very hard, to deny I loved. In the next, I saw wings, and like a great, dark angel, Ash rose from the ground. Hovering in the air above me, wings outstretched, until what he was became indistinguishable from the sky itself. His wings, the night. His eyes, what I had always secretly suspected they were, two bright stars.

Then the wings beat once, beat twice, folded in upon themselves, and Ash was gone.

On legs that shook a whole lot more than I cared to admit, I walked back to my car, climbed in, and drove slowly and carefully home.

Fourteen

Two nights later, I stood in the wings, waiting for the lights to come up on Act Two of Temptation McCoy's show. It was opening night, and the excited buzz of the audience was like a swarm of bees in my ears. So far things were going well, but the bottom line was that I could hardly wait for the night to be over.

After tonight, the contents of Act Two would no longer be a mystery. I could stop feeling like I was always half a dozen steps behind. At work, anyway. I wasn't making any predictions about my personal life. Nor was I going to think about that now. In the days since I had last seen Ash, there had been no contact with him, no more mysterious and threatening messages to pass on. But the fact that my personal vampire activities seemed to have ceased as suddenly as they had begun didn't really make me feel much better. I knew the lull for what it was: the calm before some seriously badass storm.

At least the show was going well. One thing Lucas Goldfinch's untimely demise had meant was that I was now the undisputed point person when it came to security for Temptation McCoy. I still hadn't been allowed to see rehearsals for Act Two, but that was about the only place I couldn't go. I had watched the first act from the stage-right wings. For Act Two, I was switching to the stage-left side. No real reason for this, except that I was feeling antsy. And I've never really been the sort who likes surprises.

Bibi had kicked things off. Literally. I was half surprised some of her high-fliers hadn't taken out key members of the front row. Bibi had chosen to play to her strengths, I think that was the phrase she used. She was a Vegas showgirl. As such, she was going to strut her stuff and provide the perfect counterpoint to Temptation's woman-child. Bibi had played it to the hilt, and the crowd loved every minute of it. I had never been more proud of her. She was having the time of her life, and it showed.

Temptation's first act had been just what the audience expected, a run-through of the tunes that had made her a star. She had bantered and chatted with the audience, pure Southern charm. By the time intermission rolled around, she had the crowd eating out of the palm of her hand. Act Two would be the big payoff. The last few days had seen a veritable media blitz, all of it playing up the secrecy surrounding it, the way Act Two promised to reveal a whole new side to Temptation McCoy. Ticket sales had gone through the roof. Randolph walked around looking like the cat who had just eaten an entire cageful of canaries.

As far as I could tell, the only people not thrilled to death were me and Al. Neither of us would be satisfied until tonight went off without a hitch. I pulled in a steadying breath as the houselights began to go down. The working lights backstage began to fade. Right before they went to black, I saw Dru Benson step into the wings on the far side of the stage, standing in the very same spot I occupied for Act One. *Great,* I thought. Now I had two things to keep my eye on. He had watched Act One from a seat beside Randolph. I sincerely wished he had stayed there.

I willed my eyes back to the stage. Much as I hated to take my eyes off Dru, Temptation was my priority. The stage was now completely dark. A tiny glow-tape X mark stood out clearly. This was Temptation's mark. I continued to watch it, saw the second it disappeared from view. That meant the star was in position.

Showtime.

Slowly, silently, the curtains pulled back. I heard the audience murmur, an echo of my own surprise. The stage was still completely dark. Then, in the darkness, a saxophone began to wail, the sound evoking a thousand smoky nightclubs, and a spotlight slowly came to life on Temptation McCoy. She was dressed in flowing black, her blond hair piled in elaborate coils on top of her head. As the lights grew brighter I realized she was muffled from neck to toes in a sweeping black cloak. Her eyes were enormous, the lids dusted with sparkling silver. Her mouth, a vivid slash of scarlet. Against the hot white lights, the night-dark cloak, her pale skin glowed like polished mother-of-pearl.

In the space of an intermission, Temptation McCoy had grown up.

She began to sing then as the rest of the orchestra joined the sax. It was a torch song, full of unrequited desire. Standing absolutely still in the center of the stage, Temptation sang of a passionate thirst that had yet to be slaked but could not be denied. A thirst for the one thing other women knew but she had never sampled: love.

And then, suddenly, she was no longer alone. A male dancer was with her on stage, dressed in a black bodysuit, his face obscured by a black domino mask. She began to sing to him, the physical embodiment of the passion she longed to explore. He moved behind her, his hands plainly visible against the black of her cloak as he caressed her shoulders. The cloak slid down to pool at Temptation's feet, and I swear every single person in the audience pulled in an audible breath.

For one split second, she looked absolutely naked.

She wasn't, of course. It was a bodysuit, but so cleverly designed—the color an exact match for her pale and lustrous skin—that the first impression quite genuinely was that she wore nothing at all.

The two began a dance of seduction, and again, both the audience and I got a surprise. Because instead of being pursued, Temptation was the pursuer. This was not some virginal girl, afraid of her first taste of love. She was eager, demanding. It was her partner who was coy. Coming in close, only to dance away, out of range. All of a sudden, I found myself smiling. There, on stage, was the physical embodiment of what a guy's lack of commitment felt like from a girl's perspective. *Way to go, Temptation,* I thought.

I watched as the male dancer's choreography took him to the side of the stage on which I stood, so close I could have reached out and touched him. That was when I felt it, the familiar chill along my skin, down the length of my spine. I felt my pulse rate ratchet up a notch. As the dancer propelled himself back on stage, I gazed straight across. Dru Benson was still right where he had been at the top of Act Two, standing in the wings stage right. The chill I was feeling had nothing to do with him. There was only one obvious conclusion.

The dancer was a vampire.

Okay, Candace, whatever else you do, do not *panic,* I thought. There could be another explanation. *Such as what?* I asked myself. I'd had access to every nook and cranny of the backstage area, cleared every single member of the cast and crew myself. Once all were present and accounted for, the entire backstage area had been off-limits to everyone else, locked down, tight. I knew there were no vampires among Temptation's regulars, with the exception of Dru Benson.

There's your answer, right there, I thought.

Dru Benson was responsible for the vampire on stage. At the moment, it didn't matter that I didn't know the how. What mattered was the why. What mattered was what was going to happen next. I had a feeling I wasn't going to like it much, and neither was Temptation McCoy. A sick feeling in my gut told me that the real events of Act Two had been kept a secret even from her.

I pulled my attention back to what was happening on stage. The dance of seduction was almost finished now. Both Temptation and her dream lover had surrendered to the inevitable. Their passion was too great to be denied. As I watched, he moved behind her, running his hands slowly up her body, just skimming the outside of her breasts, then tilting her head to one side. And, in that moment, I knew what would happen next. The vampire on stage with Temptation was going to sink his fangs into her neck. In front of an audience of thousands, Temptation McCoy was going to die.

I didn't stop to think. Sprinting from the wings at a dead run, I launched myself onto the stage. With a flying tackle, I took down the vampire. The force of the impact sent us both crashing to the stage floor. Temptation backed away from us with a cry, her hands at her throat. I heard a great roar as the audience surged to its feet, then heard it dim as the curtains swished closed and the lights on stage went out.

The vampire fought like a wild animal, body bucking upward, trying to throw me off. I hung on for dear life. He brought his elbow up, a quick, solid hit to my face. I saw stars, tasted blood, prayed he hadn't broken my nose. My head snapped back, my grip loosened. He was out from under me in a flash, scrambling to his feet. I reached for him. It was all but impossible to see in the darkness, my fingers slipping off the slick bodysuit he wore. He twisted away and was gone.

I got to my feet, staggered to where Temptation still stood, her pale costume making her easier to see. Her hands were pressed against her mouth. I took her by the arm.

"Are you all right?" I asked. "Temptation, answer me, are you injured?"

She shook her head. "No," she gasped out. "No."

"Come on," I said. "Let's get you to your dressing room."

Not much of a sanctuary, but it would have to do. For now.

* * *

"Lock the door," Temptation said the second I closed it behind us. "Please, Candace, lock the door."

I did as she asked, not liking the note of panic in her voice. Temptation was trembling, her whole body shaking as if she had a fever.

"I can't breathe. Oh, God, I can't breathe. There isn't any air," she gasped.

I took two quick steps, grasped her by the arm. Gently yet firmly, I eased her down into the closest chair. "It's okay," I said, striving to keep my own voice calm. I put my hand on the back of her neck. "Put your head between your legs. Keep your breathing slow and even. It'll pass. You're just upset, that's all."

"Gee, ya think?" I heard her mutter.

"There, you see?" I said. "You're feeling better already. No, take another minute," I said when she tried to sit back up. I hoped we would get that minute. I didn't know what was happening outside the dressing room door. Whatever it was, we wouldn't have much time.

"Now, sit up slowly," I told her.

"You have blood on your hands," she said.

I grimaced as I caught a glimpse of myself in the dressing room mirror. There was blood on my face as well.

"I'm sorry about that," I said, reaching for a tissue. "Sonofabitch caught me in the nose. You're sure you're all right? He didn't hurt you?"

"He didn't hurt me," Temptation echoed. "You knew," she went on, her voice almost expressionless. "You knew what he was. That's why you reacted the way you did. You knew he was a vampire."

No way to deny it and not much reason to. I tossed the bloody tissue in the trash. "I did."

She made a sound, sort of a cross between a laugh and a sob. "Do you have any idea what it feels like to be able to say that out loud, and not see you reaching for the phone to call the funny farm? Sometimes I think that's been the very worst thing of all. There's been no one I could talk to, no one who would believe me even if I did talk."

I thought of Bibi. Counted my blessings. "The ultimate form of an abuser's power," I said. "He can say no one will believe you because no one will."

This time I knew the sound she made was a sob.

"I'm sorry," she said. "I'm sorry. I've always promised myself I wouldn't cry. It's just . . ."

"I really do understand," I said. "But there are some questions I have to ask, and I don't think we have much time. Lots of people are going to be unhappy about what just happened, and they aren't going to leave us alone in here for very much longer."

"Dru," Temptation said, and I heard the way her breath hitched. "Oh, God, Dru."

I knelt in front of her. In spite of the fact that

they still had blood on them, I took her hands in mine.

"You think he's behind this, don't you?"

She nodded, as if literally afraid to answer aloud. "I could feel him," she whispered. "I wanted to run, but I couldn't. I could feel him in my mind. He wants me dead, Candace. Oh, God, he wants me dead."

She managed to hold the tears back, but in her fear and agitation, she began to rock from side to side.

"He threatens me. He's always threatened me, telling me what will happen when I've outlived my usefulness, when he doesn't want me anymore. He's been doing it since the beginning, really. But then Lucas died.

"Dru was so angry when I didn't want to rehearse. I got my way during the day, but we had a terrible fight that night. This time, when he threatened me, I told him he should just go ahead and finish me off. I think I actually told him he should shut up and put his money where his mouth is."

"Interesting turn of phrase," I said.

She gave me a wan smile. "I know the two of you didn't get off to a very good start, Candace, but Lucas was the closest I came to having a friend. When he died, I knew I would always be alone. Dru will never let anybody else get close to me again. The truth is, I'm already dead. I have been for years."

"You can't think that way," I said. "You've got to fight."

She dropped her head down into her hands. Now, at last, she began to cry, great racking sobs that shook her body like a seizure. Gone was the temptress who had held an audience enthralled. The woman in the chair before me wept like a small and frightened child.

"I don't know how to fight him," she sobbed. "I want to, but I don't know how, and I'm all alone."

"You're not alone," I said. "You have me. Tell me where his nest is, Temptation. Where he rests during the day. If you do that, I can take him out."

She gave a funny hiccup, and lifted her face to stare into mine. "What?" she said, her voice dazed. "What?"

"Even the most powerful vampires need to recharge their batteries. Usually, they nest at midday to avoid the peak of the sun. It saps their power," I said, as patiently as I could. Surely she knew this as well as I did. I was wasting valuable time.

I leaned forward, put my hands on her shoulders. "If you tell me where Dru rests, I can set you free, Temptation. I can destroy him."

"No, no!" she cried out, jerking back out of my grasp, her eyes wild. "I can't let you do that. Dru would never really hurt me. He only says he will. He needs me. He loves me too much."

I resisted the urge to shake some sense into her. But I was beginning to fear that she was too far gone. She had been abused to the point where no matter how much she talked about longing to be free, she could no longer truly imagine life without the framework the abuse provided.

"Let's say you're right," I said, as patiently as I could. "Let's say he does love you. It won't make a difference, and you know it. *Sooner or later, he will end your life.* He won't have a choice, Temptation. He'll *have* to do it. It's what he is, what he does. And I'm in danger, too, now. Have you thought about that? I gave myself away to save you tonight. I could have stayed out of it, but I didn't. I made a choice. Now, you make one.

"I can stop him from hurting you. I can make sure he never hurts anyone else. But only if you tell me where he nests."

"He'll kill you," she whispered. "He's a cold-blooded killer."

"I know that," I said. "And, no, he won't. Not if you tell me what I need to know."

For one humming instant, I was sure I had failed to convince her. Then she gave a sigh.

"It's where the detective said Lucas was found," she said. "The club, I can't remember its name."

"Lipstyx," I said as I felt my pulse pick up. I had what I needed to know now. The only question was, could I use the information in time? Could I get to Dru Benson before he got to me? Temptation had just given away his hiding place. She wouldn't be able to keep that a secret from him, not for very long.

She nodded. "Yes, Lipstyx, that's the one. There's a hidden basement. That's where he nests."

"Thank you," I said. Once again, I took her hands in mine. "Whatever happens, I want you to know I mean that."

Before she could answer, there was a wild pounding on the door.

"Temptation!" Dru shouted. Her hands jerked in mine. I gripped them tightly, holding her steady. "Temptation, are you in there? Are you all right?"

"Mr. Benson, this is Candace Steele," I called back. "Ms. McCoy is secure. She is unharmed."

"I want to see her. I have the right to see her," Dru said. "Open this door, right now!"

"I'm sorry, but I'm afraid I can't do that," I said. "I will open the door to Mr. Manelli, and no one else. If you would like to return with him . . ."

There was a short, charged silence.

"Ms. Steele," Dru Benson said at last, and I fought against a shiver at the cold fury in his voice. "You have a lot to answer for. I look forward to being present when you're called to account."

I listened to the sound of his footsteps die away.

"He'll kill you," Temptation McCoy said again.

"No," I answered. "He won't. I'm harder to kill than I look."

She glanced up at me then, her eyes weary but calm. "I dearly hope so, Candace."

Then, as I heard Al's voice at last, I released her to unlock the door.

Fifteen

"What the hell were you thinking?" Randolph Glass exploded the minute I stepped off the elevator into his penthouse. I had always sort of wondered what Randolph looked like mad. Or even if he got that way. Guess I now knew the answers to both questions. The Scheherazade's owner was literally shaking with rage. It made me grateful Al was present.

Al had only spoken once, as we began our ascent in the elevator. "I've got your back as much as I can, Nerves. But there may be limits."

"I understand," I said. "Thanks."

Al gave an unamused snort. "Don't thank me yet."

When we got to the penthouse, I stepped out first, into the full force of Randolph Glass's rage.

"I know you want an explanation," I began.

"You're damn right I do," Randolph broke in. "Stop playing the deferential employee, Ms. Steele. There's not a thing you can do to save your ass. The only reason you're here is because Al spoke up for you, and because I deserve an explanation. So let's just cut right to the chase, shall we?"

"I did what you hired me to do," I said. "I protected Ms. McCoy."

"How?" Randolph exploded. "By tackling a member of her cast on stage?"

"He wasn't a regular cast member," I said. "That's why I reacted the way I did. I wasn't allowed to watch the rehearsals for Act Two, as you know. But I did for Act One. I'm on at least a speaking acquaintance with all of Ms. McCoy's dancers. The man on stage with her tonight wasn't one of them."

Randolph took a turn around the room, pacing like a wildcat in a cage. "So what you're telling me," he said, "is that, even though he was wearing a costume that covered up half his face, it was dark, and you were nowhere near him, you decided the man who knew all the choreography for Ms. McCoy's show wasn't someone you recognized and wasn't supposed to be there?"

"In essence, yes," I said.

"It never occurred to you that he might just be someone you never met?"

"Of course it did," I said. "If I could just get you to think about things from my perspective for a moment, Mr. Glass. Two days ago, Ms. McCoy's head of security was killed in a spectacularly brutal fashion. The police have no suspect in custody, as far as I know."

Nor were they likely to, I thought. Not that this

was information I needed to pass along to Randolph.

"On opening night, I see an individual I have never seen before in close proximity to Ms. McCoy," I went on. "Beyond that, my professional instincts tell me that he's dangerous. Yes, it was dark where I was standing, but there was still enough light for me to see that I only had two options: do something, or do nothing. If I hadn't interfered and Ms. McCoy had been injured, on stage in the Scheherazade's new theater, the consequences might have been even more disastrous.

"Protecting Temptation McCoy was my first priority, a priority you gave me. I did my job."

Randolph's jaw worked, as if he were chewing words he longed to spit out. Before he had a chance to speak, the elevator pinged open and his personal assistant came into the room.

"Excuse me, Mr. Glass."

"Not now, Amy."

"I'm sorry sir," his assistant said firmly. "But I think this is a situation you'll want to know about. If I could just have a moment."

I had to hand it to her, the girl had guts.

"I'm not finished with you yet," Randolph said, giving me a look that made me feel like a bug on a pin. "Stay there."

Beckoning to his assistant, the two stepped aside. Al sidled up next to me.

"He should have let you clean up," he said. "I

didn't want to say anything earlier, but you're a mess."

There's this thing about Al that I always appreciate. He knows how to make me laugh. Even when things do not look so funny.

"It's okay," I said. "Maybe it'll impress him, make him think of me as a warrior." I fell silent for a moment, my eyes on Randolph's assistant, who was speaking to him earnestly. "So, how do you think I did?"

"Hard to tell," Al said. "Not too bad, though, all things considered. Mentioning Goldfinch was good. Makes it seem like part of a pattern. You think it is?"

"I'm not sure what I think yet," I replied. "Mostly, I just want to get through this."

With a nod, Randolph stepped away from his assistant, who got back in the elevator without another word.

Randolph waited until the elevator doors had closed before he spoke. "Well, Ms. Steele," he said. "I find there are new factors to consider."

I waited for the explanation but Randolph only gave a short exhalation through his nose.

"I had every intention of firing you tonight, Candace. Dru Benson has demanded it, and, frankly, I was inclined to agree with him. It may be that the fact that the situation now seems to be rebounding in our favor will help to change his mind. There's also the fact that, in your defense, you made several good points. The most significant one is this: You did, indeed, protect Temptation McCoy. Neither Mr. Benson nor I appreciate your methods, but I, at least, can't argue with the outcome. Temptation is safe because of your efforts.

"I am, therefore, going to present Dru Benson with the following compromise. You will return to your regular duties in the casino. You will have no further access to, or interaction with, Temptation McCoy. Are we clear on all points?"

"Crystal," I said.

"Good," Randolph answered. "Then I'll say good night to you both."

Moments later, Al and I were alone in the elevator, heading back down to the casino. "What the hell was that?" I asked. "What did he mean about the situation 'rebounding in our favor'?"

"I'm not sure," Al admitted. "But if I had to take a wild guess, I'd say that rumors about the attack you prevented have gotten out, and they're already increasing ticket sales."

"That's completely sick," I said.

Al gave me a weary roll of his eyes. "No, that's Vegas. Do me a favor. Take the rest of the night off. Go home, rest up, come back tomorrow ready to keep an eye on the floor."

"Right," I said, allowing myself to feel a few moments of sheer, sweet relief. I had deflected a vampire attack and managed to keep my job.

* * *

The first thing I did when I got home was to take a shower. I needed to wash my own blood off my face and hands, scrub the events of the night from my body.

I felt better in a change of clothes. Just your basic streets, nothing fancy or flashy. I didn't want to be memorable in any way, shape, or form. I fixed myself a sandwich, made myself eat it, downed a glass of milk, then cleaned up. I took a quick pass through every single room in the house, for the simple reason that it made me feel better, then went to the safe room to organize my thoughts.

My situation board was just as I left it. Dru Benson on one side, Ash on the other. Temptation on Dru's side of the board. I removed the card in the center, the one for the first headless vampire to be discovered in the Lipstyx parking lot. I was reasonably certain now he was not connected to the others. I replaced it with Lucas Goldfinch's card. Then I stood back, as far away as I could and still be in the room, narrowing my eyes, trying to see the board as I had the Vegas streets.

Intersections, I thought. *Connections.* Connect the dots. The lives. The deaths. Ash was responsible for Lucas's. He had as good as admitted it. But, in life, Lucas had been tied to Dru Benson. The fact that they had apparently hated each other's guts didn't matter when it came to that. Lucas was connected to Dru. He had been taken out by Ash. Did

Dru know that Ash was in town, that he was responsible? If he did, would he seek revenge?

I caught my breath. Slowly, I walked to my situation board, plucked a three-by-five card from the chalk tray, and added one last card, one last name, one last connection to the mix. So obvious that I hadn't seen it before, even though it had literally been staring me in the face. One last connection between Dru and Ash, a way for Dru to balance the scales.

The new card on the board said: Candace Steele.

Sixteen

San Francisco, a year and a half ago

I gazed up at Ash, as if, by focusing on him and him alone, I could bring the world back into focus. Turn it back into the thing that it had been before he had spoken. My chest felt funny and tight. My throat, clogged with an emotion I feared to set free.

"Would you please," I said, very carefully, "say that again?"

Throughout my reaction, Ash had kept his eyes on me, his own gaze steady.

"I'm a vampire."

I gave up, then. Dropping my head down into my hands, I gave vent to the thing that I was feeling. The emotion that could not be denied: I laughed.

"For crying out loud, Ash. Though I have to hand it to you. You really had me going for a moment."

"You don't believe me," he said.

I lifted my head. "Of course I don't believe you," I replied. Now that I had released the tension, I felt a little better, though I still didn't understand quite why he felt he needed to set up such an elaborate and ridiculous joke.

"You've just informed me that you're a vampire. A creature from medieval legend. Also the creation of a fevered, and probably repressed, Victorian novelist's brain. The fear of being buried alive, *undead,* is very real. That's not the same thing as saying vampires actually exist."

"How can I convince you?"

I was starting to get annoyed now. "You can't. And I'm not sure why you would want to. What are you really trying to tell me, Ash? That's what I want to know."

It happened so fast I never saw it coming. One moment, we were sitting together, on the bed. The next, Ash was across the room, before the darkened window. His pose, relaxed and natural, as if he were just standing there. Just an everyday man across the room from the everyday woman he loved.

Except his feet were not touching the floor.

And, from the center of his back, extending out from his shoulders so that they seemed to fill the room, fill the whole world, stretched a great pair of sleek, leathery black wings. I was off the bed, scrambling for the door almost before I knew I'd moved. I never even made it halfway. I felt a rush of air at my back, and then those great, dark wings were all around me, cutting off escape and sight, leaving only sound. I gave a cry of sheer, unadulterated terror.

"Don't, Candace," I heard Ash say. Felt his hands on my arms. "Don't be afraid. You don't have to be. I'm not going to hurt you. Please, don't fight me."

"Take those things away," I said. "Get them away from me." I could hardly breathe now. My head felt light and heavy, all at once. Spots danced before my eyes.

"Alright," Ash said. I heard a sound I couldn't quite identify, then nothing at all. "It's alright, Candace," he said. "It's only me."

Slowly, as if he feared any sudden movement would cause me to shatter, Ash turned me toward him. I buried my face against his chest, hearing the way my own heart thundered. His was silent. He had no heartbeat. He had no pulse. He did have wings, the wings of a bat to be precise.

My lover, the man I loved, was a vampire. I couldn't wrap my mind around it. It was all so unreal. Horror movie images filled my mind. He killed people, fed on them. . . .

I stepped away from him as I took that in. I was shaking uncontrollably. "So what is this, Ash? What the hell are you doing here? Are you setting me up to tear my throat out? Is that what's going on?"

"Stop it," Ash said roughly, his arms coming around me in a crushing embrace. "That's not what I want. I'll never take you against your will, Candace. I need you to believe that."

Slowly, I lifted my head and looked into his eyes. *So beautiful,* I thought. *And so strange.* Had they always looked like that, or were they like the wings, some vampire power?

"Never take me against my will," I repeated. "You mean, make me what you are."

"I do mean that," Ash said.

"You can do that, drink my blood, make me a vampire." Statements, not questions.

Ash nodded.

"Whether I want you to, or not."

Another nod. "I have that power. But it isn't one I want to use, Candace. That isn't what I want for us."

I shook off his arms, took a step back, and realized, for the first time, that I was naked. We both were.

"What do you want, Ash?" I asked.

"You," he said simply. "I want us to be together, Candace. Now. Tomorrow. Always. I love you. That hasn't changed."

"Always. I assume you mean longer than till death do us part."

He smiled then, taking me completely by surprise. "God, I love you," he said. "Sometimes I think you don't even know why."

"Just answer the question, please," I said.

A half-smile formed on his face. "For the record,

you didn't actually ask one. But yes, that is what I mean. I want us to be together, in my world. I can give you so many things, show you so much."

"And what about what I want?" I asked.

He grew still then, those silver eyes holding mine. "Are you saying you don't want me, don't love me?" he asked.

I took a deep breath. Told the truth. "No. But what you're talking about . . . I'm not even sure I have the vocabulary to talk about it. We're talking about me dying to be with you, Ash. Isn't that the bottom line? That's an awfully big step."

All of a sudden, I found I was laughing, astonished to find I still could. "Usually when people say that, they're talking about moving into a house together, not picking out matching coffins."

Ash took a step forward and enclosed me in his arms. "Don't think of it as a big step, then," he said. "Think of it as a series of small ones. We don't have to rush things, Candace. We can take them slow."

"What things, Ash?" I whispered. "What sort of things?"

I felt the tremor move through him then, the way his cock surged and pulsed. He tilted my head back, slanted a kiss across my mouth.

"So many things, my sweet Candace," he murmured. He ran the tip of his tongue across my lips, along the line of my jaw until he reached my ear. "Let me start to show you."

His kiss was gentle, a feather touch of lips across mine. Then he kissed my cheekbones, the tip of my nose, and, to my utter astonishment, made me smile. I felt the soft brush of his lips against my eyelids, the unexpected, warm glide of his tongue.

"I love you so much, Candace," I heard him whisper. "So very, very much."

And then his lips moved back to mine. Coaxing. Almost pleading. *Open for me. Accept me. Take me inside you.* I could feel the way his body trembled with his passion, with his need. I knew he would hold it in check until I joined him. I parted my lips, pulled his tongue deep into my mouth. With a groan, he lifted me from my feet, turned and took several quick steps, and laid me on the bed, his mouth never leaving mine.

As if I were a banquet, a feast that would never sate him, Ash's mouth moved down my body. He pulled first one nipple, then the other, deep into his mouth, tongue dancing across them. I felt it then, that ache between my legs that only he created, only he could satisfy. It should have been no different from what he always made me feel. But even my body seemed to know it was. For the first time, I was truly making love with Ash. Now I knew all of what he was.

His mouth left my breasts to meander across my stomach, his tongue gliding down, down, down. I felt my breath catch, my heart grow still. We both knew where this journey would end, what his destination was. And then he was parting my legs, lifting my knees so that my most secret places were open to his mouth. I felt his tongue slide through my center and I arched up, crying out. The very air around me seemed to thicken, shimmering with passion. Rippling and dancing like a mirage. Slowly, deeply, Ash stroked with his tongue, until there was no sensation but what he brought me. No need that didn't have him at its heart.

"Ash," I whispered, my head restless on the pillow. "*Ash.*"

And then, once more, he put his mouth on mine. I could taste myself on his lips, on his tongue. He reared up suddenly, and I reached to bring him back, suddenly sure that, if I didn't have his mouth on me somewhere, anywhere, I would simply die.

"Look at me, Candace," he said, and I could hear the passion in his voice. "Tell me that you want this. That you want me."

"I want you," I said, without hesitation. "I want it all."

Swift as lightning, Ash lowered his mouth back to mine, pulling my lower lip into his mouth to suck. And it was then, and only then, that I felt his teeth for the very first time. A quick, bright spear of pain, quickly over. I tasted blood, knew it was my own. Then Ash was surging forward, his cock filling my body in one, deep stroke. I made a sound I didn't recognize. We were indistinguishable, inseparable, now. My mouth, my blood in Ash's mouth.

His body, his sex, his passion feeding, stoking, driving mine. Until I could no longer think, only feel. No sensations but the ones he brought me. No world outside the boundary of his arms. I felt my body quiver, stretched taut, like the pulled string of a bow. And then I was flying, set free on a great arc of pleasure. And as I came I tasted blood once more. His or mine? I could no longer tell. It didn't matter anymore.

I slept deeply that night, my mind completely free of dreams. When I awoke in the morning, he was gone. On the pillow beside my head was a single white rose and a note with just three words. *See you tonight.* I got out of bed, wandered to the bathroom, snapped on the light. I stared at my face in the mirror. My eyes were full-lidded and drowsy. My skin, flushed. My lips looked full, the lower one, ever so slightly swollen. I looked like a woman who had spent her night sampling passion. A woman who would be ready for more.

How much more? I wondered, as I forced myself to meet my own eyes. I had learned things, done things, last night that I never imagined possible. What else was I going to discover about Ash, about myself? Just how far was I going to go?

"Hey, stranger," Bibi said, several days later. "Wait up."

I thrust my arm through the elevator doors,

catching them before they could slide all the way closed. The blousy shirt I had tossed on over a formfitting tee slipped off my shoulders just as Bibi slid into the elevator beside me and pressed the button for the ground floor.

"I've missed you at dance class this week," she said. "You're not dropping out, are you?"

"No," I said, easing the shirt back up. "I've just had some stuff to do, that's all."

Bibi was silent for a moment as we both listened to the hum of the elevator.

"I don't suppose this has anything to do with the fact that Ash is around."

"Of course it does," I said, annoyed. "Don't play stupid, Bibi. It doesn't suit you."

"Hey." Bibi held up her arms. "I was trying to be funny. Obviously a failed attempt. But for the record, this is the guy who walked out and broke your heart, if you remember."

"He had his reasons," I said.

Bibi gave an unimpressed snort. "Don't they all." We both fell silent as the elevator continued its descent, the tiny space suddenly uncomfortable. "I'm surprised at you, Candace," Bibi finally said. "Somehow, psychology degree and all, I thought you would be smarter."

That stung. "Thanks for the vote of confidence."

The elevator reached the ground floor, the doors opened, and I started out.

"Oh, for crying out loud," Bibi exclaimed. "Wait. Don't go away mad. I didn't mean to fight."

Following me out, she reached to pull me back, catching me by the arm. I gave a hiss through my teeth and spun away.

"What?" Bibi asked, her eyes widening.

"It's nothing," I said shortly, turning back around. She reached for me again, catching me by the shirt collar. Before I quite realized what she intended, she yanked it down, sliding the loose garment off my shoulders, exposing my arms. A series of diagonal lines ran along the insides of both of them. Ash and I made love every moment we were together. Every single time, there had been blood. His. Mine. Because of what he was, Ash's body didn't show the marks. But mine did.

"Oh, Jesus," Bibi said, her voice little more than a whisper. "Jesus H. Christ. What the hell have you gotten yourself into, Candace? What have you been letting him do to you?"

"It isn't what you think," I said. Furious, I shrugged the shirt back up onto my shoulders. "You don't know anything about it."

"For the love of God, Candace," Bibi said. "It looks like he's cut you. You're telling me you *let* him do that? That it's what you *want*?"

"Ash doesn't do anything to me that I don't want."

Bibi's face went dead white. "You're telling me *you* did that? You made those marks, yourself?"

"I'm telling you that you don't understand. You don't know what's going on."

"And you aren't going to tell me, are you?" she asked, her voice flat.

I pulled in a breath. "No, I'm not. I don't want to fight, either, Bibi. It's just . . . Ash and I are working something out. Until we do, the topic of our relationship is not open for discussion."

"In other words, it's none of my business," she said. To my horror, there were tears in her eyes. "I'm your friend. I fed you chocolate when you cried. I backed you up."

"I know you did," I said. "I appreciated it then. I appreciate it now. But things are different this time, Bibi. I can't explain. I'm sorry."

"So am I," Bibi said. She brushed past me, moving quickly through the lobby of our apartment building. She yanked the front door back, and I felt the cool air of another San Francisco morning. Just before she stepped outside, Bibi turned back. Now her eyes were dry.

"I just hope you don't make either of us sorrier than we are right this moment, Candace," she said.

"Don't be such a drama queen," I said.

Something like pity came into her eyes then. "Is that what you think I am?" she asked quietly. "Because to me, it just feels like I'm looking at what's staring me right in the face. And that is 'this thing I don't understand' with Ash is already tearing you apart. So just be careful, Candace. Or there won't be anyone around to pick up the pieces." She released the door and it crashed closed.

"There's really nothing to be nervous about," Ash said that night.

He was standing in my bedroom, in front of my dresser mirror, putting the finishing touches on a tie. It was a Friday and we were going out, out into the world Ash called his own. The world of the vampires. Not only that, we were going to be witnesses to an event few humans ever see, much less live to tell about. I was about to watch someone else perform the act Ash desired of me: willingly give up his or her humanity, become a vampire. Ash had described it as a sort of vampire wedding. We were dressing up.

I gave a shaky laugh as I struggled with my stockings. I couldn't seem to make my hands work properly. My fingers were trembling too much. Finally tugging them into place, I stood up. Then Ash was beside me, sliding the slim, black dress we'd purchased for me just that afternoon over my head. It fit me like a glove. But its plunging neckline left my neck and shoulders bare. The marks of the unique form of passion I shared with Ash were plain on my body. I made a soft sound, my hands fluttering in a futile attempt to cover them. Ash captured my fingers, held them still.

"Don't," he said gently. "Those who see you tonight will know those for what they are: tokens of our love, to be displayed proudly. It's the world you are about to leave behind that doesn't understand. That misjudges."

I shook my head, as if to clear it. "I'm sorry," I said. "It's just so hard. When we're together, I feel as if I understand. Then, I go outside . . ."

There's this thing about discovering a brave new world—it makes you all but incapable of living in the old one. It's probably why old explorers seldom die in comfy armchairs at home. They have to keep on voyaging.

"We don't have to go tonight," Ash said now. His tone was infinitely patient, but I thought I could detect a note of strain in his voice. He had gone so slowly, so carefully when, with every single breath I took, every single time we touched, I could feel how much he wanted me, wanted the true culmination of his desire: for me to become what he was.

"Our situation hasn't changed in any way, Candace. If you want to stop at any point, all you have to do is say so. Nothing you see tonight is going to hurt you. There are rules, I do keep telling you."

"I know you do," I said. "And I appreciate it."

Ash and I had done more than just have spectacular sex in the last few weeks. We had also done a lot of talking. From him, I learned of the existence of an undreamed of vampire world with its own rules, its own hierarchies. Not every vampire was allowed the taste of human blood. That had been one of the first things Ash had told me. That was a privilege reserved for only a few, the very powerful. And Ash was one of them. I hadn't just gone and fallen for any old vampire. I had fallen for one of the big guns.

"Candace," Ash said softly. "Look at me."

I took a breath, and met his eyes. *So beautiful*, I thought, as I had the very first time I'd seen them. The breathtaking light of the stars.

"Do you love me?" Ash asked.

"Yes, I love you," I replied. It was the truth. It was as simple as that. I loved him, even knowing what he was. I felt myself begin to steady.

"Do you trust me?" Ash inquired.

"With my life."

He leaned down and brushed his lips softly against mine. "Then share this with me, my love. Let me show you what we can have together."

Our destination turned out to be one of the old mansions in the Berkeley hills. It would command a spectacular view in the daytime, once the ever-present fog burned off. The night was clear and had turned chilly. I was grateful for the cashmere wrap Ash had purchased to go with the dress. No sooner had we pulled up at the house than a slim young man, a valet parking insignia on the breast pocket of his crisp white shirt, appeared at the driver's window. Ash got out of the Mercedes, handed him the keys. A second young man opened the door for me, his fingers just barely touching mine as he helped me from the car.

"Have a good evening," Ash remarked.

"And you, too, sir," the young man said.

Ash came around the front of the car to take my arm.

"Are they . . . you know?" I asked, as we began to climb the steps.

Ash smiled as he shook his head. "No. They're simply very good at parking cars."

"But once we get inside . . ." I persisted.

This time, Ash nodded. "Once we get inside, with one exception, everyone you meet will be a vampire." He leaned down then, gave me a searing kiss. "And I am going to be the envy of every man in the room."

"Bet you say that to all the girls you bring here," I remarked, trying without success to quell the sudden fluttering of butterflies in my stomach. Ash stopped at once, turned me toward him.

"There is no one else but you, Candace," he said, softly. "There will never be anyone but you. That's why we're here tonight."

I took a shuddering breath, trying to will myself to be calm. I couldn't quite manage it. "I'm just so afraid," I blurted out. There. I'd said it. The thing that had been haunting me for days, ever since I found out where Ash wanted to bring me, what he wanted me to see.

He reached to capture my face between his

hands. "There is nothing for you to fear here, Candace," he said, his voice fierce. "*Nothing.*" And I understood, suddenly, that he would fight for me. Fight anyone.

Within the frame of his hands, I shook my head. "That's not what I mean," I said. I felt my breath hitch, and I fought to steady it. "I'm afraid I'll let you down. That I'll disappoint you."

By way of answer, Ash bent his head. He pressed his lips to mine in a kiss so sweet it made my throat ache. Then he pulled me all the way to him, holding me close.

"That is simply not possible," he said. "You may have doubts, but I don't. I know your strength."

Unbelievably, I felt a bubble of laughter rise within me. "This really better not be one of those conversations where the guy tells the girl he knows her better than she knows herself," I said. "Because I have to tell you, they always piss me off. That is such a load of horseshit."

I felt a quiver of what might have been laughter pass through him. He stepped back and regarded me at arm's length.

"There, you see?" he asked. "That's the Candace I know and love."

"The Candace you know and love is scared to death," I said.

"There is another way of looking at this," Ash pointed out. "Do you really not see that you are the one in control? If you decide you don't want this, I could lose you forever. You're not the only one with something at stake here tonight."

I opened my mouth then closed it again. All of a sudden, I felt slightly ridiculous. Ash had always seemed so powerful, so strong. The truth was, it hadn't occurred to me that I might hold the upper hand, because what he wanted was a gift that only I could bestow. Deliberately, I stepped to him, slid my fingers into the crook of one of his arms.

"I'm ready to go in now."

The house's entry hall was high-ceilinged and spacious. My shoes made sharp, percussive sounds against the elaborately tiled floor. A young woman in a traditional maid's uniform greeted us and took my wrap. I felt the cashmere slip away, exposing the marks that had so horrified Bibi. The marks of my shared passion with Ash. I straightened my shoulders.

With Ash's hand resting gently on the small of my back, we started down the length of the hall. I began to be aware of a murmur of voices. At the hall's end, we turned to the right. Before us was a large room, whose vast proportions somehow managed to feel comfortable. In the center was a slightly raised dais, a ring of curtains drawn around it. A series of plush leather chairs, most of them already occupied, were arranged in a loose semicircle in front.

"Those are our places," Ash said, pointing to the

only empty chairs that remained. I stopped to link my arm through Ash's. The truth was, I desperately needed something to hold on to. Then I took a deep breath and stepped into the room full of vampires.

They were so beautiful, all of them. I swear that was my first thought. Like gorgeous animals, sleek, well-fed predators, and they watched me with predators' eyes. A murmur passed through them as Ash and I made our way to our places. *What do they see when they look at me?* I suddenly wondered. Did they see a specific person, as Ash clearly did? Or was I simply something that moved and breathed, a potential source of blood? All of a sudden, I was grateful not simply for the feel of Ash's arm beneath my fingers but for the marks on my body. They had a dual purpose, I understood that now. Not simply a way of introducing me into the world Ash hoped we would come to share, but the literal marks of the claim he had to me. I belonged to him, and no one else.

By the time we reached our seats, my knees were shaking. I don't think I have ever been so thankful in my life for the chance to sit down. I sank into the soft leather, feeling the way my body warmed it instantly. Ash sat beside me, a low table clustered with flickering votive candles between us. He reached across it, palm up, and I placed my hand in his. He brought it to his lips, pressed them briefly into the center of my palm. I curled my fingers around the kiss, as if I could hold it, like a talisman.

At some signal I couldn't perceive, the lights in the room began to dim. The candles were the only light now. Dozens upon dozens, on the tables, at the edges of the room, on the steps leading to the dais in front of us. Then, with a whisper of sound, the curtains on the dais parted, pulled back. A murmur of appreciation moved through the assembled vampires.

Lord have mercy, I thought.

In the center of the dais was a great circular bed, the ivory satin sheets upon it gleaming in the soft light. Then the curtains at the back of the dais parted and two individuals stepped into view, both attired in shimmering silk robes of a hue there was really only one way to decribe: the color of blood. One was a red-headed woman. The other, a dark-haired man. But I knew at once which was the vampire. The expression on the man's face was one I thought I recognized. Trepidation and excitement so bound up together, it was no longer possible to separate them. I felt Ash flex his fingers against mine and realized the hand he held had clenched into a fist. I relaxed it, turned it over to link my fingers with his.

Without speaking, the figures on the dais moved apart, the vampire to the front of the bed on the left side, her human lover, on the right. They met at the foot of the bed, turned to face each other. I saw her give him what looked for all the world like an encouraging smile. With fingers that trembled visibly, the man reached for the sash at the vampire's waist, untied it, and eased the robe from her shoulders. It slid down her body to lie in a great crimson pool at her feet.

She had the kind of body men fantasize about. Long-legs, her hips and torso slim, her breasts full and lush, the nipples dusky. Her own hands steady, she unbound her lover's robe, pushed it back. As it fell away, I felt my body start to tingle as a murmur of approval and appreciation ran through the assembled vampires.

His body was marked, just as mine was.

She took him by the arm and turned him toward the assembled guests. I saw the sheepish grin that spread across his face at the quick, spontaneous smattering of applause. Saw, too, the way his cock began to stir, as if to signal that his body understood, that it welcomed and anticipated what was to come. And, in that moment, I understood, too. She was going to complete the journey they had begun together, make him what she was, in the midst of the act of love.

The guests grew quiet again as he turned toward her, ran his hands across her shoulders, down her arms. She lifted them up, placed them around his neck, then leaned in close. Brushing her breasts against his chest, nipping, teasing at his mouth with teeth and tongue. I felt Ash's fingers tighten on mine.

Mouths fused together now, the couple tumbled backward onto the bed. My heart began to beat in hard, fast strokes.

Hands a blur of motion, they stoked each other's passion. *So fast. So fierce. So hot,* I thought. More than just a race to the finish, a race to whatever lay beyond. She sprawled across him, mouth ravenous on his, arms stretching his straight out to the sides, then releasing them to slide like liquid down his body. She used her tongue. She used her teeth, until her lover was writhing on the bed, literally begging for more. She slid back up to straddle him, poising herself above his jutting cock. His hands reached for her, gripping her hips. Then, head flung back, breasts flushed with passion, she sank slowly down. He gave a groan, and I swore I heard the assembled vampires give a sigh.

This was the secret of arousal, I thought. The certainty of what was to come. The mystery of when it would arrive. The knowledge that, each time, it would be different. How far would you travel away from yourself? Could you go so far you could never come back?

"Now," I heard him say, his voice thick with need. "Now, for the love of God."

With a suddenness that left me gasping, she leaned over him, her body covering his, and sank her teeth into his throat. He gave a great cry as his body spasmed upward in what I swore was pleasure, his hands crushing her to him as his cock continued to thrust. For an endless series of moments, they stayed locked together, each feeding the passion of the other. Then, slowly, his body settled and grew still. His hands slipped from her body to lie prone, palms facing up. And still, she straddled him, her teeth locked into his throat. He stopped moving, entirely.

And then there came one crystal moment, a moment entirely without sound. In it, I realized I was the only one breathing. In all that assembly, I was the only one who was truly alive. In the next, the female vampire threw her head back, her lover's blood staining her mouth. One beat passed, then two, and then I heard him make a sound. Not of pain or fear, but of need and desire.

As if his cry had been a signal, she drew one sharp and red-tipped fingernail across one perfect breast, and the blood streamed down. Then, gently, she reached down and brought his mouth to her breast, for all the world like a mother guiding a beloved child. So that he might drink from her as she had drunk from him, so that he might become what she was. On her face, a look of exaltation, of ecstasy so pure and elemental it seemed an intrusion to watch. I closed my eyes. An image of Ash and me, together, flickered against the inside of my eyelids.

This was what Ash wanted for me. For himself. For us. This passion. This ecstasy. This end of all earthly boundaries. If I gave myself to him like this, when we performed this act we would belong together, forever. There would literally be no place we could not go.

I opened my eyes.

Spent now, the two vampires lay together, the ivory of the sheets stained crimson with their mutual blood. As gently as they had parted, the curtains surrounding the dais whispered closed. This stage of their existence was over. The new stage was yet to come.

Ash was silent all the way home. As if knowing, instinctively, that I needed time to absorb what I had seen, what I had felt. He didn't touch me, not even to help me into and out of the car. It wasn't until we stepped into the elevator of my apartment building and he leaned across me to push the button for my floor that his hand brushed against my arm, the touch of his skin searing as a brand. Startled, I stepped back, and I realized then the need he had been holding back, holding down, keeping prisoner, deep inside him. Only I could set it free.

In that moment, I knew that I had made up my mind.

What I had just witnessed had been the most electrifying experience of my entire life. I wanted it to be mine. I closed the distance between us in one small step. With a groan of need, he pulled me into his arms.

Mouths fused, feeding a hunger so ravenous it

could never be satisfied. I felt his hand slide straight down my belly to my crotch. I parted my legs, then captured his hand between them, rubbing against him in utter abandon. Nothing else mattered but what he brought to me, what he would bring.

Now, my mind screamed. *Don't wait. Do it now. Give me that ecstasy. Make me yours.*

As if he understood, his lips left mine, trailing a stream of pure fire across my face, down my throat. I thrust against his hand, arching my neck up, a bare and open invitation. Just for a moment, I felt him pause. Then, with a growl as feral as any animal's, Ash bit down. I felt my body jerk, then settle into the rhythm he established, as he began to draw the blood from my body in the same slow, deliberate pace he used to pleasure me when we made love. His hand between my legs, his mouth at my throat, pulling, releasing, stroking. Until I no longer knew where I ended and he began, was no longer certain it mattered anymore. I could hear the blood rushing in my ears and let myself drift on its swift current. It would take me to the only place there was left for me to go.

First my feet and then my legs went cold. I could feel my knees begin to buckle as the strength left them. My legs refused to hold. I began to fall, sliding toward the floor of the elevator, and knew real pain for the very first time. The sudden, horrifying jerk of Ash's teeth, fastened into my throat, were all that held me in place as he continued to suck.

What is it they say happens right before you die? Your life passes before your eyes. In that moment of pain it seemed to me that I saw myself for the very first time that night. Not pledging my devotion to my lover, but willingly giving myself over to my own assassin.

Unless I did something to prevent it in that second, I would have no seconds left. I was going to die.

I began to fight then, desperately trying to twist away, to break Ash's grasp upon my throat. My life had become a horror, a nightmare of blood and fear and pain.

"Ash," I tried to gasp out, and didn't recognize the sound of my own voice. *"Ash. Stop. No!"*

He moved both hands to cup my arms, trying to hold me still. I knew the truth then, that he would never let me go. As if from a great distance, I heard the elevator chime its arrival on my floor. The doors slid open. I slid my arms up between us, palms flat against his chest, and pushed with every ounce of force that I possessed.

I felt the flesh in my throat tear, felt a bright and dazzling pain shoot through me. And then, against all odds, I was free. Stumbling backward out of the elevator, blood streaming down my neck. I took four stumbling steps backward, twisted one ankle, and fell hard, slamming my back against the hallway wall. My knees gave way once more, for good this time, and I slid slowly down.

But I kept my eyes on Ash, standing absolutely still, framed by the open doorway of the elevator, my blood dripping from his face, his own eyes on mine. And in them I read an expression that, from someplace far away, in the part of my mind that still functioned, I realized that I had never seen there before: surprise.

Then the elevator chimed once more and the doors slid closed, hiding him from view. I closed my own eyes and wondered how long it would take me to die.

Seventeen

Las Vegas, present

I waited until just before noon, the sun a disc of gold in the piercing blue of a cloudless sky. As I selected the weapons I profoundly hoped would help me put an end to Dru Benson forever, I felt absurdly as if I had somehow wandered into an old western. High noon. Only one choice: Go out there and meet the evil, head on.

I kept my weapons simple. The slim, silver stakes I favored, two through my upswept hair, one each in the special sheaths I'd had made for them on the outside of my boots. A vial of holy water around my neck. It wouldn't be enough to kill him, but, taken full in the face, it should be enough to blind him, maybe slow him down. Now I could only hope that Temptation was right, that Dru nested somewhere in the bowels of Lipstyx, and that I could get to him before he managed to recharge.

The trip to Lipstyx didn't take much time. Once again, I parked several blocks away. There was no reason to announce my presence by leaving my car in plain view in the parking lot. I reached the club doors only to find them locked. Not surprising. Lipstyx was a nightclub, after all.

I kept walking, my gait even. I was just an ordinary gal out for a midday stroll. And if my stroll just happened to take me on a full circuit of the building, so what? Big things had happened here lately. Surely I was entitled to do a little gawking. As I walked I pulled a pair of thin latex gloves from my back pocket and tugged them on. There wasn't any sense in leaving behind any more of myself than absolutely necessary.

I spotted my opportunity about halfway around the club. The back door was locked, but just beyond it was a window set high up in the wall. It was the sort you sometimes see in a college dorm, the kind that has a long-handled catch on the inside that pushes the window out and open. *A bathroom window, most likely,* I thought. It was open, just a crack. Not only that, it was right above a Dumpster. I cast a quick look in both directions then boosted myself up.

To say the fit was tight is something of an understatement. Once through, there wasn't much on the other side to break my fall. I ended up crouching on the windowsill, carefully maneuvering to change direction, then clinging to the ledge, the metal digging painfully into my gloved fingers. I let my body extend to its full length before releasing my hold. I hit the tile floor with a thump that made my ankles tingle, but it stopped after a minute or two.

I had done it. I was inside.

At night, Lipstyx managed to make itself look colorful and sexy. In the daytime, it just looked down and out. The air stank of sweat and spilled liquor. The floor was ever so slightly sticky, as if the cleaning crew had yet to do its job. I covered it in a quick circuit, looking down. But I could detect nothing out of the ordinary, no seams that shouldn't be there that might reveal a hidden trapdoor. I stood still for a moment, trying to decide where to look next. Then, on impulse, I turned a slow circle, and, as I did so, I closed my eyes. I kept turning until my instincts told me to stop.

When I opened my eyes, I was facing the bar.

I moved toward it, ran my fingers across the top, down every inch of the front, then stepped behind. A rubber mat ran the length of the counter, no doubt to make things easier on the bartender's feet at the same time it caught errant spills. It was truly disgusting, but I knelt down, rolled the mat up. Beneath it I found what I was looking for: an oblong seam in the shape of a door. It had a metal ring, designed to fit flush to the wood. I inserted two fingers through the ring, gave a tug. The door swung up, on soundless hinges, revealing half a dozen wooden steps. I eased the door all the way open and left it that way; there was no sense cutting off my only means of escape myself. Then, snapping on a flashlight, I started down.

Beneath Lipstyx was a single open room, as large as the club above. The beam of my flashlight sliced through the gloom, but I hadn't gone all that far before I realized I didn't need it after all. A subtle light seemed to pervade the whole room. I couldn't identify the source, but I was grateful not to need the flashlight. It meant I had both hands free. I snapped it off, returned it to my shoulder bag, kept moving forward. The sense of unreality grew with every step I took.

You have got to be kidding me, I thought.

It looked like a movie set, an Ed Wood movie set, one where every single item had been borrowed from someplace else. Cobwebs thick as lace dripped down from the ceiling. If I saw one three-pronged wrought-iron candelabra, I saw a dozen. I completed my traverse of the room. There was an organ in the far corner. The only thing missing was the Phantom of the Opera. No vampire nest on earth really looked like this, I thought. Surely I'd been had. The whole thing was a put on.

I was just trying to decide who I was more pissed off at, Temptation or myself, when I felt the hairs on the back of my neck stir, a tantalizing brush of cold. Quickly, I spun around. Ridiculous as the room looked, there was something here. Someone here. I just hadn't found him yet. Where was the cold coming from?

I began to move back the way I had come, sliding one of the silver stakes from my hair as I did so. In the far corner, opposite the impossible organ, I found what I was looking for. A coffin made of highly polished dark wood, sleek and unadorned. Just Dru Benson's style. Now all I could do was hope that he was actually inside, dormant.

I took one more step and watched in horror as, soundlessly, the lid began to open. I had time to take one shuddering breath before it *thunked* to a halt, and Dru Benson sat straight up, his neck swiveling toward me, his dark eyes seeking mine. I skidded to a stop.

"I've always wanted to do that," he said in a tone that suggested he was confiding some secret I might actually want to know. He laughed then, and the room rang with the mocking sound. If I hadn't wanted to kill him before, I sure as hell did then. "Oh, how I wish you could see the expression on your face, Candace. It is absolutely priceless."

Still chuckling, he climbed nimbly out of the coffin. "I certainly do have to hand it to you," he said. "You've been affording us quite a bit of amusement for several days now. I can't remember when we've had so much fun, in fact."

"*We?*" I echoed. "I don't suppose you would care to elaborate on that."

His grin was positively wicked. His eyes danced with unholy delight. He took a step toward me. I took two gliding steps away.

"Of course I would," he said. "You don't think we went to all this trouble only to leave you in the dark, did you? That would be no fun at all. We want you to know everything, before the end."

"There's that plural thing again," I said. I figured I didn't need to ask him to elaborate about what he meant by *the end*. That was clear enough.

He made a face, as if annoyed that I was rushing him, and all of a sudden the cold spiked, completely off the charts. I was looking right at him, staring right into his handsome, wicked face. He hadn't moved at all. But suddenly I was so cold my bones ached with it. A terrible suspicion began to snake its way through the back of my mind.

"The look on your face has changed," Dru observed. "But then you always were quick. I said so, right from the start. But not quite quick enough, were you, Candace?"

The attack came then, completely without warning. One moment, Dru was standing in front of me. Dru and Dru alone. In the next, a figure seemed to come from nowhere, appearing behind him as if it had literally risen straight up from the bowels of Hell. I saw two pale hands reach to twist his neck brutally to one side. And then its teeth were fastened in his throat.

Dru Benson never made a sound. He stood absolutely still, first the expression, and then the color draining from his face until there was nothing left at all. He was a cipher. No longer human.

Most certainly, he was no longer alive. It was over so quickly I couldn't have interfered even if I wanted to.

Temptation McCoy released him and he dropped to the ground.

I'm not quite sure what I did then. I'm pretty sure I made a sound. Some inarticulate expression of dismay and disbelief. I had thought I was so smart, so strong. But I had gotten it wrong, right from the beginning. And now I had a terrible feeling that my strength would fall short as well. I was face-to-face with a vampire so powerful I hadn't even been able to imagine that power.

I was never going to make it out of this place alive.

"He was right about one thing," Temptation said. "The expression on your face really is priceless."

"You," I said, finding my voice at last. "It's been you, all along."

"Well, obviously," Temptation said. "Though that does sound a little pathetic, considering how long it took you to figure things out. You not only needed to see me end Dru before you understood he was the drone, you needed directions to find us. I mean, if I hadn't all but drawn you a map to his supposed lair . . ."

I felt a spurt of red-hot anger then. She had played me. Messed with my mind. The thing I hated most, because I feared it most, even more than dying.

"Fuck you, you stone-cold bitch. You played me, and now I'm going to make you pay. How does that sound?"

"Like a last desperate stand," Temptation said. "But that's alright. It shows you know the truth."

"And what's that?"

"Oh, honey," she said, in that sweet Southern voice. "You don't really want me to say it right out loud."

I lunged then, the hand already holding the silver stake punching out in front of me, even as my other hand reached for a second one. She sidestepped in one single, fluid motion, bringing her own arm up in a backhanded blow. I caught it, full in the face, staggering backward. Felt the blood stream from my nose. I didn't take the time to wipe it away. Instead, I dropped into a crouch as we began to circle each other in a movement as old as time. Two combatants. Cat and mouse.

"You don't really think you can hurt me with one of those little things, do you?" Temptation asked.

"Why not?" I replied. "Silver is silver. A powerful vampire is still a vampire. The math is on my side."

"But you have to stick it in me first, don't you, sugar?" she said. "You're never going to get the chance. You won't even come close. Face it, Candace. I am just too much woman for you."

I caught her blur of motion, just in time. I feinted right then spun away, not quite fast enough. I felt her grasping fingers tangle in my hair then gain a hold. She yanked back viciously, so hard I heard my neck crack with the strain. Stars danced before my eyes. I gave a cry of pain and fury all at once, slashing down and back with my left hand, meeting only open air.

As suddenly as she seized me, Temptation let go. I spun toward her and we both danced backward, out of reach. I was panting now. She wasn't even breathing hard, but then I suppose that was to be expected, considering she didn't actually breathe at all.

She grinned at me suddenly, baring those perfect white teeth. "You know," she said, her tone almost conversational. "I think I'm going to enjoy drinking your blood. I may even keep you around for a while. I'm going to need a new drone, now that I don't have Dru."

This time the icy chill seemed to clamp itself around my heart. To exist like that would be my worst nightmare come true.

"Not a rat's chance in Hell. I'll take myself out before I let you do that."

"You mean you'll try."

She darted forward, so suddenly and swiftly she was no more than a shadow. And I was reacting, forcing my body to do the opposite of what it wanted. Leaping forward to meet her, the fist clutching the silver wand sweeping up and out, then slashing down. I felt my arm drag as the sharp tip of it caught. Heard a sound that, to this day, I cannot describe. It seemed to slice clean through my skull, piercing my brain like a spike of ice.

And then she was upon me. The weight of her was on my back. Frantically, I spun around, took four staggering steps, and slammed us both into the closest wall. Temptation held on. I pitched forward, then slammed back again even as I felt her teeth bite into my throat.

My body spasmed, my neck arching upward in an entirely involuntary reaction to the pain lancing through me. Temptation made a sound like an animal, a wild and hungry dog. Spots dancing before my eyes, breath rattling in my throat, I brought my arm up, stabbed backward with the silver, felt it connect.

With a roar of fury and pain, Temptation released her hold on my throat. I staggered forward, staggered away, one step, then two, before my legs gave way and I went down hard on all fours. I forced myself to roll over, to face my adversary as she loomed over me.

Temptation McCoy wasn't so beautiful now. I hadn't gotten enough silver inside her to finish her for good, but I'd caught her where it mattered most to her. In the face, twice. The first, a great, glancing slice. The skin on that side was already blackened, peeling away. The rank smell of rotting flesh filled the room. My second, desperate backward stab had caught her just beneath one eye.

"You filthy little bitch," she screamed. "Look at what you've done. I am going to eat your heart out. You are going to beg for death before I'm done."

She threw back her head then and screamed, an utterly inhuman sound. Her body began to ripple and buck. Her arms stretched then contracted. Her hands curled into claws. Her torn face became something I no longer recognized as human, though embedded deep within it were a woman's eyes.

"I am going to own you, do you understand me?" she cried. The sound of her voice seemed to eat the very air around me, leaving nothing to breathe. "Everything you have, everything you are, is going to be mine. I am going to take your secrets, to feast on your brain. I am literally going to eat you alive."

I didn't have enough energy to waste on a reply; it was taking all my strength just to pull myself to my feet. I was determined not to go down without a hell of a fight. *Come on,* I thought. *Come straight at me, you inhuman bitch.*

She screamed again, a great cry of rage, and obliged. With a scream of my own, I rose to meet her, both fists extended together, silver pointing upward.

She was gone.

Winking out as if she had never existed. *No!* I thought, suddenly. Desperately. *No, no, no!* I swung in a circle, my arms outstretched to make myself as wide as possible. Nothing. *Nothing.* Then, all of a sudden, I realized where she must be. I stopped, my arms dropping to my sides, and looked up.

Temptation McCoy hovered in the air above me like some great, ruined angel, a being from after the Fall. Great leathery wings had erupted from her back. Her face was blackened and contorted. And all around her, oozing from her like some evil miasma, was the greatest cold that I had ever known. I could feel it sink into my body as if it had a corporeal presence, numbing my limbs. Numbing my mind. Somewhere, inside my head, a voice was screaming at me to move; forward or back, it no longer made a difference as long as it was away.

I stayed right where I was.

Temptation's power, a power great enough to misdirect me into thinking Dru Benson had been the vampire, not Temptation herself, now held me in place as effectively as a nail driven into wood. There was a sound like the soughing of wind through tall trees as, slowly, she settled to the ground and her great wings folded out of sight.

"You see how powerless you are?" the thing that was Temptation McCoy inquired, its voice mocking. "And you thought you were so smart, so special, with your built-in vampire radar. I made you from the second I saw you, Candace Steele, but you never saw me coming. And Dru was the perfect patsy. He fulfilled all your fantasies, your fears, so nicely."

She moved a little closer then, the still-beautiful eyes in her ravaged face staring straight into mine.

"You have no idea what I am," Temptation said, her voice simple and straightfoward now. And I knew we both recognized the truth. "The kind of power I can exercise over you. I can make you stop breathing with a single word. I can make you take your own life, or anybody else's. You will never belong to yourself again, Candace. That's a promise. From this moment foward, *you are mine.*"

I felt it then. A thought, a hope, a prayer, was trying to rise from somewhere deep inside me. The one, the only, place Temptation hadn't yet conquered, for the simple reason that it hadn't occurred to her to look for it. I might not have looked for it myself if her words hadn't reminded me.

Ash, I thought.

I couldn't belong to Temptation, would never belong to her, for the simple reason that I already belonged to someone else. I belonged to Ash, as he belonged to me. Temptation could strip everything else from me, but this one thing, she could not take. I had already given it, of my own free will. She could not take away my love.

Ash, I thought once more. And then, again, *Ash.* Three times, in all, like an incantation, a charm, a magic spell. *I love you. I never stopped. I know that now. I'm only sorry you don't know it.*

I had thought that the pain and betrayal had bled the love from my heart. They hadn't. They had only driven it underground. Fear had kept it there, until, in my hour of need, like a phoenix rising from the ashes, it had lifted itself up. I loved Ash. I believed that he loved me. Temptation might hold sway inside my brain, but she would never rule my heart. The knowledge wouldn't save me. Nothing on earth could do that now. But at least I knew the truth. Against all odds, even the ones I had stacked against myself, I loved and was loved.

I watched Temptation close the final distance between us. She didn't even bother to take the silver from my dangling hands. What was the point? I wasn't even the possibility of a threat, not anymore. She stepped in close, opened the mouth that was no longer quite human, and ran her tongue across my bloodstained face. I couldn't even shudder.

"Your blood tastes sweet, Candace," she said. "Like icing on a cake. It's going to take me a very, very long time to enjoy it all."

"*Candace,*" I thought I heard a voice say. A voice I loved. A voice I recognized. Ash. Now I could see him, just over Temptation's shoulder. I might have thought that I was dreaming, my great need for him calling him up, if not for Temptation's own reaction. I saw her body start, her eyes go wide. She spun around, hissing like an animal that believes another predator has come to deprive it of its kill.

"Back off," she snarled. "This one's mine."

"No," I heard Ash's voice say, clear as a bell this time. And suddenly I felt heat roar through me as, with the uttering of that single syllable, the sound of Ash's voice pushed back the cold of Temptation's power over my mind.

I raised my left hand, stepped forward, and drove the silver home. Propelling it with such force that the entire length of the wand was buried in her body. My fist thumped against her back. Temptation gave a cry that could have shattered bone. Another vampire would have been gone in an instant, but I had been right about one thing. Temptation McCoy was strong. She staggered away, dropped to one knee, and then suddenly, she looked human once more. Tears streamed down her once-beautiful face.

"Why?" she said, her eyes on Ash. "You're one of us. I don't understand why."

"You made a mistake," Ash said, his tone almost kind. "You tried to take what cannot belong to you. She is already mine."

On legs I wasn't altogether sure would carry me, I moved to her, then knelt down at her side.

"I would say I'm sorry," I said. "But the last thing you hear on earth should not be a lie."

I ran the second wand of silver straight through her vampire's throat. I had time to see a thing I swore was relief rise in her eyes before her power shattered forever and Temptation McCoy crumbled into dust. I closed my eyes then and let the darkness take me. Just before I hit the ground, I felt the strong embrace of Ash's arms.

Eighteen

When I opened my eyes, I was in my own bed, the covers pulled up around my shoulders. I was lying on my side. The blinds were down but angled up and open so that the room was filled with light. My left hand rested on the pillow beside my head. Slowly, carefully, as if a sudden movement might break me, I flexed it. There was no pain and no sign of blood. I pushed myself upright, then twisted so that I could lean against the headboard and sit up. Ash was sitting on the end of my bed.

Experimentally, I cleared my throat. "Hi."

"Hi, yourself."

He looks so tired, I suddenly thought. As tired as I felt.

"You brought me home?" I asked. "Cleaned me up?"

He nodded.

"So that means you were there, at Lipstyx. I didn't imagine it. You came. You knew I needed help."

"I did," Ash said.

I pondered for a moment, decided it was better

to know than not. I had had enough of being kept in the dark.

"How?"

Ash was silent for a moment, his fingers toying with one of the ridges in my chenille bedspread.

"I heard you," Ash said at last. "I heard you call. In my heart." He lifted his hand then, as if he thought I would protest that statement. "I know you're not convinced I even have one. But I swear to you that it's the truth, Candace. I knew you were in danger, knew where to find you, because of our love. You needed me, you called to me, and so I came. I had to come. I didn't have a choice."

"I wasn't going to argue," I said.

He looked up then, an expression I couldn't quite decipher on his face. "No?"

"I thought of you," I said quietly. "Right before I knew Temptation was going to do her worst. And all I could think was that, no matter what she did, she wouldn't win after all. Because you were inside me, you always have been, and she couldn't touch you. She couldn't touch us. And then, suddenly, you weren't just a thought. You were actually there, and your presence distracted her just enough for me to take her out."

"Silver," Ash said. "Good choice. I take it you've been doing some reading up."

"I was always good at research."

I thought I saw him smile. "They give degrees in vampire studies?"

"I think you have to audit."

"I have a question."

I tried a smile of my own. "Only one?"

"For now. You said *us,* Candace. She couldn't touch *us.*"

"Those are statements," I said.

"*Is* there an us?"

"I think there must be," I answered slowly. "Of some sort. I don't know what to do about the way I feel about you, Ash. That's God's own truth. I don't even know what all of it is, half the time. But I do know this: Most of it is love."

He closed his eyes then, and I saw the emotion in his face. "Love. You love me," he said.

"I do," I answered. "But I hope you'll understand if I say it doesn't always make me jump for joy. Too many things have happened for that, though I have to think what happened today has evened the score."

He opened his eyes. "I wonder," he said, as carefully as if he were stepping through a minefield, "if I might ask you to do something for me."

"Depends what."

"I want to hold you," he said simply. Stealing away my breath. My heart. "I want to feel you in my arms because it is your choice and your desire."

Across the length of the bed, we stared at each other. And suddenly I recognized the thing that was in his face, the expression I had been unable to identify before. It was hope. My love gave hope to a man who was no longer alive. I lifted one hand, fingers extended toward him. He slid forward and enfolded me in his arms.

I felt his body shudder as he took me in, pressing gentle kisses to the lids of my eyes.

"I thought I had lost you," he murmured. "That I hadn't gotten there in time and she would take you from me."

"No," I said simply. "I'm yours."

"Candace," he said. "My sweet Candace." And then he put his lips on mine. I made a sound, half sorrow, half joy, and kissed him back. Of my own free will. Of my own desire. This was the thing that had saved me, that what I wanted as much as my own life was to be in Ash's arms.

He brushed his lips across my face, ran his fingertips across my skin, light as feathers, soft as down. "This," he said, "is what I've wanted from the moment I saw you."

He loved me like a revelation. I thought I had known what he had to give, all the flash and fire. But the slow burn of this was a thing I had never even thought to imagine. Never dreamed it was a place that existed, let alone a place I could go. Slowly, delicately, he carried me onto a great rolling wave of desire. Until I lost the world outside his arms. There was only Ash. Only me. Only our love. I felt him fill me, then move within me. Both of us complete, both whole. And then I lost even the world, as my body flew, straight out over the void, and the only stars to guide me were the ones in my lover's eyes.

A long time later, I came back to myself. I was lying with my head on Ash's chest, his arms around me. I felt his fingers stroke through my hair, the gentle, loving way a parent strokes a child's. Without warning, I felt my eyes fill. *This is what I want,* I thought. What any woman, every woman, wants. To lie quietly beside the one she loves. Loving Ash seemed so very simple. It was anything but. And I knew, in that moment, that if I didn't send him away now, I never would. I would keep him and give up myself.

Before I could so much as blink to hold them back, the tears spilled down. I watched them fall onto his body, make their way across his chest. What do you do, when love isn't enough?

Ash's hand stilled, suddenly. If he had been human, I would have heard him catch his breath. "No," he said, as if he knew precisely what was in my thoughts.

"This is never going to work, is it?" I asked. "It can't work."

"Candace, I can't believe you're going to do this." His voice was ragged. "Not after . . . Not now."

I sat up then, brushed the backs of my hands across my cheeks as something hysterical pounded against the inside of my chest, desperate to be let out. A laugh or a sob, I honestly didn't know which.

"So you're saying what?" I asked. "That I should wait for a better time? There is no better time for us, Ash, and you know it. That's the problem."

"No, it isn't," he said at once, sitting up in his turn. "The problem is that you deliberately refuse to accept the obvious. It's the fact that you struggle against it that's unnatural, Candace. Not the fact that I want you to join me."

"Join you in darkness," I said. "In drinking human blood. In being a vampire."

"What I want for us is a new way of being together. It doesn't have to be a horror show," he said. "We're not all like Temptation McCoy."

The sound escaped me then, a sob, straight from the heart. I knew the truth, and it might set me free. It would also tear me apart.

"Yes, you are. Because sooner or later it all comes down to just one thing, Ash: It comes down to blood."

I took his hand then, pressed it to the center of my chest, as he had once done with mine, a very long time ago it seemed now.

"What do you feel?"

His hand jerked. I held it steady. "You know damn well."

"I want you to say it," I said.

"Your heart."

"My heart beats, Ash. My blood pumps. *I am alive.* That's what I was fighting for in that basement. Not just to win, but to stay alive."

"It's not that simple and you know it, Candace," he shot right back. "There are many ways to live, and to die. You think being a living, breathing drone to something like Temptation is better than spending eternity with me?"

"No," I answered steadily. "Of course I don't. But I also don't accept that those two extremes are my only choices. I want to keep *my* life. Just the way it is, human and vulnerable but completely alive."

He moved then, sliding his hand from mine. He turned away, swung his legs over the side of the bed, and stood. I let him go. I had started this and I would finish it. I wasn't going to call him back. There wasn't any point. In silence he moved to the end of the bed, pulled on his clothes.

"I don't think you'll be seeing me for a while, Candace," he said. "You've made your choice. You know how to reach me if you change your mind."

"I don't," I said.

He walked to the bedroom door, pulled it open. "Yes, you do," he said.

Then he was gone.

Nineteen

The discovery of Dru Benson's body in the basement of Lipstyx, coupled with Temptation McCoy's mysterious disappearance, made the headlines for a solid month. Eventually, though, the story began to fade away, as it became clear that no answers were likely to surface. There were two main theories about what had happened. One was that, for reasons unknown, Temptation had killed her manager herself then gone on the run. The second was that her masked assailant on opening night had tried again and met with more success the second time. In this scenario, Dru had been killed while trying to protect the star.

In neither case was there a clear motive. No ransom note has ever been found. Neither has Temptation McCoy.

The Sher and Randolph lost money hand over fist, but, strangely, Bibi came out of things alright. Without Temptation, Bibi's opener got expanded to a full-length show. She even made the marquee, her name up in lights. With no star to protect, I returned to my regular gig, working the casino floor.

After careful consideration, I decided not to bring Al up to speed on the fact that Temptation was a vampire. She had caused more than enough trouble. I just didn't see the need to spread it around.

I haven't seen Ash since the night he saved my life, but I'm reasonably certain he's still around. He came to Vegas for me, he said, to win me back, to finish what we had begun. Things are a long way from over between us. Sometimes I wonder when I'll see him again, sometimes I don't.

Oh, who the hell am I kidding? I think about him all the time. Wondering if I did the right thing. Then. Now. I don't know the answer. Sometimes I think I never will.

But I do know one thing. I enjoy being alive. I intend to do everything in my power to make sure I stay that way to a ripe old age.

Some days I actually manage to convince myself it's going to be enough.

Read on to catch a glimpse
of the next seductive book in the Candace Steele
Vampire Killer trilogy

Luscious Craving

It gets cold in Las Vegas at night, especially if you are alone.

But after working all night in a casino designed to resemble a hyped-up *1,001 Tales from the Arabian Nights,* called the Scheherazade, shlepping drinks in instruments of torture masquerading as high-heeled shoes, fending off ass-pinchers, watching newlyweds lose their nest egg on a single roll of the dice, sometimes, the cold, thick darkness is exactly what I crave.

Tonight was one of those nights.

Besides, I'm used to being alone.

"G'night, Candace," the night doorman said as I left the Sher through the employee exit that leads to the parking garage. "You have a nice day, now, young lady."

"Same to you, James," I replied. Every female under sixty is a young lady as far as James is concerned. Rumor has it he was hired by Bugsy Siegel when the mob arrived in the desert to make Vegas what it is today. Followed closely by a second rumor which claims that James started the first one himself.

I waited until I could see my car, then hit the button on my remote to unlock the driver's side. I got in, then drove home slowly through the neon streets. I didn't turn the heater on. This is the hour when the night is at its coldest, at its darkest: the hour just before dawn. The time that normal, everyday people dread, when their eyes suddenly fly open in the darkness and it occurs to them to wonder if this will be the day when the sun declines to rise.

I never worry about this myself. When you've seen the things that I have, you know the truth: Truly major shit doesn't give a damn about the time of day, and it sure as hell doesn't go by anyone's alarm clock. If it's coming at you, about all you can do is duck. Or run. And even then, chances are more than a little good it's going to get you anyhow.

I pulled into my driveway, killed the headlights, then switched off the engine. *What is up with you tonight, Steele?* I wondered. *Since when do you get off being all film noir?*

I twisted around to face the backseat, reached for a long wool coat I always keep there, in case of emergency or for precisely the kind of impulse I intended to follow now. I pulled it toward me, got out of the car. I'm always careful not to slam the door behind me. Most people are asleep at this hour, after all. I locked the car, tucked my keys into my back pocket to nestle against my driver's license, draped the coat over my shoulders, then began to walk. My feet made absolutely no sound against the sidewalk.

Down my street, past another, and suddenly, it's there before you: the Mojave Desert, nestling at the feet of the Spring Mountains. You can smell the desert long before you get there, just the faintest tang of sage in the air. It can find you when you least expect it, even on the Strip. Las Vegas is pure boomtown, spreading into the desert in a constant invasion that lasts for miles. But the desert is a worthy adversary. It does not give up. Between the condos and the malls and the brand-new developments that seem to sprout up overnight, the Mojave is always there.

It was exactly what I needed tonight.

I found my favorite spot, a small hollow in what, later in the day, would be the shade of a boulder. I sat down, letting the coat fall back behind me. I pulled my knees up to my chest, wrapped my arms around them, and gazed upward. You have to know how to look to see the Vegas stars at night. But I was good at it. I ought to be. I did it often enough. A bittersweet pleasure, a test I insisted upon giving myself. I closed my eyes, then opened them again. The stars were still there, and so was my reaction to them.

Where are you tonight, Ash? I thought.

Ashford Donahue III, the man I loved. The vampire I hated. Just my luck that he was both. The first time I met him, I could have sworn the stars were in his eyes. The last time I saw him, he was walking out. He had sworn not to come back. If I wanted him, it was my move. And I hadn't made it. Not in six long months. On nights like this, I wondered why. Nights like this made me want to forget the pain, the past, the blood. On nights like this, I still wanted Ash. The taste of his skin. The feel of his mouth.

"What you're doing is dangerous, you know."

At the sound of a voice beside the boulder, I jumped a good half mile. Then came up in a single, fluid movement, my hand automatically reaching for the silver chopsticks I use to keep my wild and crazy curly hair in place. Hair adornment and vampire protection all in one. *What Not to Wear* would be so proud. Or not.

"Ash! What the hell are you doing here?" I demanded, even as my heart performed a series of painful flip-flops. I am not particularly proud of this, by the way. I have fought against my feelings for Ash, over and over, long and hard. I've lost every single time.

"I should ask you the same question," he said, stepping out from around the boulder. "You're starting to develop patterns, Candace. That can be dangerous, you know."

"Do you watch me, Ash?" I asked now. "Is that

what you're saying? If I want you, I have to come to you, but in the meantime you like to watch?"

"Dammit, Candace," he said, and he took a step closer. He was standing beside me now. In the predawn darkness, his eyes seemed to kindle with their own light. He truly did have the stars in his eyes.

"You want me to say it? All right: I want you. That's why I watch you. That's why I'm here. I'm willing to admit my need. I always have been. All you do is fight me."

I felt a strange madness seize me then. Out in the desert, beneath the light of the stars. I took a step closer, watched Ash's eyes go wide.

"And if I stopped fighting?" I asked, my voice low and husky. "Not forever. Just for tonight. What would you give me, if I stopped fighting you, Ash?"

Almost before I finished speaking, he gave his answer. I think we both knew what it was going to be.

"Whatever you want."

I took a second step, and then a third, until our bodies touched. "You," I said. "I just want you. You're all I've ever wanted."

He bent his head then, put his mouth to mine, and the world exploded in a shower of sparks. Ash's hands were on my breasts, trailing fire in their wake. There was no patience in his touch. Other nights were for explorations, for going slow.

Not this one. On this night, Ash and I desired one and the same thing: to take what we wanted.

He brought his hands together at the front of my T-shirt, fisted them, then tore the shirt apart. I wasn't wearing a bra—one of my simple pleasures after an evening in the ridiculous, velvet push-up number I wore while on duty at the Sher. Ash growled, low in his throat, filling his hands with my breasts like a greedy child. Pushing them together, then up toward his mouth. The action pulled me to my tiptoes. Another moment, and I would lose my balance.

"Hold on to me, Candace," I heard him gasp, as the movement of his tongue shot the fire straight down to my legs. "Hold on."

I put my hands on his shoulders, and felt the world fall away as Ash lifted me, to lie me down. His hands a blur of motion against the fastenings of my jeans, and then I felt the cool desert air on my legs as he drew the jeans down and off. The silk panties I wore went right along with them. I felt the rough texture of the wool coat beneath my shoulders, beneath my rump. I lay back, gazing up at him. I was completely naked; Ash, completely clothed.

He leaned over me, bringing his lips to mine for a lingering kiss, then stroking a hand straight down the center of my body. I watched it, a cool, pale white against my tanned skin, both saw and felt the way my body tightened at his touch. When his fingers reached the triangle of curls between my legs, Ash stopped, his eyes on mine. In them, a question. Slowly, my eyes never leaving his, I slid my legs apart, then bent my knees, tilting my pelvis up. Offering myself, opening myself to this lover as I did for no one else.

"What do you want, Ash?" I asked.

"You."

"Then take what you want."

He leaned down, pulled my knees onto his shoulders, and kissed me, openmouthed. Tongue thrusting deep inside me, then sliding out to slick across my clit, fingers tightly gripping my butt. I writhed against him, all but helpless in my need.

"Ash," I gasped out. "Ash, I want . . ."

I heard him laugh then. "I know what you want, my sweet Candace. I always know what you want. The only problem is, you can't always have it."

He put his lips against my clit, then, vibrated them wildly, even as his fingers slid inside me. In and out. In and out. Faster. Deeper. Harder and harder. Until I heard myself give a hoarse cry of pure pleasure. Felt my body arch up, pull taut. And then I was coming, the world shattering around me, the sky above, a sea of shooting stars.

I sat straight up in bed, my bedroom echoing with my own cries of passion. The sheets were a tangled mass at the end of the bed, my legs spread open, wide.

God, I thought. *Oh, sweet, merciful Jesus.*

I sat up, pulled my knees to my chest, hugged them tightly, and told myself I would not cry. *A dream. It was only a dream,* I chanted, over and over. So vivid, even in my own bedroom I believed that it was real, a literal slice of my own life. The passion so potent, I had actually climaxed. But it was only a dream, a dream I had summoned up myself. Of passion fulfilled, and unfilled. Desire sated but never satisfied. After six long months of silence, six months of relative peace, I had awakened from a dream of Ash where all it had taken was just one look for me to throw myself back into his arms.

"I know what you want. The trouble is, you can't always have it."

As if I didn't know. As if he hadn't taught me that himself.

Damn, damn, damn, I thought. *You are not going to do this, Candace. Do you hear me? You are going to put a stop to this, right here. Right now!*

I had wasted enough of my life agonizing over things I couldn't have. It wasn't a long list, but Ash was sure as hell at the very top. Well, I was finished with that bullshit behavior. Done. No more. I released my knees, swung my legs over the side of the bed, and stomped to my window and threw the curtains open. Bright morning sunlight streamed into the room, making my eyes water. I stayed at the window, gazing out upon the bright, clear winter day, until my eyes were as dry as bone.

Only then did I turn away, set off down the hall. *I'll run a shower,* I thought. As hot as I could stand. I would wash the dream of Ash from my body even if I had to scald it off. Then, like a phoenix rising from the ashes, I would begin again. Build anew, again. Never mind that I had made myself such promises before. This time, I would make them stick. I would make new choices, stick to my guns.

But even as I gave the hot-water faucet a vicious twist, I wondered: How could I build anew when my foundation was the same as it had always been: a broken heart?